A Passionate Promise

As I nodded, I sensed Alastair's eyes on me, and when he released my waist I reached out and took his hand, marveling at my boldness.

"You need not worry any longer, my dear," he said in a soft voice as he pressed my hand warmly. "I shall not let anything happen to either you or Lili. My word on it."

I could tell he thought I had taken his hand because I was afraid, and I knew I should say nothing to enlighten him. This attraction I was beginning to feel so strongly was one-sided, and I did have my pride. It was something I had always been able to depend on. I did not intend to let it fail me now.

Coming next month

A LADY OF LETTERS
by Andrea Pickens

The Earl of Sheffield respects the political commentator known as "Firebrand," but has little patience for Lady Augusta Hadleyr. But how would he react if he discovered they were one and the same?

"A classy new addition to the ranks of top Regency authors." —*Romantic Times*

0-451-20170-1/$4.99

ONCE UPON A CHRISTMAS
by Diane Farr

After a tragic loss, Celia Delacourt accepts an unexpected holiday invitation—which is, in fact, a thinly veiled matchmaking attempt. For the lonely Celia and a reluctant young man, it turns out to be a Christmas they'll never forget....

"Ms. Farr beguiles...." —*Romantic Times*

0-451-20162-0/$4.99

MISTLETOE MISCHIEF
by Sandra Heath

Sir Greville Seton cannot abide women who work as companions. But when he meets his cousin's companion, the lovely Megan Mortimer, the Christmas spirit allows him to embrace the greatest gift of all....

0-451-20147-7/$4.99

To order call: 1-800-788-6262

The Wary Widow

Barbara Hazard

A SIGNET BOOK

SIGNET
Published by New American Library, a division of
Penguin Putnam Inc., 375 Hudson Street,
New York, New York 10014, U.S.A.
Penguin Books Ltd, 27 Wrights Lane,
London W8 5TZ, England
Penguin Books Australia Ltd, Ringwood,
Victoria, Australia
Penguin Books Canada Ltd, 10 Alcorn Avenue,
Toronto, Ontario, Canada M4V 3B2
Penguin Books (N.Z.) Ltd, 182–190 Wairau Road,
Auckland 10, New Zealand

Penguin Books Ltd, Registered Offices:
Harmondsworth, Middlesex, England

First published by Signet, an imprint of New American Library,
a division of Penguin Putnam Inc.

First Printing, September 2000
10 9 8 7 6 5 4 3 2 1

Printed in the United States of America

PUBLISHER'S NOTE
This is a work of fiction. Names, characters, places, and incidents either are the product of the author's imagination or are used fictitiously, and any resemblance to actual persons, living or dead, business establishments, events, or locales is entirely coincidental.

Chapter One

The village was just as poor and mean as the others we had seen on our journey across France, but instead of dashing through it, scattering mongrel dogs and the occasional scrawny hen in the speed of our passage, we had been forced to stop.

It was close in the carriage, but I felt no desire to step down and walk about until we were free to continue on our way. I didn't like the angry voices I could hear, the crowd that had begun to assemble, the uneasy feeling I couldn't stifle that warned of danger. I was alone. My cousin had left the carriage earlier, to see what the problem was. I wished he would return. I knew I would feel better then, even though he was hardly a heroic figure.

I made myself sit back on the lumpy leather seat. This carriage was the only one we had been able to purchase in Calais. The French were not anxious to oblige the English, but one could hardly blame them for that. Only a short time ago we had been enemies, intent on destroying each other. Now they had lost, their beloved Napoleon banished to Elba. It was only natural they hated us still.

I looked out at the dusty street and caught the eye of a peasant woman. She was emaciated, her face lined above her ragged clothes, but considering the toddlers that clung to her skirts, I knew she was probably close to me in age. There was hatred in her stare and it startled me. As I watched, she stooped to pick up some stones. Hastily I turned to the other window, where more peasants stood mumbling among themselves. One old man with the face of an angel raised his fist to me and spat at the carriage. I could feel the two grooms up behind shift uneasily on their perch and I wished we were gone, rumbling down the road toward Nancy, this ugly, hateful village left far behind.

Still, I told myself stoutly, there was nothing to worry about. The grooms were both armed, as was the coachman. We had brought these servants from England with us, although the courier we had hired was French. And then there was my cousin. Surely even he must have a pistol.

I wondered what he was doing. How could a man like him manage, surrounded by surly peasants who wished us harm? I heard his voice then above the others, speaking rapid, idiomatic French. But it was not his command of the language that amazed me, no, it was the ease in his voice. You would have thought him at his club in London, sharing a jest with his fellow members.

One of the angry Frenchmen was comparing the ancestry of another to the donkey hitched to his cart. The other, not to be outdone, claimed his adversary had a lot in common with the pig that lay lifeless at his feet. My cousin was objecting to both descriptions.

"Oh, surely he cannot be compared to the pig, my good man," he said. "I see hardly any resemblance at all. He is much thinner."

A torrent of French ensued. I was happy to see the woman who had picked up the stones had turned toward the argument, even pressing forward in her interest.

"It does appear you all might have one good meal from it, however," my cousin continued as I struggled to translate his patois. "Now, do stop this jabbering, both of you."

I was surprised. I had never heard my cousin raise his voice from the bored drawl he generally affected. The peasants must have been surprised as well, for the argument ceased abruptly.

"Of course my carriage caused the accident," he

said. "No doubt our arrival startled the donkey and the pig and they, er, collided. You must blame the haste with which I travel. I am for Vienna to meet with Talleyrand."

A murmur rose from the crowd and I heard the revered name of Napoleon's former minister of foreign affairs on many lips. How clever of my cousin to mention him, I thought. The tension almost seemed to flow away.

"Ah, take this gold piece and buy yourself another pig. I am correct in assuming you are the owner of the unfortunate animal? As for you, sir, for the fright you and your donkey have sustained, here is another guinea. Now, if you will just move the pig, we will be on our way. Harris, come here and help. What a charming child, madame. Your grandson? He must have a penny for himself, he is so handsome."

Still talking, still dispensing coins and opinion, my cousin made his way back to the carriage. The cart and pig were cleared out of the way and the grooms jumped up behind again. Still, I did not take a deep breath until we had left the village behind. And I do not think I imagined a stone that thudded against the carriage, thrown by a peasant who had not been won over by easy charm, gold, or Talleyrand's name.

As he settled back, my cousin removed the pistol he was carrying under his coat and put it in a pocket on the door.

"I forgot to inquire, coz," he said. "Is it too much to hope you also have a pistol? And that you know how to use it?"

"I do, to both questions, but it is in my trunk."

"Typical. What good does it do us there since your trunk is strapped to the top of the carriage?"

"I know, don't scold," I told him as I smoothed my gown to avoid his sardonic smile. I noticed my hand was trembling and it annoyed me. I had been cool and collected during the incident, yet now, when all danger was past, my mouth was dry and I was shaking badly.

"I commend you for remembering Talleyrand," I

told him. "Surely that was a stroke of genius, he is so well-loved here."

"It was brilliant, wasn't it? I did think to elaborate and give them a recipe for roast pig I meant to claim Talleyrand's own chef gave me, but we did not have time. Just as well, I suppose. Escape was our main concern, not cuisine."

"It was bad luck the donkey and pig were there," I made myself say lightly.

"Bad luck?" he drawled. "I hardly think luck had anything to do with it. Hand me the map case, there's a good girl."

Puzzled, I did as he had bidden me. I even forced myself to swallow my questions as he spread the map of France out over his knees and bent to track our route with one elegantly gloved finger.

"Yes, here we are, and not that far from our destination. Close enough to dispense with our escort. What say you, coz?"

"The courier? But he was engaged to guide us as far as the convent and see to our safe return as well."

"Indeed. But if you remember, he went ahead of us this morning and we have not seen him since. He was supposed to locate a suitable inn where we could stop and change the horses, eat, and rest. I saw his horse behind a wine shop in that sorry spectacle of a village we just escaped. I rather think our courier planned the incident with the pig and the donkey. Luckily we made good time, and *he* did not have enough of it to arrange which peasants would slaughter us for our money and clothes and horses."

"You think they intended to kill us?" I asked, horrified.

"Consider their situation. They are hungry. Their children cry for food, and most of their sons and husbands have not returned from the war. If they ever will. There is no one to bring in the meager harvest but some old men past their prime. Winter can be brutal for those who have not prepared for it.

Wouldn't you kill to save your children from starvation?"

I nodded, for I could not speak.

He rapped on the roof of the carriage and it slowed obediently. I was glad we had traveled so far from the village that there was nothing to be seen around us but woods and an empty field. When the trap opened, the coachman was ordered to take the next right turning.

As we set off again, my cousin explained, "The courier will expect us to travel straight on to Nancy, where we had planned to stay the night. He will not expect this detour, nor will he believe we could complete our journey in one day. You are up to the travel, ma'am? I do not overestimate your fortitude?"

How polite this second cousin of mine I hardly knew was, I thought as I reassured him. Always so solicitous, so careful of me, such a *gentleman.* And yet I did not think Alastair Russell was a man overly concerned with the well-being of others, no, not even women who might be in his care. It seemed to me he was merely playing a role, much as an actor might on the stage, and once again I wished there had been someone—anyone!—else I might have called on in my need.

"Do tell me why the husband of this distant relative of yours felt he had to leave his infant daughter in a convent so inconveniently located after his wife's death, coz. When I think how this country is positively littered with holy retreats, I do wonder at his choice. And what were they doing in France anyway? France was our enemy even in 1801."

"My mother once told me this Thora and her husband, a Thomas Martingale, preferred the continent to England. He was an artist, much taken with the scenery of Lorraine. They should have come home long before England and France were at daggers drawn, but they did not. They had lived here long enough that people were used to them. And then, of course, Mrs. Martingale was unable to travel. I believe she is buried somewhere near the convent."

"I trust you will not feel obligated to search out her grave," Russell murmured as we both grasped the side straps when the carriage lurched into a deep hole. "The sooner we are gone, the better. Something tells me this journey is ill-begotten. I get an itch on occasion, and I've learned to trust that itch. Now it tells me we are in danger here. And next time the peasants may be better organized. Next time we may have no warning. And we are only four men and a woman whose weapon is out of reach."

"I bow to your premonition, sir," I said. "To be truthful, I've no liking for the journey myself."

I did not continue. I had used all my powers of persuasion when I had enlisted Alastair Russell's help in London. Now it was not necessary to enumerate all the reasons it was important to fetch this distant relative from France. And I had felt it safe to do so, for Napoleon had been banished to Elba and peace was at hand.

The carriage slowed and turned into a narrower road, and the horses slowed to a trot. I made myself relax. We were close. It would not be long now.

"Perhaps we should consider returning another way," I said, idly looking out at the fields we were passing. This was a lovely part of France. I could see why artists would admire it, study it, commit it to canvas.

"Absolutely," Russell agreed. "I was about to urge you to travel on to Austria. There can be no safer place than Vienna now the Congress to sort out the peace is assembled there."

"Vienna? But . . . but it is almost autumn. I've no desire to spend the winter in a foreign country. Have you?"

"No, when all is said and done, I prefer London to any other city on earth. But I do not care to put myself in jeopardy to return to it, no, even though I will be without most of my wardrobe if we travel on."

I thought of the heavy trunks strapped to the roof of the carriage. Only one of them was mine. Indeed, it had been necessary to come without our personal servants, my cousin had been so insistent on his weighty baggage. Was there anyone vainer than Alastair Russell, I wondered? I stole a glance at his profile. I had heard that profile was enough to make sensible women throw caution to the wind and themselves at his feet, and I could well believe it. I had never seen a handsomer man. Tall and slim but with broad shoulders and well-muscled legs, he had the face of a Greek god under carefully groomed blond hair. His eyes were deep-set and piercing, a startling clear true green in color. I had never seen eyes like them, nor any man to equal him for looks. In London he was admired and cosseted, and emulated as a true leader of fashion. If Alastair Russell was heard to drawl he found puce a tiresome color, you may be sure bolts of that shade languished on the shelves of all the capital's best tailors.

I would have preferred someone more valorous, a man better known for his prowess with saber and pistol than lapels and cravats, but I had had no choice. The letter from the Reverend Mother had urged me to come immediately. My young relative, she said, must be removed from the convent without further delay.

Beside me, Russell straightened up as we passed some small farms. In the distance I could see a stately chateau and I wondered if its owner had escaped the terror that had been the French Revolution. Then I held my breath when we came to a small village that was no more than a few buildings and an inn set at a crossroads. Alastair rapped on the roof again and the coachman pulled up. It was very quiet. Even two dogs that were sprawled in the dust did not move. For a moment, I wished it might remain so. Then a boy came running from the stable to take charge of the horses, and Alastair got down to give him instructions. The owner of the inn came out to greet us and assure us that of course food would be prepared and an excellent wine brought for our enjoyment. Relieved by this welcome, I allowed a groom to hand me down the steps. I stretched as unobtrusively as I could, for I was stiff from the long morning's travel.

We did not linger at the inn. The wine was superior, but the food, although well-cooked, was scanty and the accommodations poor. I was disturbed we could not change the team, but my cousin assured me the beasts we had would see us safely to the convent.

It was almost dusk when we came to the abbey we sought at Blamont. Besides being a very welcome sight, it was serene and peaceful. Through the elaborate tracery of the gate in the high stone walls that enclosed it, I could see the abbey consisted of several large buildings connected by cloisters amid the spacious grounds.

The nun who finally answered the bell would have sent us away, but Alastair was having none of that.

"We have come a long and weary way, Sister," he said. I was amused to see the nun was staring at him, mouth agape. Her orders had not made her immune to a man of Alastair's stamp, unless, of course, she thought she was having a confrontation with an angel.

"This lady is Cornelia, Countess of Wyckend. She has come to fetch a young relative of hers." He turned to me and asked in English, "What was the girl's name again, ma'am?"

"Lillian. Lillian Martingale."

"Ah, *oui, oui,* Lili!" the nun cried, clasping her hands and looking so pleased I wondered what the girl could possibly have been up to, she appeared so anxious to be rid of her.

A torrent of French ensued, of which I caught about every fourth word. Fortunately, Alastair was more fluent. When he spoke to me again, his smile was wry. "You are welcome in the abbey, coz, but I—and our servants—have been banished to a cottage outside. I'm afraid you'll have to manage that small portmanteau of yours."

"That will be no problem. It's not heavy," I told him as I stepped down and smiled at the nun, so neat in her gray habit and white wimple. "We shall not stay long, after all."

As the carriage moved away, I could see the men's guest cottage only a slight distance away. It looked well-cared-for and there was a stable close by. Hopefully there would be food and drink for the men, and the team. It had been a long day for all of us.

I saw the sister was careful to lock the door in the gate securely before we proceeded. She also insisted on carrying my bag, and I was free to walk along admiring my surroundings. The lawns of the abbey grounds were smooth green velvet, the late-afternoon shadows long across them. Ahead of us the church loomed, the golden cross high above it catching the light. Beside it there was a prominent bell tower. The entire setting was magnificent yet serene and full of peace. I told myself there were a great many worse places to grow up.

"Reverend Mother will not see you tonight, lady," my guide explained as she ushered me through a portal into the main building. "It is too late. She is at prayer. Here is the guest dining room where your meals will be served," she added, indicating a room to the right. "We have no other guests at the moment. This way, please."

Together we climbed a steep flight of stairs to an upper hall lined with closed doors. The nun opened the nearest one and stood back to let me enter. The room was small, narrow, much like a cell. It contained only a single bed covered in crisp white, a washstand, and a *prie deux*. Some pegs along the wall served for clothing. I was glad tight spaces did not unnerve me.

"I will have some hot water sent to you. Please come to the dining room when you are ready, lady," the nun said as she set my portmanteau down, bowed, and left me. I was sorry about that. I would have liked to question her about Lillian, or Lili as she was called here.

Left alone, I opened my portmanteau before I went to the one window to admire the view. Suddenly a deep-toned bell in the tower began to ring the angelus—three strikes and a pause three times, then many minutes of continuous ringing. The bell seemed to resound within me, its clamor deep and comforting, and for the first time since I had set out on this journey, I felt at peace and at ease. And safe. I only regretted that those feelings, of necessity, had to be so fleeting.

Chapter Two

I was permitted to see the abbess the next morning after I had had breakfast and she had celebrated Mass with the rest of the convent. We studied each other carefully as I entered her private rooms and curtsied. Although I am not a Catholic myself, I understood the courtesy due this woman who had been elected to her high office for life by her nuns. She was a woman in late middle age with a serene face and a direct, unsmiling gaze. That gaze swept over me without condemnation, but I was suddenly conscious not only of the crumpled condition of my traveling gown but of its fashionable cut and luxurious fabric. And of the handsome hat I wore as well, which suddenly seemed not only out of place but whimsical. What Reverend Mother saw in my face seemed to reassure her, for she nodded before indicating a seat near her desk.

"But of course," she said, speaking English as if she knew somehow I was not fluent in French. "I would know you for Lili's kinswoman anywhere. You are much alike, Countess."

"Truly?" I asked as I settled my skirts. "It does not surprise me. Most of the women in my family bear a resemblance. It is the shape of the face, I believe, and oh yes, the widow's peak in our hair."

After a few courtesies, asking about my journey and bemoaning the state of a world at war, the abbess folded her hands on her desk and said, "I am glad you were able to come so promptly, ma'am. It has become imperative Lili be removed from the abbey."

She paused as if to give me time to comment. When I did not, she nodded as if in approval before she went on, "We have not heard from her father in over a year. I fear something may have happened to him."

I could not help the stab of anger I felt. "And only for that you have summoned me this distance, Reverend Mother?" I asked. "The family would have been glad to pay any sum you require for Lillian's keep, if you had only told us of it."

She waited patiently until I was finished. "You misunderstand me, ma'am. The dowry Lili brought with her as an infant was more than adequate. And if you were of the true faith, you would know we would never banish a sister for her poverty."

I was ashamed as she went on, "The situation is much more serious than mere money. You see, Lili does not have a vocation."

I must have looked confused, for she added, "It was understood when she came to us that she would be raised in the faith even though her parents were not Catholic. It was only this agreement that made it possible for us to welcome her and assume her upbringing. But in spite of our best efforts, the child does not wish to live her life as a *religieuse*. I assure you, this failure on my part weighs heavy on me."

"I see," I murmured, not knowing what else I could possibly say. I had thought the girl might have an incorrigible temper—I had even been prepared to discover she had taken to slipping out of the convent to meet handsome stable boys even at the tender age of just thirteen. I was not prepared to find she had decided a cloistered life was not to her liking. "I am sorry," I added. More than you can possibly know, Mother, I added silently.

She inclined her head. "She is young to make such a decision, but she is adamant. And however much I may regret her decision, I am aware only a blessed few are chosen for this path. Since it is so, however, it is best she leave us and enter the world. There are many girls at this particular time who wish a place here. True, their relatives see it as a sanctuary, but to one with a true calling, it is a summons that cannot be denied. With Lili gone, we can accept someone who has been waiting to join us for a long time."

She rang a small bell on her desk. "You do agree to take her with you? See to her care?" she asked as the door opened and a nun stood waiting for her order.

"Of course," I managed to say although my throat was tight with emotion. I had come to France for just that purpose, yet now it was upon me, I dreaded what lay ahead. I knew it would be difficult.

The time I spent waiting for Lillian to appear seemed endless to me. I asked questions about the convent and its inhabitants, inquired how long it had been in existence, and requested information on the saint it had been named for. The abbess regarded me with an air of amused detachment, as if I were no more than an entertaining child on her best behavior. It annoyed me. Still, I told myself, it does not mean anything. It is only that I am English and a heretic in her eyes. How reluctant she must be to entrust her stubborn lamb to such as me and how hard for her to have to acknowledge defeat. In spite of myself, I felt real admiration for the young girl who had been able to remain steadfast before what had to have been the Reverend Mother's considerable powers of persuasion.

I heard the tentative knock plainly. I had been waiting for it, my nerves on the stretch. I held my breath as the abbess bade the girl enter, but it was a moment before I could turn and face her. When I did, I was barely able to stifle a gasp. It was as if I were looking into a mirror at a younger version of myself or my sister, Phillipa. Of average height and slim, the girl wore the simple gray gown of a postulant but without the veil to hide her black curls. I thought how stunning she would look in a habit with that pronounced widow's peak just showing beneath the white wimple.

"My child, here is a kinswoman of yours come to take you away," the abbess told her, still speaking English. "She is the Countess of Wyckend. You may greet her."

The girl moved forward hesitantly, her blue eyes never leaving my face as she did so. She looked a little frightened and I made myself smile at her. "Madam, I bid you good day," she said in English in a clear soprano as she curtsied. I was glad she was bilingual. At least *that* would not be a problem.

"I am happy to meet you, Lillian," I told her, proud my voice did not reveal the turmoil I was feeling.

This girl presented all kinds of problems, not the least of which was her safe removal from France. And then what? I asked myself. I could not house her in London, nor could I take her to Wyckend, and most assuredly my father would not welcome her in Berkshire. As for other relatives, who would be suitable? And agreeable, I reminded myself. Lillian Martingale had been raised in a convent. She knew nothing of the world and its ways. And the world of Regency England was, when all was said and done, not only sophisticated and demanding, but, some would say, wicked. It made no excuses for its immorality, its excesses, its indifference. It would devour her and laugh as it did so. Yet since Lillian had refused to join the convent where she had always lived, as I am sure we had all expected her to do, there was nothing for it but to find her a husband when the time came. After she had learned everything every other sweet young thing had spent years acquiring: how to talk and dance and flirt, how to greet her elders and those of every rank, how to smile and control her temper, how to write a neat hand and sew and knit and manage a household and an estate—oh, the task was mammoth! I myself was not capable of educating her, even if I had been inclined to do so. I was, after all, only twenty-six and I had problems of my own. I put all these decisions from my mind, for there were other things of more importance to consider just then.

"We shall leave as soon as possible," I told her, and from the emotions that crossed her face, I could tell such a course left her torn between mournful remorse and elated anticipation. Something would have to be done about that much-too-expressive face.

"I was accompanied here by a second cousin of mine," I went on. "A Mr. Alastair Russell." As I spoke his name, his handsome face came to mind and it was all I could do not to groan. Lillian would be awestruck, overcome. There was no chance she would be immune to that masculine beauty and handsome physique, the easy charm and devastating smile. No one else had ever been. And I would be willing to wager she had never seen any males other than priests or elderly farm workers. It would certainly present a problem.

"I must see him and make the arrangements," I made myself say. "Perhaps it would be better to leave early tomorrow? At dawn? But Alastair will know what is best."

"Be sure and let me know of any special needs you may have, Countess," the abbess said. "There is little to be had in the countryside, but we would be glad to provide you with food and other supplies.

"Run along now, Lili, and make ready," the abbess instructed her charge. To my surprise, the girl ran to her instead and knelt at her feet, her head bent as she asked for her blessing. Her voice was choked with tears but that was understandable. She was, after all, about to leave the only home she had ever known, the only people who had shown her love. Of course, she was upset, even though she herself had chosen this path. Turning aside to allow her some privacy, I wondered at the courage it must have taken at her age to decide to leave in the face of what had to have been an equal determination that she stay. There was more to Lillian Martingale than met the eye. The child evidentally had backbone. I approved.

I was not to see her again until we left. After we parted outside the Reverend Mother's apartments, I assumed she went back to the convent proper while I set off to inspect it. It was still very early. I did not care to disturb Alastair, for I knew he rarely rose before noon in London. This journey had been taxing enough for him.

The same nun who had admitted me at the gate joined me and became my guide. She showed me the church first. It was lovely, its tapestries and stained glass glowing with color against the gray stone walls. There was a not unpleasant odor of incense and burning candle wax in the air.

Leaving the church, I was soon confused by the sheer number of rooms. Parlors, a library, extern chapel, refectory, kitchen, infirmary, and numerous cells for the nuns. There was even a bindery and a scriptorium. I was delighted to finally sit down on a stone bench in the garth, a lovely square garden with a fountain that was enclosed by the convent buildings. Over on one side two nuns knelt to weed a flower bed, and overhead I could hear some birds chirping contentedly in the boughs of the fruit trees. It was completely peaceful although I was aware the life of a busy convent was going on all around me. During my exploration, I had seen several nuns, and although all of them had bowed in acknowledgment, no one had spoken. There had been no sign of Lillian although more than once I had felt eyes on my back. But when I turned, there was no one there. Still, I was sure my progress was being watched. By my new charge? Or by young postulants here? I did not know.

At last I excused myself and walked to the cottage where Alastair and the servants were staying. I found him at the table, the remains of a hearty breakfast before him. The elderly woman serving him was beaming and blushing in delight at his appetite. Another conquest for the debonaire Mr. Russell, and I was sure he had done nothing at all to inspire it. A picture of

Lillian's innocent face crossed my mind as I took the seat Alastair held out for me, and I frowned.

"You were not given such a munificent repast, coz?" he asked as he went to pour me a cup of tea from the pot on a side table. "Shall I order you more?"

"I am fine," I told him, stirring the tea. The convent certainly seemed to have an abundance of good food. I reminded myself to ask for extra for the road as the abbess had suggested. It would save us from having to stop along the way.

"You have seen the girl?" Alastair asked idly as he regained his seat.

"An hour or so ago. She is very young for thirteen. Very innocent."

"Do I detect, oh, just the merest whiff of a warning in your tone? I do assure you, coz, I have no interest in the infantry. Far from it. Indeed, I find anyone under the age of twenty tiresome."

"Do you? I am sure Lillian will not find you tiresome, however."

He shrugged, those green eyes of his dancing with mischief. "I cannot help that, but you may be sure I shall be quick to dampen any ardor the chit shows for me. I intend my role to be that of a kindly elder person. Why, I shall be positively avuncular, just you wait and see."

With this I had to be content as he changed the subject to discuss the journey we would undertake on the morrow.

"I still think it wise for us to travel to Germany. It is only two days or so to the border, but as you remember, many days through the heart of France to reach the coast at Calais again. We must also consider that there is a good chance our former courier will be looking for us. He may well have enlisted others to help him. The thought of facing an armed band of ruffians intent on robbing and slaughtering us leaves me feeling positively unmanned, however brave you may consider yourself to be, ma'am."

"You think he might be hunting for us?" I asked. "But why? How?"

"Think, coz, do. He knew we were bound for this convent. I expect he is in the neighborhood at this very minute and he will not be in a—how shall I put it?—*pleasant* mood since our earlier escape."

He rose to fetch the map case and spread it out on the table before me as I hastily moved my teacup. Leaning over my shoulder, Alastair said, "You can see how close to the border we are situated here. And since we hired the man to see us safe back to the port, he will not expect us to head east. I suggest we leave at ten tonight. No one would expect us to travel in the dark, either."

"But how shall we find our way?" I began before I paused and said, "Forgive my stupidity. Of course you have found another guide for us, haven't you?"

He went back to his seat. "I do so admire your quickness, coz," he said. "It makes it a pleasure to converse with you.

"Yes, as you surmised, the good Berthe who is taking care of me here has a nephew. He was crippled in Spain yet bears no animosity toward the English that a few gold coins can't erase. He can sit up beside the coachman while we trail his horse. He knows every road, every turning, for miles. There is also a half moon. By daylight when he will leave us, we will be far from Blamont and the convent. And even if you do decide to go home directly, we can travel through Germany to Belgium and the coast. It will be longer, but infinitely safer.

"Tell me about the girl. You have seen her? Will she be tiresome, prone to nervous spells, or always at her prayers?"

"I've no idea. We only exchanged a few words. I think you will be pleased at her beauty. I was startled to discover how much she looks like all the women in my family. But you shall see. To my relief, she speaks excellent English with little accent."

"Just enough to make her intriguing to the more impressionable young gentlemen someday," he said.

"She is only just thirteen, Alastair," I reminded him. "Thank heavens, for she has much to learn before she is ready to be presented."

"Who will instruct her? Where were you planning to take her in England?"

"That is a problem," I admitted. "There is no one suitable in her father's family. I do not believe I mentioned it, but Thomas Martingale was not gentry, never mind *haute ton*."

"I suspected as much. I've never heard the name. But surely among her mother's relatives . . . ?"

"Thora Edson was the only child of an only child, more's the pity. If only her mother still lived! As the girl's grandmother, she would be the perfect guardian."

He did not say anything. Was he wondering why I myself did not assume responsibility? Before I could defend myself, he went on, "What about your sister—Phillipa, isn't it? And your brother George? I seem to remember he has a large number of children. What's one more to him and his wife?"

"George has twelve children, and Ellen is to present him with another token of her affection shortly after Christmas," I said tartly. "I would not subject any young girl to the life of an unpaid nursery drudge, and I am sure that is what she would become. As for my older sister, poor Phillipa! Her husband is in bad health and commands all her attention.

"I believe there may be some second cousins somewhere in the north country. Yorkshire, or Northumberland. I set my man of business to looking for them before we sailed. I hope he will have good news for me when I return to England."

Alastair did not look up from the spoon he was toying with. As he turned it, it flashed silver in the light.

"So, since there is no one waiting breathlessly for her, there is no reason we cannot go on to Austria. It might be amusing, don't you think? I understand Vienna is crowded with the elite of every nation as the diplomats try to forge a peace."

"It is not fair to you, to keep you from home and your friends," I protested.

I thought his mouth tightened for a moment, but I could not be sure. "I've a reason for preferring exile right now," he said. "A small matter, nothing of concern," he added, in case I might be so gauche I wouldn't hesitate to question him further. I nodded and changed the subject. Alastair Russell and I had little in common. We had seldom met even though both of us made our homes in London. I cared nothing for his exalted circle of society and he, surely even less for mine. I knew he would consider my friends a tiresome group of eccentrics and bluestockings. We were complete opposites even though we were related. But then our lives had taken us down very different paths.

"Very well, let us go to Austria," I said. "I hope there will be some competent dressmakers there, for I have but little with me. As you must surely be aware, coz."

His brows rose. "More censure?" he teased. "But the flimsy gowns women are wearing are easily made while there is no one on the continent I would trust to tailor a coat for me, or make me a pair of boots. How fortunate I thought to bring evening clothes!"

I swallowed a biting remark. How typical he had done so, rather. And who else would have thought such garments necessary for traveling through a foreign country to a convent and back?

Alastair was speaking again and I made myself concentrate. "I assume the girl has a great need for clothing as well? Yes, we cannot have her drooping about in gray and black even if she is not out. We had best stop in Strasbourg before we leave France. There is sure to be something suitable there for both of you, and I know how you ladies adore French fashion. Besides, we will need additional servants, a valet and a maid."

I had nothing to say in reply that would not show him my scorn for his dandyism. I had no doubt Alastair would cut a dashing figure in Vienna and break a good many hearts while he was about it. I vowed young Lillian's heart would not be one of them.

Chapter Three

It was full dark at ten that night when the carriage pulled up to the convent gates, where a trembling girl and I waited in silent anticipation. Remembering what I had been like when I was younger, I was sure Lillian Martingale must think this all a tremendous lark. Indeed, I might have thought so myself even now if I had not been so concerned with our late courier and his possible band of cutthroats.

Still, I was almost certain I heard a sob that was quickly muffled, and I wondered if Lillian was having second thoughts. I hoped not. It was far too late for that. And just the idea that I might have a weeping, reluctant girl on my hands—and Alastair's, horrors!—was daunting.

The grooms quickly loaded our baggage in complete silence. Like me, Lillian had only a small portmanteau. I found it sad to think that it contained everything she could call her own—the substance of all thirteen years of her life. She was wearing a heavy gray hooded cloak. I was glad of that. The nights were growing chill even though the days still held summer's warmth.

As Alastair handed me into the carriage, I looked up and saw a dark bulk on the perch beside the coachman. The plump Berthe's accommodating nephew, I was sure.

It was eerie how quiet it was as we set off at a slow walk. Seated beside me, Alastair confided he had had the horses' hooves muffled with cloth, and the tack as well. Across from us, facing back, Lillian sat huddled in a corner of the carriage, next to the baskets of food the nuns had given us. She did not move and she did not speak. I had tried not to frighten her when I explained why we must travel at night, but I was not sure I had succeeded. I could not see her, nor could she see me, or I would have smiled to encourage her.

I managed to doze at times through that long, dark night. I hoped the girl was able to sleep. I had wrapped a lap robe over her earlier, conscious of Alastair's amused gaze as I did so. Let him think what he chooses, I told myself as I settled back in my own seat. I am responsible for Lillian Martingale now.

When I woke sometime later, the sky was lightening ahead of us. I could just make out the pale oval of the face across from me. Lillian was fast asleep. How fortunate the young are that they can sleep anywhere.

Turning, I saw Alastair was also awake. "We seem to have made good our escape, coz," I murmured so as not to disturb our sleeping companion.

"Yes, but I must say that conjuring up a vision of the courier's face when he discovers his quarry has flown is all that has sustained me throughout this endless, uncomfortable night," he replied, sounding more than a little tart. Then remembering his manners, he added, "And you, coz? You are content? I would prefer we only stop when good Berthe's nephew leaves us."

"I am quite all right," I told him, sitting up to straighten my hat. I am not generally concerned with how I appear, but for some reason I knew I looked a sight and wished I might do something to repair that condition. Thinking it over, I decided this sudden interest in myself must stem from my cousin's always immaculate appearance. I had not the slightest idea how he managed it, and without his valet's assistance, too. But ever since we had started our journey, I had never seen Alastair disheveled and his linen was invariably crisp and fresh. I knew such order should be applauded. Unfortunately all it did was make me cross. Because you are such an untidy mess, I scolded myself as I tucked a stray curl behind my left ear.

Alastair had nothing further to say, and I kept my own counsel as well. Perhaps he did not enjoy conversing before breakfast. I believe many gentlemen do not. I suddenly wondered how Lillian would react when she first had a good look at her protector. Part of me almost looked forward to it in spite of my anxiety, and when the time came, I was not to be disappointed.

It was light enough for me to see her when she stretched at last and yawned hugely before she opened her eyes. For a fleeting moment she stared blankly as if confused about who we were and where she was. Then, remembering, she smiled at me a little. As her eyes went to Alastair's face, I held my breath. Her eyes widened and her mouth fell open to gape in astonishment at the vision before her. She did not move. I swear she did not even breathe. Fortunately, Alastair was looking out the carriage window and so missed this first, devastated reaction. I was glad it was so, for sitting there vacant-eyed with her mouth agape made the girl look half-witted.

"I see you are awake, Lillian," I said in a normal voice to allow her to gather her wits. "Allow me to introduce my cousin, Alastair Russell. He is no relation of yours, of course, but he was kind enough to bear me company on the journey."

"And see to your safety," the gentleman added. Bowing a little, he said, "How do you do, Miss Martingale?"

"I—er—Mr.—ah, um—I—er, very well," she stammered. I did not dare look Alastair's way lest I laugh. And although he had himself under firm control, I detected a hint of laughter in his voice when next he spoke.

"It appears it will be a fine day. I am sorry it was necessary to steal away from the convent as we did. I trust you have not been too inconvenienced, miss?"

"No, no—that is, er, of course not, I mean . . ."

I was about to step in and untangle this incoherent

speech when she took a deep breath and said with quaint dignity, "Please forgive me. I do not think I am really awake yet and it is making me stupid. Give you good day, m'lady. Mr. Russell."

I wanted to applaud, but I only said, "This is exciting, isn't it, Lillian? I daresay you have never been this far from the convent or I would ask you if you have any idea where we are."

She didn't bother to look out the window. "I've never even been outside the walls before," she confessed. "And I've never ridden in a carriage. It is very elegant, isn't it?"

Alastair shifted beside me, and before he could tell her exactly what he thought of the old, badly sprung vehicle, I asked her how she had generally spent her days.

She told us of her studies and her duties. Her recreation had consisted of walks around the garth. I was horrified. The convent sounded just like a prison to me. A safe place, to be sure, but a prison for all that. Before I could comment, Lillian excused herself, saying she had been most remiss to forget her morning prayers.

Both Alastair and I concentrated on looking out our respective windows. Fortunately, Lillian prayed in silence.

A short time later, the coachman pulled up at the side of the road and Alastair went to confer with our guide. I saw he was a tall, thin man with a bad limp. As he rode away on the horse we had trailed behind the carriage, I suggested Lillian and I get down and see if we could find a brook and refresh ourselves while the men set out breakfast and the team rested. We were on our own now, and I said a prayer myself that our former courier would waste a lot of time searching for us in quite the wrong direction.

We arrived in Vienna two weeks later. To be accurate, we arrived *outside* Vienna then. Alastair had decided we would put up at an inn a few miles from the city while he went on to investigate the situation. Later, when I discovered how crowded Vienna was, how there were not even the meanest rooms to be had, I applauded his foresight.

We were much easier with each other by that time. Our stay in Strasbourg had broken all barriers between us. Of course, Lili had a lot to do with that. She was a delightful girl, proper and quiet one minute, excited and enthralled with her first taste of the world the next. She managed to keep both Alastair and me amused, challenged, and thoughtful—an interesting combination.

She protested the clothes I bought her, insisting she did not need them and she would not like to be a burden. It was not until Alastair told her he would become quite depressed if he had to continue in the company of a convent girl dressed all in gray that she capitulated. Because, of course, just as I had feared, she had tumbled into love with him. I thanked God every night the man treated her like the child she was. One time we were alone, Lili confided that she had never dreamed there were men like Alastair, and now that she had seen any number of other masculine specimens, she was sure of it. He was unique.

So along with the simple gowns I acquired for myself, and the ballgowns Alastair insisted I must have, I bought Lili any number of pretty pastel muslins, and even a pale pink silk with puffed sleeves and ribbon rosettes tucked in its flounces for best. Alastair was with us when we shopped, and when he caught Lili admiring a cherry red wool cloak with a hood lined in white lapin, he purchased it for her. She tried hard to dissuade him, for it was expensive, until he pointed out how selfish she was to deny some poor needy girl the warmth of her gray cloak. Only then did she agree.

He also bought her an unusual scarlet trunk, to carry all her new clothes. It was banded in shiny black with brass hinges and studs, and a whimsical brass design on its domed lid. It even had a brass plaque for her initials. She adored it. In fact, that night when I went to bed in the room we shared, I found her sleeping with the cloak laid over a chair close to the bed, the trunk beside it. It was as if she feared these precious items might disappear while she slept.

I was easier as soon as we left France and entered Germany. We had seen nothing more of our nasty courier, but I could not rest easy until we were beyond his reach. The long journey did not seem as tiresome, nor the carriage as uncomfortable, with Lili along. The tidy German villages with their hearty peasants in native dress enchanted her, and if the weather was fine, we often stopped to eat at midday beside a tumbling stream.

Lili had an endless number of questions, but she was sensitive enough to know when they became tiresome. To our surprise, we discovered she was fluent in German as well as French and English, and she confessed she had also begun to study Italian. The convent had given her an education that far surpassed anything she might have had as a young English girl. She could discuss geography, mathematics, philosophy, and religion with ease, although to be honest, she had a very narrow view of the latter subject. I know it pained her that both Alastair and I were the heretics the nuns had taught her to shun. It was only after a long discussion one day as we rumbled down a country road in Austria that she came to accept that other beliefs could be as valid as her own. "Truly," I said, holding her eye, "it is intolerant to think otherwise."

She hesitated, and I was reminded that I had discovered she had a very stubborn nature. Now, she was torn between the urge to serve as a missionary and bring us both into the true faith, and the slight possibility that perhaps we were, after all, right. Now we were, Alastair and I, the two most important people in her limited world. We had become close, the three of us, and such was our intimacy, she called us both by our first names.

One evening after she had gone to bed and Alastair and I sat on in a private sitting room before a cozy fire, he asked what I intended for the girl.

"Suppose there is no one at home to take her," he said, surprising me by sounding almost worried it might be so. "What then? I do not think a school the answer."

"Heavens, no," I agreed. "She has enough learning, some might even say too much. And I could not bear to see her shut up in a rigid routine again. What she needs, of course, is a family life, a home where she can learn all the frivolous things a girl needs to know."

He cocked a brow at me. "I am sure I do not need to know what those might be. Pray do not enlighten me, coz."

As he admired the ruby color of the glass of port he held to the light, he added, "You might consider a cursory explanation of how babies arrive in the world, however. Or, at the least, inform her such things should not be discussed with gentlemen."

I was shocked. "You don't mean she has asked you about it?" I demanded.

"No, indeed. We chanced to see a man kissing a pretty barmaid this afternoon on our walk, and she wondered aloud how long it would be before the girl had a baby. I imagine the nuns taught her that foolishness. But it will not do, ma'am. She must know more than that for her own protection. Would you find it awkward to tell her the truth? It is surely not my place to do so."

I thought about it. At last I said slowly, "No, I don't think so if it came at the proper time." I laughed then, putting my head back to rest it against the cushioned chair. "My, how my life has changed!" I said.

He smiled at me. "How did you live it before?"

"Simply—quietly—*sedately,* I suppose would describe it. I managed my home, saw my friends, read a great deal, and wrote letters, did needlepoint, visited my relatives. You know a lady's routine, I'm sure."

He did not comment and I was grateful. I was sure he thought it sounded dull. I had not thought so before this journey, but now I wondered if I would think so when I returned.

"I knew you were never a lady much interested in society," he remarked. "Is that because the earl was such a recluse? And even if he were, why do you continue on the same path? You are out of mourning now, I know."

I hesitated. I did not care to discuss my marriage with Alastair Russell and I did not know how to tell him that. "Ogden was not exactly a recluse," I said. "He simply preferred country life. But what of yours, coz?" I concluded, turning the tables neatly, or so I supposed. "How do you pass the time?"

"Point taken, ma'am. We do not discuss your marriage," he said easily. "As you know, I live in the forefront of society by choice rather than chance. What else is there for a man like me? I have no lands to oversee, no business to conduct. Do not pity me, if you please. I am sure I would find either occupation a dead bore. No, I manage to amuse myself, perhaps sometimes even others, and one day is much like another.

"Do you find Lili as refreshing as I do? She is like a deep breath of Alpine air, don't you agree?"

I nodded, but I had noted the change of subject. Point taken as well, Mr. Russell, I thought. For some reason you do not care to discuss your personal life either. I wonder why?

Later, when I went off to bed, I remembered his words and I did pity him. Was there nothing more important than amusement for him? Could he truly be happy living such a frivolous existence? I was reminded how different we were, this distant cousin and I. And where I would be the first to admit I found him a more interesting man than I had suspected him to be, and had almost always enjoyed his company, I knew, like Lili, that a year from now, Alastair Russell would have returned to his world, leaving me to mine without a single regret.

Chapter Four

Lili and I spent a pleasant day at the cozy inn we had found outside Vienna, after Alastair had driven away in our battered carriage. After breakfast, Lili ran off to investigate the village, and visit the church to pray while I busied myself with more practical matters. There was our laundry, some hose to be mended, and a letter I must write to explain to my man of business why I was not returning to England immediately as I had planned to do.

As I sat at the small table in our bedchamber under the eaves, trying to cut a new point on the old quill provided, I realized this delay was more beneficial than detrimental. For remaining in Austria where we were unknown, living on the fringes of whatever society there might be here, would be a respite from what I knew awaited us at home. Besides, I told myself as I dipped my pen in the inkpot, it will give Lili time to become accustomed to the world outside the convent walls. Truly, the more I considered it, the more grateful I became to Alastair for suggesting it.

That afternoon, Lili and I set off for a walk. We were armed with stout staves and a small pack containing some fruit and a stone bottle of water. Lili insisted on carrying the pack. I did not ask, but I was sure she was making up adventures in which she was featured as the heroine as we strode along. Surely the little brook we crossed became a raging stream from which she had to rescue me after I carelessly fell in. And the dog who barked at us even as it wagged its tail and came to be petted turned into a rabid beast she had to fight off with her stave until it ran howling away. There were times Lili made me feel positively ancient.

An hour or so later, we rested at the top of a hill we had just scaled. There were no houses to be seen, no neat farms, only a rustic bench beside a roadside shrine. Someone had left wildflowers before its crude carving of Mary, but they were withered now. Lili knelt to pray before she discarded them and set out to find more.

I closed my eyes, my face lifted to the warm sun. There was an underlying bite to the breeze that stirred in my hair and cooled my cheeks. I was reminded it was almost October.

I heard Lili humming as she came back so she did not startle me when she sat down beside me on the bench, her legs spread out before her. It was a pose she had adopted with glee, for she had never been allowed to sprawl at the convent. I hadn't the heart to tell her that sprawling was unbecoming for a young lady. It was difficult, for Lili was half a child still. Sometimes she acted as if she were ten, other times, twenty. Right now, I discovered, I was to be visited by the younger version.

"When do you think Al-as-tair will return, ma'am?" she began. "He did not tell me, but surely he will be back for supper, don't you think?"

"I've no idea," I said idly, still with my eyes closed. "He must find us somewhere to live while we are here. Vienna is probably crowded with all the diplomats and heads of state come to attend the Congress. He even mentioned he might look for servants. You know he was not pleased with the French ones we interviewed in Strasbourg."

She giggled. "I remember. He said he would prefer not to be shaved by someone holding a sharp razor who might also still hold a grudge. He is so, how do you say, *droulé,* isn't he?"

"Droll," I instructed. "Speak English, please."

"I never learned the word. The sisters did not find many things droll."

I thought she sounded pensive and I opened my eyes and said, "Lili, are you content? Are you ever sorry you left the convent?"

Her eyes were wide as she turned to face me, and she shook her head so hard the black curls that covered it bounced. "Oh, no, dear ma'am, never!" She thought for a moment, then added, "Well, of course I miss the sisters, even the routine. It was so, so safe and predictable. And I especially miss Sister Marie Margete—she was a special friend—she liked to laugh, too. But I would not have missed meeting you or traveling here, and Al-as-tair, oh no, not for anything."

Her sigh spoke volumes. She had always given Russell's name full emphasis on all three syllables. Sometimes I thought she did so so she might linger over it, and not for the first time I was glad she was so young.

Reminded of Alastair's story of her reaction to a young couple kissing in a doorway, I drew a deep breath and said, "Do you know how babies are born, Lili?"

"But yes, of course. I watched once when the kitchen cat had kittens, eight of them. The sisters didn't know I did that," she added, truthful as always.

"That is not quite what I meant," I said, wondering how to get from the ending to the beginning and from animals to people.

"Don't worry, dear ma'am," she said cheerily. "I promise I won't kiss anyone until I'm married and that is a long time ahead. Years and years and years."

I gave up, coward that I was. But as long as Lili thought a kiss produced a baby, there was nothing to worry about. I stole a glance at her profile. She had acquired a dusting of freckles across her nose. It made her look as young as I reassured myself she was. And I intended to keep a close eye on her, make sure she was safe wherever she ended up. She would be all right. I would see to it.

* * *

We were just returning to the inn when a glorious carriage pulled by a team of matched grays thundered by us and came to a halt at the inn door. Somehow I was not a bit surprised to see my cousin descend the steps a groom had hastened to let down for him. The coachman and both grooms were all attired in pale gray and silver livery. The grooms were well over six feet and almost as handsome as Alastair. Lili's eyes were as large as the silver buttons on their jackets, and her mouth hung open in astonishment.

"Al-as-tair!" she cried, waving frantically. "Wherever did you get the carriage? And why have you been gone so long? Oh, do tell us everything!"

He did not speak until we had reached him at the inn door. "I shall be delighted to tell you whatever you want to know, Lili, but I do not intend to announce it to the entire world."

Since the village street was deserted except for a fat yellow cat sleeping in a windowbox, this was surely an exaggeration, as Lili was quick to point out. Still, she held her tongue until we were alone in our private parlor.

"And you, Countess? You have no interest in the carriage? Or what I discovered?" he asked me after a long drink from the mug of cider he held.

"Of course I do, but I'll not encourage any more of your masculine glee at teasing us. Besides, you'll have to tell us sooner or later lest Lili burst."

The girl let out an enormous breath and we both laughed.

"Do tell us, Al-as-tair, please?" she begged, rising to give him her best curtsy and peeping up at him under her lashes as she did so. I decided there was little I would have to teach Lili about flirting. It seemed to come naturally to her.

"The carriage belongs to an acquaintance of mine from London, a Mrs. Alva Potter. She came to Vienna for the festivities and took a house there. It is a very large house in the best part of town on Johannesgasse, very near the Hofburg Palace. Mrs. Potter is there alone. She was delighted to, er, offer us her hospitality for as long as we care to enjoy it. Indeed, she would not take no for an answer."

I wondered what he had had to promise the woman in return for all this generosity, but with Lili still there, I could hardly ask. Thinking this over, I realized I couldn't ask even if she weren't. I could tell from Alastair's amused green eyes he was well aware of my dilemma.

"Alva is expecting us to join her this evening for dinner," he went on at his most urbane. "I suggest you both run along and see to your packing. Alva tried to send a maid or two but I was able to dissuade her. The grooms are loading my trunks right now."

I did not listen to Lili's excited chatter as we packed our things. Instead, I searched my mind for a recollection of anyone I might have met in London by that name. I could not do so, and I was sure I had never read it in the court news in the newspapers. Stranger and stranger, I thought. Was Mrs. Potter a diplomat's wife, perhaps? But no, I reminded myself as I fastened the strap of the case and set it outside the door to be taken down to the carriage, my cousin said she was alone.

Suddenly I was sure the woman must be some conniving female intent on getting Alastair in her clutches. I was positive she was young and beautiful in a hard, fierce way. A widow as I was, but not content with that state, and superbly turned out in the best fashions with stunning jewelry. I was quite prepared to hate her.

The carriage was so luxurious Lili was struck dumb by it. Seated facing back as had become her custom, she ran a reverent hand over the pale gray velvet upholstery that covered the plump, comfortable seats. She is a blonde, I told myself. Not an ordinary blonde, mind you. No, a clear, silvery blonde. I noted the silver vases containing fresh flowers that were fastened to the sides of the carriage, the soft cashmere lap robe folded on the seat beside Lili. Where had she found such a prize? I wondered.

"Alva insisted on bringing her own carriages with her," Alastair explained, as if he had read my mind. "And teams. And servants. All of them, indoors and out."

"She must be very wealthy," I said, trying not to sound impressed.

"She is. Perhaps as rich as Golden Ball. Perhaps even more so."

"My wretched memory," I said lightly. "I do not remember ever hearing the lady's name before."

"I would be surprised if you had," he said, a tiny smile curving one corner of that perfectly sculpted mouth.

"Al-as-tair, are these vases real silver?" Lili whispered. He assured her they were before he began to point out the spires and turrets we could see ahead as we approached the walls that encircled Vienna. Once we entered the gates, our progress was slow for the streets were crowded. So crowded I realized this Mrs. Potter was a godsend. There didn't appear to be room for even another mouse in the Austrian capital.

At last we reached a large house set among others like it on a wide, tree-shaded boulevard. As I left the carriage on a groom's arm, I saw a beautiful girl a few houses away about to mount the front steps. She was accompanied by a dark, frowning man, but she smiled at us before they were both admitted to the house.

"At last! You are here at last! Oh, I know I should have waited inside but I could not bear to do so, so please do not pull caps with me for it, Russell," a high, hurried voice exclaimed.

Surprised, I turned to see a tiny older lady in a fussy deep blue silk gown peering up at me. The jewels she wore would have excited a queen's envy. To my astonishment, she smiled widely as she curtsied before she threw her arms around me.

"Dear Countess!" she said as she backed away. Her voice was a purr of satisfaction. "I am so delighted to see you, I cannot tell you. And this is the young relative you are befriending? Too good of you, I'm sure. I hope she appreciates your gracious condescension.

"You there, Alvin, ain't it? Start removing the baggage at once. The countess will need her clothes. Dear ma'am, you must allow me to send you my own maid until you have a chance to acquire one of your own. Or better still, let me do that for you. Yes, that is what I shall do, first thing tomorrow! I'm sure I can find one you'll like—superior yet accommodating.

"Oh, why are we standing about here? Let us go inside. I've wine or tea laid on if you prefer it. What?" she demanded as Alastair held up a hand to stem the endless flow.

"Breathe," he said softly. "If you don't, ma'am, I fear you might expire."

She stared at him for a moment, her lower lip pouting, but just when I began to think she was so angry she would send us all on our way, she began to laugh, a deep belly laugh that was astounding coming from her tiny frame.

"Too much, ain't I?" she asked when she was able to do so. Taking my arm, she led me up the marble steps, snapping orders over her shoulder as she did so. A number of servants were assembled in the front hall when we entered, and they bowed and curtsied in unison. Surely this wasn't for me. Mrs. Potter must be even more eccentric than she had first appeared, demanding endless homage.

"This is my butler, Cranston," she told me, indicating a plump white-haired man with a cold gray eye. "He's been with me ever since I lured him away from the Duke of Harfield's employ. You may depend on him, Countess. Here's the porter, Briggs, he's called. And my housekeeper, Mrs. Deevers. The rest of 'em, well, you've no need to be filling your brainbox with all *their* names."

Beside me, Lili shifted her feet and I sensed she was having a hard time not to laugh. I did not dare look at her lest I disgrace myself by laughing first.

Mrs. Potter, after pressing us to take refreshment and being firmly denied, led the way up a wide, curving staircase, talking all the while. Alastair, I saw, disappeared into what I assumed was the library.

"I assure you, your ladyship, Vienna ain't a bit what I expected, and it's so full, you'll stare. A perfect crush, ain't that what all you society ladies call a crowded assembly?" she asked, turning slightly toward me. Not waiting for a reply, she went on, "I suppose while you're here, you'll be gay to dissipation. Heaven knows there are parties without number, night after night. Balls and soirees, receptions, dinners, military reviews—oh, those are held during the daylight hours, of course, and . . .

"Here is your room, Miss Martingale. Just ring for the maid if you need anything. The countess will be at the front of the house, down this corridor."

Lili looked at me with pleading eyes, but before I could say anything to reassure her, our hostess took me away. She was like a small but powerful wave, sweeping everything before it to strand on the beach. I promised myself I would return to Lili as soon as I was free of Mrs. Potter, for I knew she had never slept alone before.

"Here you are, Countess," that woman said gaily, throwing open double doors and giving me a little push so I would precede her. I could not help gasping, but far from offending her, it made her beam with pride.

"Yes, it's something like, ain't it?" she asked as she followed me inside. "I had it done up right when I took the place, in case, you know, I should have visitors. And I'm so glad I did, for now you're here. The Countess of Wyckend, my, my!

"Do you like the dressing table? The bed hangings? I ordered them especially . . ."

I stopped listening and just stared. The room was very large, so large the enormous poster bed hung with scarlet satin and ornamented with gold braid and fat tassels was almost lost at one end of it. The bed was heaped with pillows of various shades of red, from palest pink to deepest scarlet. One side of the room was almost entirely floor-length windows, covered with sheer cream underdraperies and finished with cream satin that had an overall pattern of delicate scarlet embroidery. I could almost picture a roomful of poor seamstresses bent over their hoops, straining their eyes for hours on end to produce it. There was a tufted satin chaise longue as well as any number of sofas, chairs, and tables. The wall was covered with cream pleated silk, and a gorgeous oriental rug was as silky underfoot as it looked from a distance. Priceless crystal and porcelain ornaments were on every surface, and there were flowers everywhere—luscious pink, white, and red roses in huge bouquets perfumed the air. The dressing table Mrs. Potter was so proud of was an elaborate piece of furniture made of some sort of pale wood I did not recognize. It had an inlay of mother-of-pearl. Over it, the large oval mirror had an ornate gilt frame in the Baroque style. I spotted a handsome escritoire and even, to my astonishment, a pianoforte and some music stands. Did the woman envision me giving morning musicales here in my bedchamber? Good heavens.

I realized Mrs. Potter had not spoken for some time. She stood waiting, hands clasped to her breast, for me to say something. I thought the room dreadful in its opulence, but I managed to say, "How very impressive, ma'am. I—I am rather overwhelmed."

My hostess beamed and nodded. "Yes, it's that all right, ain't it? Impressive, if I do say so myself! But come, my lady, come see the dressing room . . ."

She grabbed my hand and hustled me over to another set of doors, which she flung open with a flourish. By now I was prepared for anything so the large green marble tub set up on gilded claw feet on a platform did not astound me, nor did the mural of cherubs and nymphs in a garden that covered the entire ceiling. There were more flowers here, thick towels and perfumed soaps and creams, and yet another chaise.

In case I was so exhausted I could not get to the one in the bedchamber, I wondered? Two maids who were unpacking my portmanteau and trunk curtsied deeply.

"When all your other trunks arrive from London, there'll be plenty of room for the contents," Mrs. Potter told me, showing me an elaborate armoire with its many drawers and shelves. Not caring to disillusion her about the extent of my wardrobe, I only smiled faintly.

"Now, I'm sure you want to have your bath and rest, dear Countess, so I will leave you. Dinner will be served at eight unless you prefer a later time. No?

"I understand from Mr. Russell your acquaintance does not know of your arrival, and you would prefer to keep it a secret for now. And he tells me you very much dislike having your name bandied about. That, no doubt, is why I have never read of you in the society columns. I'm sure I don't understand you, ma'am. If it were me, well, I'd be sending the footmen bearing my cards flying by now. But I'm not of the aristocracy."

She paused for breath and I said, "Thank you, Mrs. Potter. You have been very kind and I do appreciate it, not only for myself, but for my young relative. She has only recently left the convent and is apt to be overwhelmed by life outside its walls."

Alva Potter nodded sagely. "Best you keep an eye on her, m'lady, for all she's only thirteen," she said. "Them convent gels tend to snatch at the bait early, if you take my meaning. Must be all that holiness makes them anxious. But no more now. We'll have plenty of time to gibble-gabble. So, as the Frenchies would say, *"Adieu, madame la comtesse!"*

As she flitted away with a final wave of her hand, I wished she would not attempt to speak French. Her accent was atrocious. I would have to warn Lili so she would be prepared.

I asked the maids to bring bath water and went to the windows of my bedchamber to stare down into the street. What had Alastair called it? The Johannesgasse? Perhaps Lili could tell me what that meant. As if recalling her had conjured her up, she knocked on my door then and, a moment later, put her head around it.

"Oh, good," she said, coming in and running over to me. "I wasn't sure this was your room, ma'am."

She looked around for the first time and stood speechless.

"Well!" she said minutes later. "I never thought there was anything like this here. My word, is that a pianoforte?"

"It is," I said as she went and struck a few notes.

"My room is very fine, too, but not at all this rich," she confided next. "The maid who waited on me is nice. She's sixteen and she tells me Vienna is very exciting. Will we be able to explore it tomorrow, do you think?"

Before I could answer, she picked up a delicate shepherdess figurine and I held my breath. Lili could on occasion be rather clumsy. I suspected it was just her age and she would outgrow it. Now, however, I was glad to see her put the figurine down carefully. "I could never live here," she whispered, as if afraid someone might be listening. "I would be sure to break something.

"But I didn't come about that," she added, taking my hand to peer up into my face. "I came to tell you I do so appreciate all you are doing for me, I do! I didn't need that Mrs. Potter to remind me, and in front of all the servants, too! It is too bad!"

Her blue eyes were flashing with emotion and I hugged her for a moment. "Of course you didn't, goose," I said lightly. "But if you should forget to be properly humble and grateful at least four times a day, I'll be sure to remind you of it, just see if I don't."

Chapter Five

I wore a plain muslin gown to dinner, one I had bought in Strasbourg and particularly liked for its simplicity. I could tell Alva Potter questioned my taste. She also remarked my lack of jewelry. Unconscious of her rudeness, she went on, "Oh, silly me! Of course you have left it all in the vault at Wyckend, haven't you, Countess? Not liking to travel about on foreign soil with old family treasures? You must borrow any of mine you like, ma'am. I insist on it."

I tried to look properly grateful. Mrs. Potter was resplendent this evening in a gown of bright gold damask edged with beautiful lace. She wore emeralds with the gown—a necklace, ear bobs, and bracelets. A truly enormous diamond wedding band adorned her left hand while the right sported a huge emerald and diamond ring. I wondered she could lift her fork.

"Overuse of jewelry is now considered rather *déclassé* in the *ton,*" Alastair murmured as he signaled for more wine. "The countess is correctly attired for dinner *en famille.*"

Our hostess flushed and I wished he had not spoken. She was so anxious to please us, so thrilled even to have us under her roof, it seemed the height of unkindness to mock her. I could tell Lili thought so too, in spite of her initial dislike of the woman, for she was looking askance at Alastair. He chanced to glance at us just then, and his brows rose. "I have said something amiss?" he inquired, his voice haughty.

"No, no, of course not, sir!" our hostess hastened to say. "I appreciate it when you set me straight. I hope the Countess of Wyckend will do so as well, for I know I have a great deal to learn if I am ever to be accepted in the *ton*."

I almost choked on the piece of meat I was chewing. Alva Potter wanted to join society? But that would never be, and I knew it as well as I was sure Alastair did. The *ton* had recently gone so far as to condone marriage between one of their own and a wealthy cit, but that was out of necessity, not magnanimity. Money was a necessary evil and it unlocked many doors, especially those with impoverished aristocrats crouched behind them.

Dinner seemed endless after that. It consisted of many courses and removes, and there was entirely too much food for only four people. By the time the desserts and savories had made their rounds, Lili was drooping in her seat. She was not used to late hours, for the nuns went to bed early and were at Mass at dawn. It had been hard for her even on the road when we rose early of necessity. Now she would have to get used to people not leaving their rooms until late morning.

I sent her yawning to bed right after dinner. Only a little later in the drawing room I could tell Mrs. Potter would have been happy to join her, for she was having the greatest difficulty hiding her own yawns. When I excused myself, saying I was weary from traveling and wanted an early night, she rose quickly as well.

After I had been undressed and the maid had finished brushing my hair, I looked for something to read. But Alva Potter evidently had not considered literature a necessary part of her decor. I watched the traffic below on the boulevard for a while, making up stories about the people in the carriages that passed. Then I smiled. I was acting no older than Lili.

I was just about to extinguish the candles when I heard a strange sound and turned to see a door I had not noticed before in the wall that separated my room from the one next to it. The door opened, and moments later, Alastair Russell came in, a bottle in one hand and two glasses and a corkscrew in the other.

"And just what do you think you are about, sir?" I demanded as he put his burdens down on a table near the windows, as nonchalant as you please.

"Joining you for a glass of port, ma'am, and some conversation unedited by our eager hostess."

He seemed to sense I did not consider this an adequate explanation, for he added, "I had to find out if you are content here, ma'am. I do assure you, this was the only acceptable place to be had."

"Of course I am content. Just look at this room," I snapped.

"Please. I am trying hard not to," he murmured as he opened the wine. "I suppose I have seen others in equally bad taste but I have succeeded in putting them from my mind. And why, do you suppose, did she choose scarlet and gold?"

"Because it's regal-looking?" I suggested, sitting down and tucking my feet under the chair so he would not notice my slippers. I was very conscious of my robe, the hair loose on my back.

"I am sure you are right. It's the sort of thing that would appeal to her," he said as he poured two glasses and handed me one of them.

"How do you know Mrs. Potter, sir?" I asked as he sat down opposite. I was resigned to a cozy chat now. I knew if I pointed out how improper his visit to my room was, he would only stare at me, then look amused I was so provincial. "She does not seem the kind of woman you would include in your circle of friends."

"Nor is she. She has been trying for a long time to get me to assist her in her attempts to storm the citadel that is the *haute ton*. I told her there was no hope for it, but she refuses to give up. She feels that with the amount of money she has to squander, she is sure to be welcomed, just as soon as she has learned the correct way to behave. Behavior, you and I, you see, can teach her."

"Am I supposed to be instructing her in return for my accommodations?" I asked, indignant he had made such an arrangement without my knowledge.

"No, no. It is enough for Alva that the Countess of Wyckend is in her house. She's a terrible snob, you know. Even worse than I am. It is why I've always refused to be a party to her plans until now. Although in candor I must admit there was a time when I was in need of a large sum of money that I was sorely tempted. Fortunately, a horse I had wagered on romped home in front of his fellows and it was unnecessary.

"This wine is not at all despicable, is it?"

"It is excellent, as were the wines at dinner. But do you mean to tell me you would really have taken money for something you knew would have no chance of succeeding? Letting the woman think she had a good chance of seeing her dreams come true? I do not believe you would be so base, sir!"

"Then you are being incredibly foolish. I am not a nice man. Why did you think I was?"

He had to see the distaste I did not even try to hide, although it did not cause him any remorse. Indeed, he smiled as he added, "In a way, you might say I would have been performing an act of kindness, for while La Potter was engaged in self-improvement, she would have been happier than ever before. But I see you do not agree with me. Pity."

We sat silent for a moment, then Alastair set his glass down and leaned forward to take my hand in both of his. "Come on, then, dear coz," he said softly. "We've a way to go together, you and I, before we reach home again. May I suggest you relax your high standards until that time? I am sure we will deal much more successfully together if you do. Besides, we cannot leave this house. There is nowhere else we can go. And Alva would probably wail to the heavens if we tried it."

I was very conscious of his nearness, the sleeping house around us, the look on his handsome face, even the sensation of having my hand held warm in both his large ones, and I pulled away in confusion.

"What did you do with the servants we brought with us?" I asked, more to change the subject than from any real concern for them. I was too unsettled to think of others just then.

Alastair reached for his glass again, to my infinite relief. "Alva has hired them. I thought it best to keep them handy, just in case."

"And they are English and we couldn't just strand them here in a strange country with no way to get home," I added.

He raised his glass in a salute. "As you say. I give you permission to finish my sentences and make them more conformable, if it will make you feel easier about me."

Before I could comment, he went on smoothly, "How do you think Lili will do here in Vienna? From gossip I've heard from Alva, I gather it is even more licentious than London."

"I'll keep a close eye on her, never fear. Tell me, how did you find Mrs. Potter here?"

"It was the most amazing thing. I had intended to go to Robert Stewart's headquarters—Lord Castlereagh, you know. He heads the British delegation here. But as chance would have it, we had stopped so I could ask a policeman directions, and Alva just happened to be passing in her carriage. I heard some female shriek my name, and when I turned, she was leaping from the carriage to run toward me. You do see how direly she needs proper instruction, ma'am? If for nothing more than to keep her from causing horses to bolt?

"Well, when she learned of our predicament, mine and the *Countess of Wyckend's*"—and here he winked at me—"there was nothing for it but we must come to her. She even insisted I follow her home so she might show me the accommodations and help her decide which room should be assigned to you."

"This was *your* choice?" I couldn't help asking. I

was amused by his tale. I could almost see the tiny woman flinging herself from that gorgeous carriage to accost the tall, elegant Mr. Russell. I wanted to ask if anyone from the *ton* had chanced to witness the encounter, but I restrained myself.

"No, actually I chose a lovely blue and white room, but Alva would have none of it. She claimed it was one she had not redecorated—which I already knew—and she wouldn't put a baronet's wife in it, never mind a countess. I gave up. It was easier, and I admit a certain cowardice when it comes to determined females.

"More wine?"

I looked down, surprised to see I had finished my glass. Shaking my head, I thought of something else. "It was good of you to tell her I did not want my name bandied about and did not intend to join society here."

"Tell me, why do you shun it so? I have never understood it. You are a handsome, young woman full of spirit and intelligence. What makes you hide yourself away as you do?"

"I've never really considered why," I said lightly. "I suppose it's because I've never been part of it. I lived in the country until I married at eighteen, and—"

"You did not have a Season?" he interrupted, sounding stunned.

I shook my head, busying myself with putting my empty glass down on the table beside me. "No, it was impossible for various family reasons. And as I told you, my husband did not care for town. We lived almost continually at Wyckend."

He shuddered. "I believe I've heard the earl's mother still lives there, isn't that so? Lord, she must be ancient by now."

"Sarah, the dowager countess, never leaves the place. She is eighty and she still possesses all her faculties."

"Unfortunately?"

"Alastair, you ask the most impertinent things," I

remarked as lightly as I could. "How do you manage to escape others' wrath?"

"Audacity almost always carries the day. And do you know, people are generally so surprised to be confronted, they tend to answer. I've found it the only reliable way to get at hidden secrets."

He paused, as if considering probing further, and I decided then and there that I would not be tricked into indiscretion, no matter how hard he tried.

"To return to the question of joining society here, may I suggest you give it a try? Who knows? You might like it."

"We'll see," I said before I raised my hand to hide a nonexistent yawn. "I wish you would go away, sir. I'm tired," I added as I rose so he would be forced to do so as well.

As he bowed, I said, "Do take the glasses and bottle with you, please, Alastair. I'd just as soon not start Mrs. Potter's servants to gossiping about midnight bacchanals."

He shrugged and picked them up. "I suppose as a gentleman I don't mind being accused of it. But I must say it does look rather bad for you, ma'am."

"How?" I asked as he walked toward the door. He turned to give me a mocking grin. "Well, with the evidence in my room, it appears you sought *me* out, instead of the other way around. Tsk, tsk. Terribly bold of you. I don't know what the world is coming to."

He laughed and disappeared, the door closing a moment later with a decisive click.

Alva Potter had summoned another of her carriages, this one an open landau, to take us for a drive around Vienna the next morning at eleven. Supposedly this was to show me, and Lili, of course, the city, but I suspected it was to show Vienna the countess she had acquired.

The streets were crowded with people from all the nations present. I saw more different military uniforms than I had ever imagined existed. Lili was especially taken with some Russian Cossacks in their belted shirts, wide white trousers, and tall fur hats. I recognized only a few people from home, and I was reassured. Perhaps I might go about here. It might even be fun to dance with Alastair at a gala. In the white ballgown, I wondered? Or was the sea-green more becoming? Alastair had chosen that one for the color and the cut of the bodice. He had been an exacting gentleman to shop with, always discarding this gown or that for what I considered trival, unimportant reasons. I had to admit, however, those gowns that won his approval were stunning. Should I wear my hair up or down? And would Alva Potter really insist on loaning me some of her jewels? Or course I would say no, but I had to admit those emeralds last evening had been outstanding . . .

I made myself return to earth when my hostess ordered her coachman to halt before the gates of the Hofburg. Handsome carriages went in and out of those gates, each one evaluated by Mrs. Potter, who seemed to know the identity of most of the occupants.

"There's any number of them German princes here, almost two hundred of 'em, I hear," she told her astonished audience. Lili's mouth was slightly ajar. I reminded myself to speak to her about it again.

"There, see that black phaeton with the scarlet wheels? That belongs to one of the Swedish delegation, Prince Hanson. His wife is the most beautiful blonde! Oh, now we are in for a treat!" she added, pushing her spectacles up her nose as she sat up straighter. "That coach just leaving the gates belongs to her Highness, the Empress Maria Ludovica. See how everyone bows to her. Poor, poor lady."

"Why do you say that, Mrs. Potter?" Lili demanded, almost falling over the side of the landau in her eagerness to catch a glimpse of royalty.

"Little pitchers have big ears," Mrs. Potter told me, nodding sagely. "Must remember that. No, never you mind, missy. And don't be asking questions all the time. It ain't becomin', you pushing your way into the conversation between me and the Countess. Not becomin' at all."

Lili stared at her indignantly, but she held her tongue. I knew how impulsive by nature she was, how she longed to argue this, but her convent training stood her in good stead. After a moment, she lowered her eyes to her gloves and bit her lip.

We saw a whole parade of other notables before Mrs. Potter had had enough. As we drove away, I wondered if this was something she did every nice day, for here, even if she were not precisely in the stream of nobility she admired, she could pretend she was. Only one couple, a rather vulgar woman and her meek husband, had stopped to talk to us. I had been introduced with considerable flourish and it was "Countess this" and "Alastair Russell that" until the couple took themselves off. Alva Potter wore a contented smile as they did so, for now the names of her prominent guests were out. Lili was quite rosy when I glanced at her. She was obviously having trouble containing her laughter again.

She had gone out early to Mass this morning with the young maid assigned to her, to the Stephansdom, Vienna's impressive cathedral. At breakfast she was full of her admiration for this church, its glorious stained glass, its soaring, vaulted nave, and its beautiful altar and chapels.

"I would not have missed it for the world, dear ma'am," she finished, the hearty breakfast she had chosen neglected in her enthusiasm. A footman at the sideboard smiled at her. Lili was well on the way to becoming a favorite here, I could see. I was glad of it, glad the young maid had taken her fancy. It would make it easier to leave her to her own devices whenever it was necessary to do so, although I reminded myself she must always have a servant, preferably a footman, to accompany her when she went out.

We were alone at the table. Alva Potter had gone to visit an employment agency to interview abigails for me, and I was sure Alastair, delighted to return to his normal habits, was still abed.

"Al-as-tair said we could drive out to the Vienna Woods someday soon," Lili went on. "And Brigitte, the maid, you know, says there is a marvelous park here called the Prater. Everyone goes there every afternoon to drive or stroll. She says there is even a carousel and Russian swings for the children. I would love to see them. Even though I don't know what they are, they sound like fun, don't they? Oh, I am so glad we came here!"

I was beginning to agree with her and it had little to do with the sumptuous display of crystal and plate before us, the sunlight streaming past the damask draperies, or even our unorthodox yet luxurious accommodations. It was different here, far from home. I felt free of restrictions, free of the necessity of considering everything I said, did—and even thought. Free of standing back on the sidelines watching others enjoy themselves.

There are those who claim travel is broadening. I knew now that was so and I knew something else as well. It was liberating, too.

Chapter Six

We drove out to the Prater with Alastair that afternoon. Mrs. Potter did not accompany us. Indeed, the hall seemed ominously empty when I hurried down the stairs, pulling on my gloves. My new maid had delayed me. She was French and very grand and it was easy to see why Alva Potter had chosen her, but for all her airs, she was not competent. I had had to tell her she would not suit and redo my hair after she left me muttering French phrases I decided it was just as well I could not translate.

The porter held the door for me, bowing low as he did so. Beyond him, I could see Lili and Alastair waiting for me on the flags beside Mrs. Potter's handsome landau.

As Alastair handed me into this vehicle, I said softly, "I rather thought our hostess would like to join us, sir. She has another engagement?"

He looked at me, one corner of his mouth twisting in a sneer.

"I imagine she is laid down on her bed with a cold compress on her forehead," he said, not bothering to lower his voice as I had so the servants could not overhear. "I was forced to speak sharply to her," he went on as we set off. He raised his top hat to a carriage passing us from the opposite direction. I looked at it carefully, but I did not know the occupants.

"It really is too much, ma'am, I told her, to be expecting to live in our pockets. You did have the pleasure of the countess's company this morning, I believe? Well, that will have to suffice for today."

"That was cruel of you, sir," I scolded, sotto voce still. I was glad Lili was so intent on admiring the scenery.

"It is best to begin as you mean to go on," he insisted. "Really, she does have the privilege of housing us, does she not? To expect more is too, too demanding. And common."

Lili interrupted then to ask the name of a large building we were approaching and I settled back on the seat and adjusted my parasol. Alastair Russell was impossible. There was no reasoning with the man. Still I had to admit it was pleasant, just the three of us longtime traveling companions out for an afternoon excursion.

When we reached Vienna's famous park on its island in the Danube, I could see it filled the same place in Austrian lives that Hyde Park did for Londoners, and at the same time of day as well. I had no idea what it was like during the morning hours, of course, but now, at five in the afternoon, the broad *allée* was crowded with all manner of riders, carriages, and strollers, all intent on what I had heard called "The Grand Strut," parading their finery, greeting their peers, and snubbing their inferiors. I thought the scene like a handsome painting, the rich green of the grass, the brilliant colors of the ladies' gowns as they moved from light to shadow under the wide chestnut trees that lined the promenade, the more somber array of the gentlemen who attended them serving as a neutral backdrop. Everywhere there were uniformed men as well, the brass of their epaulettes and buttons flashing in the sunlight, the medals on broad masculine chests making a brave display. Surely every hero of the Napoleonic Wars had come to Vienna for the Peace Congress. I wondered who could be left in the field as I watched them click their heels and salute each other, or bend over a blushing lady's hand.

We took a complete turn before Alastair suggested

we get down and walk about. Lili was delighted. I knew she wanted to inspect the carousel close-up, perhaps even go for a ride. For a moment I stared at her happy, expectant face, those glowing eyes and soft lips parted in a little smile, and I felt a wave of emotion. The poor child, to have lived so sheltered all her thirteen years that this little expedition could seem such an enormous treat. I told myself I would make it up to her.

Alastair declined to accompany her to the children's section. Tucking my hand firmly in the crook of his arm, he assigned one of the grooms to see to her welfare. I could not resist looking after her as she hurried away.

"There is no need to worry about the child, ma'am," he told me. "It is no more necessary for her to live in our pockets than Alva Potter."

We were soon involved with meeting and greeting those acquaintances of Alastair's who had come to the Congress. To be honest, I was disconcerted there were so many of them. Somehow I had thought the occasion mainly a diplomatic one, but now, as Alastair presented this one and that, I saw a great many of London's *haute ton* were also present. Surely Mayfair must be thin of company this autumn.

"Ah, yes, I thought I saw you earlier, m'lord. Are you acquainted with my cousin Cornelia, Countess of Wyckend?" he said. Then later on: "Mrs. Framington, your servant, ma'am. Now where did you find a muslin the exact shade of blue as your eyes? I vow it is devastating, ma'am."

I saw the interest in their eyes, could almost read their thoughts as they wondered who I was to him and why I was here. Some of the younger ladies looked daggers at me, jealous of my escort, while the cleverer ones pretended they had been waiting only for the privilege of meeting me before they begged to be permitted to call. Cynically, I realized how short those calls would be if Alastair Russell was not also present to receive them. But of all the people we met that afternoon, only one old lady who summoned us both to the side of her carriage knew me, and then only as the Earl of Wyckend's widow.

"Where's Sarah?" this *grande dame* demanded, barely acknowledging Alastair's bow. "What are you doing here, gel?"

"I am sure the dowager countess is at Wyckend, ma'am," I said evenly, careful not to look at my escort. "As for me, why, I am here to enjoy the Congress."

"Hmmph. Does she know you're gallivantin' about with this prime beau?" she demanded. She spared a glance at Alastair then and her face reddened as he swept his hat from those glorious golden locks and bowed deeply, as if to thank her for a compliment she had never intended.

"Mr. Russell is my cousin, ma'am," I said as coldly as I dared. "You must excuse us. Friends await us."

Old Mrs. Parmeter said no more, but I could feel her snapping little black eyes tight on my shoulder blades as we walked away.

"Relax," Alastair instructed, bending closer till his lips almost touched my hair. I knew he did so to annoy the elderly lady and it was all I could do not to pull away. "Horrid old crone!" he continued. "Why on earth does she think she has the right to censure you? Even question you at all?"

"She is a crony of my mother-in-law's," I managed to say.

"And as such, belongs to an earlier generation who made their sons' wives slaves to do their bidding?" he asked. "Doesn't she realize that now, as a widow, you may do as you please? See whom you please? Even take a lover if you please?"

"Well, I don't please to do any such thing," I snapped, glad a bend in the *allée* removed us from Mrs. Parmeter's malignant gaze. "But now she will write to the dowager and make up some tale, and I will receive a royal summons to the country to explain myself."

"How fortunate you are not at home to receive such a missive," he told me, drawing me to one side to let a harried nursemaid and her charges run by. We were close to the carousel now and I looked around for Lili, upset I had forgotten her so completely this past half hour. It was several moments before I realized she was not in the crowd watching the children go around, but one of them. I saw she was seated on a large white horse, grasping the brass pole before her with one hand while she held tight to her bonnet with the other. When she saw us, her face lit up and she let go of her hat for a moment to wave to us. I thought she looked about ten years old as she did so.

"Isn't it strange?" I said, almost to myself. "Sometimes you would swear Lili is a woman grown and then, in a twinkling of an eye, she reverts to childhood."

"She is a delightful girl and not at all the burden I was sure she would be," Alastair said. "I shall recommend convent training for the daughters of all my friends. It is far superior to those schools we have in England for the education of young ladies. As far as I can tell, those establishments merely encourage the chits to think they have musical talent and teach them to fall in love with the drawing master.

"But that training might make it difficult for her to find a husband when the time comes for it," he added. I must have looked at him askance, for he went on, "There are not many men who want an educated wife with thoughts of her own. No, they choose a silly widgeon they can teach to echo their own opinions. I'm sure you know the type. Forever prefacing their remarks with 'Well, *Percival* says' or '*Percival* believes . . .' Too tiresome."

I admit I felt a stab of pleasure. He could not include me in their number at any rate.

The carousel drew to a slow halt and the music stopped. I saw how reluctantly Lili left her white steed with the red saddle and flaring nostrils, its gold painted mane. The groom helped her off the platform and she ran toward us.

"Oh, that was grand! I had such fun," she called, even before she reached us. I saw several people turn to look at her and I felt uneasy even though the groom was close on her heels. I told myself I was being ridiculous. Lili was perfectly safe here among the other children. And what, after all, was the danger? Surely it was only her convent background that made me worry for her. She was so naive, so trusting. Too trusting.

As we set off back toward the waiting landau, Lili swinging my hand as she confided all the details of her ride, I suddenly remembered she carried no money. There was no need for it since Alastair or I paid for everything. Perhaps the groom . . . ?

"How did you pay for the ride, Lili?" I asked, determined to see the servant was reimbursed.

"It was the happiest thing!" she told me, still smiling. "I don't have a sou, of course, and neither did Henry. I asked him," she explained, looking confused as I frowned at her. "But there was a gentleman nearby who insisted on paying for me. Why do you look at me that way?" she wailed, stopping to wring her hands. "I have not displeased you, have I, dear ma'am? I would not do so for the world!"

"Which gentleman? Point him out to me," I demanded as I turned back to the carousel.

Lili searched the grounds. "I—I do not see him now," she said, hiding a sob. "I did try to protest, but he would not take no for an answer. He said it would give him pleasure to see me enjoying myself. And I—I did not think it was so very bad."

"Perhaps he was there with his own children? His grandchildren, even?" Alastair asked casually.

"Yes, he was old," Lili admitted. "But not that old. He was alone, watching the children and smiling at them. He was a nice man, wasn't he, Henry?"

Thus appealed to, Henry flushed bright red. Alastair

waved him away, and I could see he was delighted to leave us.

I made myself take a deep, steadying breath. I was furious, yes, but I was also frightened. Frightened at what might have happened in the short time I had neglected my charge. And if anything had happened to Lili, it would have been all my fault. Even if she did not know any better, heaven knows I did. I saw she was close to tears, her blue eyes huge in her white face. Even her hands were trembling in her distress, and I made myself hug her close for a moment.

"What you did was very wrong, Lili," I told her with my arm still around her thin shoulders. "You must never take anything from strangers, especially strange gentlemen. You cannot know what they might have in mind, and it is dangerous to be beholden to them. Everyone is not good and kindly. Some people are evil. They would hurt you. Promise me, right now, you will never, ever, do such a thing again!"

She promised, but I saw she looked rebellious now, and I wondered at it. I did not have to wait long to discover why. Safely seated in the landau again, heading back to the Johannesgasse, she said, "But I do not understand you at all, dear ma'am. Surely you cannot really believe people are evil and want to hurt us. I don't believe it, I won't!"

"The world is not like the cloister, Lili," I told her, holding her eyes with my own. "You have led a sheltered life among religious women devoted to serving God. They are good, of course. But don't you see that if the world was as good, there would be no need for nuns to renounce it? No need for convents with their high stone walls? No need for retreats?"

I saw she looked thoughtful and I decided I had given her enough to think about for one afternoon. Beside me, Alastair looked idly at the passing streets. He had contributed very little to the discussion. But surely he must agree with me, I told myself. As a man, he knew only too well the dangers I spoke of.

When we reached the house, Lili excused herself at

once, to curtsey and run up the stairs. I was sorry she felt uneasy with me, sorry I had had to upset her.

"A moment, coz?" Alastair asked, indicating the empty library.

He closed the door behind us before he said, "Yes, what you said was reasonable." He studied my face for a moment and I was surprised at his intensity as he said, "Still, you did cut up rather sharp at the poor little thing. I wondered at it. I wonder still."

I thought furiously for a moment before I said, "In this instance I believe I was right to do so. Lili knows nothing of the world. And as we are both aware, the world is not a nice place, especially in the larger cities like Vienna and London. Why, I have heard there are even kindly old women who wait at the inns where coaches from the country come in, to prey on young girls alone come to town to seek work. Before you know it, they are whisked off to bordellos, their lives ruined."

"Very true. Lili, however, is not likely to fall among such procurers. She's too young."

I did not reply. Instead I said, "I'll see she has some pocket money when she goes out so she might buy herself an ice or a pretty ribbon if one catches her eye. I'll not have her beholden to strange, *kind* gentlemen."

Alastair bent closer. His clear green eyes seemed to see entirely too much, but I dared not look away. "Now what, I wonder," he said softly, "happened to you to give you such a dislike of strange men? Dare I ask?"

"You may ask all you like. I have nothing to say except I have heard things, and in one case, observed for myself man's scheming and perfidy. Believe me, Alastair, I do not intend to make Lili fear men, for to do so would be to do your sex an injustice, but I must make her more circumspect."

I turned to the door, proud of how I had acquitted myself. "You dine in tonight, sir?" I asked over my shoulder.

"Did I forget to tell you? Tonight is the night of the weekly ball at the Hofburg Palace. I have procured tickets for us. We shall dine here early, then attend the ball." He seemed to sense the question hovering on my lips for he smiled as he added, "No, of course La Potter is not invited. She did not even badger me, for she knew it was impossible. I do warn you, however, she will interrogate you tomorrow to a fare-thee-well, so be prepared."

I nodded, but my mind was already busy trying to decide which of my gowns to wear, and whether it would be possible to borrow Mrs. Potter's own abigail to do my hair.

I need not have worried. Mrs. Potter was more than generous, bustling in and out of my room as I was dressing, full of suggestions and various accessories she begged me to try. I was able to refuse a towering sweep of ostrich feathers dyed bright green by saying it would not go with my gown, and I would not let her have the maid sew on a number of flounces "to fancy you up," as she put it. I could tell she thought my sea-green ballgown very plain with its severe lines and modest tucks. And although I did accept an emerald necklace and delicate ear bobs, I refused to consider a matching tiara that was so ornate it was downright vulgar.

"But my dear, you are a *countess*!" my hostess exclaimed, disappointed I would not take it. "If I were a countess, I would wear a tiara all the time."

I had a sudden vision of the lady fast asleep and snoring, with a large tiara set crooked on her head, and it was all I could do not to smile.

"Truly, ma'am, tiaras are generally worn only on state occasions with red velvet and ermine," I instructed her as kindly as I could. "You know, for coronations and the like."

"Paltry stuff, I say," the woman sniffed. "And what's the good of having a title if you can't let the world know you do?"

I turned away so the maid could begin to arrange

my hair. "Indeed, there's very little good to it at all," I said softly.

Fortunately Alva Potter did not hear such a radical remark, for she had suddenly remembered a beaded reticule she was sure would be just the thing to complete my ensemble and had hurried off to fetch it. Her maid and I avoided each other's eye until she returned bearing her hideous prize. Of coquelicot silk, it was covered with a design of birds and flowers in vivid blue and gold and purple. I was hard put to conceal my revulsion when I refused it, and it was all I could do not to laugh out loud when Mrs. Potter muttered that perhaps 'twas just as well she wasn't a countess, if being one meant you had to dress as plain as a vicar's wife.

Chapter Seven

It was an education to observe my cousin Alastair that evening.

From the time we arrived at the palace and joined the throngs making their way up the broad staircase to greet the Austrian emperor and empress, to our last farewell, he was a perfect example of the correct behavior of one of London's premier beaux. His manner was either witty and pleasant—to his equals and betters—or cool and distant to those below him in status and rank. As for the inferiors, he not only did not even acknowledge their existence—he appeared not to see them at all. Not that he was rude. He would have been horrified to be accused of that, for he was, when all was said and done, a gentleman. But no encroaching mushroom intent on presenting a young daughter for Alastair's approval could have mistaken the ennui with which Mr. Russell raised his quizzing glass to inspect the girl, the tiny yawn he hid as he did so, or the bland dismissing remark he delivered in such a careless monotone. And if, as happened once, such tactics did not discourage the man immediately, he was not above issuing a dismissal before he turned his back and strolled away. Alastair Russell had standards to uphold and he was well aware of it.

On his arm, I was treated with deference and a keen interest. Those I had met in the Prater that afternoon reclaimed our acquaintance with glad cries and happy smiles, while others, less fortunate, meeting me for the first time, did so with every semblance of awed delight. I did not know whether to laugh or cry, for it was all so ridiculous. When I said so to Alastair as he led me out for the opening dance, he nodded. "Of course it is. But you must admit, it is a pleasant experience to be lionized. Enjoy it, coz. I always do. And when you reach a point where you want to throw up your hands in disgust, just think how uncomfortable it would be to be outside society, snubbed and ignored."

I could say no more for the music began then and we were swept up in a lively polonaise. To my surprise and delight, the emperor and empress led the dancers through this ballroom to the next, just as huge, then out to the hallway and up a grand staircase. The dance ended in the royal audience room with the orchestra striving manfully to accompany us. The staircase was a special challenge, but Alastair and I acquitted ourselves well, unlike some others who stumbled or faltered and had to withdraw. Alastair was a magnificent dancer. Naturally.

"I would not have thought you could perform the dance so well, coz," he remarked at its conclusion as he accepted two flutes of champagne from a hovering footman and I fanned my heated cheeks.

"Now what am I to make of that statement, I wonder? It does not sound like a compliment exactly, still . . ."

"I only meant that for one who has spent most of her short life in relative obscurity, I had not expected such grace and deftness. We shall have to see how you perform the waltz."

"Ah, never even hint at such a possibility, dear sir," I cried in mock horror. "Now I shall live in abject terror that I might miss my step, or worse, tread on your gorgeously polished evening pumps. I declare, I shall be nothing but trepidation from this moment on, all my pleasure in the evening fled away!"

"You are being very silly, ma'am. As if my opinion of your behavior mattered to you. I know better," he remarked just before some friends of his interrupted us. I do not think he was upset at me, for a little smile hovered at the corners of that handsome mouth of his. I smiled in return.

I danced with several other gentlemen that evening. Indeed, Alastair was right. It was pleasant being one of the belles at the weekly Hofburg ball, frequently begged for a dance and treated so reverently. I would have been a most unusual female not to enjoy it to the hilt. And so I did. I also waltzed with Alastair, not once but twice. It was an exhilarating experience, and later, I warned myself I must not lose my head over it, or his smiling attention. He was my escort, and as such would behave scrupulously, always solicitous of my welfare, always careful to see I was not tired, or too warm, or in need of refreshment. It was nothing but common courtesy, and in my heart I knew it. I must not start making up stories, as Lili was so wont to do, pretending Alastair felt a warmer regard for me than just cousinly affection. At twenty-six I was too old for such flights of fancy.

It was sometime after the lavish supper had been spread for the guests' enjoyment in one of the larger rooms that all my pleasure in the evening disappeared as if it had never been. Alastair and I had just left the company of the Marquess and Marchioness of Wendover when his attention was claimed by a gentleman we had not met before. Not caring to intrude, I turned a little aside, wielding my fan gently, for the rooms were growing warm. And then I saw him and it was all I could do not to cry out. In shock. In revulsion. In terror.

I made myself take several deep, steadying breaths as I stared at him, unable to take my eyes away. I could tell by the erratic beat of my heart, the cold clammy feeling of my skin, and a sudden light-headedness that I was close to fainting, and I was determined I would not disgrace myself in such a way.

It had been a very long time, years and years in fact, but there was no question in my mind that the ordinary-looking gentleman in the bottle green evening jacket some little distance away was the same man I remembered. Indeed, I knew I would never forget him if I lived to be a hundred. As if aware he was being stared at, he looked around then and caught my eye. He only bowed a little, as if to a stranger. Could it be possible he had forgotten? Possible he did not recognize me? I was indignant as well as horrified and I turned my back on him abruptly. Alastair caught me at it and looked a question. I knew my cheeks must be blazing.

"It is so warm here," I said before he could question me. "Is there no place we can get a breath of air?"

"Of course," he murmured. "Unbearable things, balls. The heat of such crowds, so many candles . . ."

He continued talking lightly as he led me from the room and up a staircase away from the party. It was quieter on the next floor, and cooler, although not by much. We went down a wide hallway to a small sitting room at the end that had a pair of French doors opening on a balcony. When I would have stepped outside, he held me back.

"I've no idea if that balcony is safe, coz," he warned. "This is a huge old pile, you know, and who knows in what repair? And I've no intention of ending up splayed all over an Austrian courtyard. Not my style at all. What happened back there in the ballroom to upset you, by the way?"

His sudden change of subject was unnerving, and without thinking, I answered honestly. "I saw someone I knew from long ago," I told him.

"Obviously not someone you loved and revered."

His tone was wry. Although he had not asked another question, I felt compelled to go on. "No, I detest the man. For very good reason. I am sorry he is here. I have avoided him all these years, and I would have preferred to continue to do so."

"I see no reason why you still can't," Alastair said, to my relief not looking at me but out over the lights of the city spread below us to the countryside beyond. "Who is he? I shall contrive to arrange it."

It was then I felt the need for caution. "There is no

need for you to bother, coz. I doubt I will have any occasion to meet him. And if I should, in a general way, you know, I shall merely snub him. I am sure I will be able to manage that. After all, I have had an excellent instructor in the art of dampening unwanted pretension this evening to serve as my guide."

He did not reply for a moment and I found I was holding my breath.

"Very well," he said at last. "We will not discuss the man. However, if he should become a problem to you, I trust you will take me into your confidence, something you are obviously loath to do now. I am not without the resources to deal with such a situation, and as your cousin, I find I insist on serving as your protector in this, as in everything. It is, after all, why you brought me along in the first place, is it not? Why you are paying me such a munificent sum of money?"

I was shocked. We had not referred to the money since we had reached an agreement in London several weeks ago. When I had first approached Alastair and asked for his assistance, I had treated the matter like the business arrangement it was. And when he had agreed, I had turned over the amount we had agreed on as payment, as well as a large sum necessary for our journey. We had not referred to it again. Until now. I wondered I should feel so hurt he would mention it again. Perhaps because I felt we had traveled beyond that business arrangement to friendship, and now he had let me know it was no such thing?

"Of course," I made myself say through suddenly dry lips. "I shall do so, I promise. If the need arises, that is, not that I expect it to. Shall we return to the ball now? I find I am feeling much more comfortable. By the way, how long do these occasions go on? It must be almost three in the morning."

He replied and we discussed the ball as we retraced our steps. I wanted to excuse myself then and seek a room set aside for the ladies until the ache in my throat disappeared, but I made myself remain by his side until a young gentleman asked me to dance for the second time. He seemed to feel dancing attendance on me might somehow cause some of Alastair's polish to rub off on him. I did not disillusion him.

We did not get home to the mansion on Johannesgasse until after four in the morning. Neither Alastair nor I spoke on the short journey. I leaned back on the gray velvet carriage seat, my eyes closed as if in exhaustion, and Alastair gazed out the window beside him as if fascinated by the quiet Viennese streets. We parted with only a word as well, and I made my way up the stairs, praying Alva Potter had not waited up for a firsthand impression of the evening's festivities. If she had, I told myself as I tiptoed down the hall, I would be forced to be rude, hostess or no.

But no one was awake except for her maid, who was waiting to help me undress and brush out my hair. After she left me, I found myself staring at the door that connected my room with Alastair's. I knew he would not come through that door for a glass of port and some whispered conversation. Not tonight, he wouldn't.

I went over to the window and pulled the draperies aside to stare down into the street. Nothing moved there, not even a stray cat. All the good burghers of Vienna and their wives were fast asleep. I envied them their peaceful dreams.

I wished I had been able to tell Alastair everything, even though I knew how impossible that was. It had been a secret for too long, a secret that involved other members of my family as well as myself. A secret I was not free to reveal to anyone, for hadn't I promised on my honor I would not?

I sank down on the chaise then, rubbing my temples to relieve the tension I felt.

How long ago had it been? Thirteen years? Fourteen? It was amazing how little he had changed in all that time. Of course, if I had been closer, I am sure I would have seen some of time's ravages—a few wrinkles perhaps, a broken vein or two, some gray hair mixed in the chestnut brown.

Such an ordinary man he had been—so ordinary still. No one would ever have bothered to look at him twice. And no one, amused by his sudden, blinding grin, his happy laugh, and enticed by his light careless conversation, would have been able to discern how evil a creature he was. Satan's own, my grandmother had called him. She had been right.

Was it really possible he did not remember me or my family? Had he put us from his mind as easily as that? Well, no matter how that angered me, I, who had spent how many years in deep regret and barely contained rage—it did make it easier for me. I was the widowed Countess of Wyckend now, not little Cornelia Wakefield of Berkshire, the second daughter of Sir Reginald Wakefield. I was a countess with a proud name and estate and a considerable fortune. Someone to be reckoned with, not a minor baronet's daughter of little importance. And there was Alastair Russell to contend with besides. No, I was well-equipped to deal with the man I had seen this evening, if it came to that at last.

For a moment I toyed with the idea of bringing him down, exposing him even. I had the money to make that happen. But I knew I could never do it. For if he was exposed, the secret would be as well, and I could not do that, to Phillipa especially. She had given up so much for me. I could not ask her for more.

At last I rose and went wearily to bed. Dawn was not far off, although from the patter of rain I could hear striking the panes now, I knew it would be a misty gray morning at best. I told myself it did not matter as I turned over on my side and pulled the silken coverlet to my chin. A rainy day would suit my mood exactly.

Chapter Eight

I was not belowstairs until almost noon. My sleep had been troubled, full of strange fragments of dreams that ran into each other and made no sense at all. I felt leaden and heavy, quite a different creature from the woman who had gone to the Hofburg ball and danced the night away.

I had been sure Alva Potter would be waiting to pounce on me, impatient to hear about the evening's festivities, and I had braced myself for the encounter. To my surprise, it was Lili who came from the library to intercept me as I crossed the hall.

"If I might have a few minutes, ma'am?" she asked in a stiff little voice.

I looked at her carefully, ashamed I had forgotten her so completely. She did not look as if she had slept well either, and it was obvious from her red-rimmed eyes she had been crying recently. I fancied I could see the tracks of tears on her cheeks.

We went into the library and I shut the door behind us after informing the butler I did not care to be disturbed—by anyone.

"I must beg your pardon, ma'am," Lili began, not even waiting until we were seated. "My behavior yesterday was disgraceful. To question your advice, to argue with you, and after all you have done for me, too. I am so ashamed!"

Her tears welled up again and I took her in my arms for a hug. "Come now, Lili, it was not so bad," I said, to encourage her. "Everyone has a difference of opinion occasionally. And I was at fault, too."

She leaned back against my arm to search my face, as if to make sure I was sincere.

"Yes, I was. I should have given you some pin money so you would not have had to take a stranger's. Now that was wrong of you. I have not changed my mind about that. But come, let us sit down. Now we are alone there are things I must tell you."

She looked mystified, but she obeyed willingly enough. For myself, I wished we might have this chat some other time, when I was feeling more the thing, but that was not to be.

"I could not speak freely yesterday, when Alastair was with us," I began, not quite sure even now how I was going to go on. Then I steeled myself and continued, "It would have been bad enough if your benefactor had been a woman, but to be accepting favors from a strange man was asking for trouble. Now, all men do not wish us harm, but some of them do. And it is those few you must always be on your guard against. Men like that can be perfectly charming one moment, and demons the next, demanding payment for their kindness and tearing it from you if you refuse to give it up willingly."

I searched her face as I spoke, looking for some sign she understood what I was referring to, but to my chagrin, she only looked perplexed. It was then I told her the truth about babies, forever banishing the lovely myth that it only took a kiss to produce a child. I cannot begin to describe how awkward it all was. I had not realized how strained the words would sound, how hard it would be to say them aloud to a young girl who had no idea what went on between a man and a woman.

"So you see, Lili, that is why I was upset with you yesterday," I concluded. "Suppose that man had suggested you go for a stroll? Promised you an ice? Suppose he had contrived to get rid of the groom? Men are strong. You would not have been able to fight him, and he would have forced you. It is called rape. I am told it is ugly and painful and humiliating."

She was frowning now, and still looking puzzled. When I asked her what confused her, she said, "But I don't understand. I have seen women and their children. They look so happy! And men and women together, talking and laughing. Why would women behave that way if being with a man was so awful?"

"It isn't generally," I said quickly, anxious to dispel any notion she might have formed that lovemaking was an undesirable thing. "When you love a man, and he loves you, ah, then it is different. Because you want him. Because you are in love. But you must wait for that love, guard yourself until it comes."

"I see," she said slowly. "Why, I had no idea! It all seems very strange and awkward, and I am having trouble believing it happens. And I can't imagine *wanting* someone to do that to me. But maybe that is because I am young. Maybe when I am older I will feel differently about it. Do you think I might, ma'am?"

I could tell she had very real doubts about it, and I hid a smile as I assured her I did.

"I wonder if the sisters know about this?" she asked next. "But if they did, that would mean they *lied* to me when they told me about kissing. I can't believe they would lie."

I told her the good nuns had probably been as uninformed as she had been, for I could not bear for her to lose her faith in them.

To forestall any more questions I would rather not answer, I changed the subject by asking her if she had gone to church this morning with her maid. It was still raining, harder now. I could see we were destined for a day spent indoors.

In anticipation of Mrs. Potter's interrogation, I had brought my workbasket down with me, thinking to do some embroidery while she questioned me. Lili followed me to the morning room, where we found our hostess waiting impatiently.

She had a million questions, or so it seemed, and

she was especially enthralled by my description of the empress's gown.

"And, I daresay, she was wearing a tiara, eh, my dear Countess?" she asked archly as I threaded my needle with some delicate coral silk.

"A small one, yes. She is an empress, ma'am, not a mere countess, and she was presiding over an entertainment given in her own palace."

"Was the emperor in uniform?" she asked next.

I described his white jacket and tight breeches, the broad sash and medals he wore. Lili was as enthralled as Mrs. Potter. In fact, the two of them reminded me of small children crouched close to your knee while you spin them a fairy tale.

I then told them of the gay polonaise that had been danced through the rooms and up the stairs. Lili clapped her hands in delight as she pictured it. Mrs. Potter was not so sure such romping suited her ideas of royal dignity. But she soon forgot to be affronted and demanded to know what various ladies had worn, their jewels and accessories. I complied as well as I could. I also described the decorations, the ballroom decor, the sumptuous supper we had enjoyed.

"Did you dance every dance, ma'am?" Lili asked when I paused for breath.

"Just about," I said as I set another stitch. "For some reason, being in Alastair's company made me popular. But perhaps it was because I avoid society at home and was therefore a fresh face that made me so sought after."

"No, no, I am sure being escorted by Al-as-tair made the difference! He looked so splendid in his evening clothes, didn't he?" Lili demanded before she sighed.

"He's not for the likes of you, gel," Alva Potter told her, her harsh, prosaic accents destroying any dreams Lili might be cherishing. "No need to think he'll wait for you to grow up and be his bride. Mr. Russell has better fish to fry. In fact, I'd be surprised if he ever marries at all."

She had risen as she spoke and now was smoothing the front of her ornate morning gown. "No, he'll die a bachelor, you mark my words. He's as good as married already, y'see. To himself!"

She was still chuckling as she left the room and went down the hall.

"Whatever did she mean by it, ma'am?" Lili demanded, stooping to pick up some silks that had rolled off my lap. "You can't be married to yourself."

I thought Mrs. Potter had been cleverer than I would have supposed possible. For it was true. Alastair's preoccupation with himself showed he was his main concern. It was a marriage of sorts, if you will. Still, I knew how Lili worshipped the man, so I only shrugged and said I hadn't the slightest idea what she had been talking about.

I spent the day with Lili. I made great strides with my embroidery, and I read and wrote letters, to my friends and to my man of business. Alastair had not asked for more, but I am sure the purse I had given him for expenses was growing light. After all, we had not planned to travel to Austria, nor spend any time here, so I asked that an additional sum of money be sent to me, care of Alva Potter.

I admit I also spent the day waiting. Waiting to see Alastair so I could study his face, listen carefully to his inflection, try to discover if he were angry with me because I would not confide in him. But I waited in vain, for there was no sign of him all day, and he dined out that evening as well. I envied him his friends. Several hours of Alva Potter's company could be trying. So trying I excused myself almost immediately after dinner and went upstairs in Lili's wake as she took herself, yawning, to bed.

I had provided myself with a book from the library earlier, one of the few in English to be found there. I knew I would not be able to sleep at this early hour, and disturbed by the amount of time I had spent thinking of Alastair today, and waiting for him, I had decided reading might give my mind another direction.

The book was not very interesting, however. Supposedly a novel, it seemed more a discourse about travel on the continent in the early 1700s. I had a chuckle or two over the mannerisms popular then, and the clothes worn that seemed very unwieldly, especially for women, and I made myself persevere.

I heard the hall clock strike eleven, then twelve. I sensed the household was settling down for the night. I had not heard Alastair come in, and I wondered if he intended to make a night of it somewhere else. From what I could tell, he had had a number of almost blatant invitations to do so last evening. A Mrs. Harrison, for example, a bold brunette with flashing dark eyes and lips fresh from the rouge pot, was especially broad in her hints. Had he gone to her? I hoped not. I told myself piously that Mrs. Harrison did not look any better than she should be.

Then there had been a Lady Florence. She was a delicate, ethereal blonde dressed in a gown of palest blue. She had whispered in Alastair's ear for a long time. I had not been able to read anything in his expression. However, I would have wagered anything you like the lady was not discussing the weather, the state of war-torn Europe, or the impossibility of finding and keeping good help. No, indeed.

I put the book down and rose to pace my enormous room. There I was, thinking of the dratted man again, I scolded myself. What difference did it make to me if he spent the night in some eager lady's arms? He was nothing to me. He never had been and he never would be. But oh, it had been lovely being friends with him on our journey together! I had never had a male friend, not really. My brother George was ages older than I, and all I remembered of him during my childhood was his disapproval of my escapades and the lengthy sermons he delivered which echoed those thundered at me by my father. No, all in all, I had had few pleasant experiences with gentlemen.

As for my husband, Ogden, the Earl of Wyckend,

I could never think of him as a friend. As a business associate, perhaps, but a friend? Never.

But Alastair and I had shared a number of laughs together, and occasionally long conversations of great interest. And he had not treated me as an ignorant woman with more hair than wit. He had a way of making one feel important, listening carefully as if the ideas one put forward had real merit and deserved to be considered carefully.

I wished he were different, though. I wished he weren't so "married to himself," as Alva Potter had put it. It made it seem that his concern, when he showed it, was only an act.

I did not call a maid that evening, but undressed myself and washed in the cold water left in the pitcher. I hung up my gown and tucked my slippers away in the armoire. As I did so, I saw the sea-green gown I had worn last evening, and I spread out the skirt to admire it. A faint whiff of my perfume rose from the folds. It really was a pretty gown, and it became me. Alastair had told me so again when . . .

Damn it! I could not seem to get the man from my mind! Hastily, I shut the cupboard doors and marched off to bed. I was just about to climb in when I heard a faint voice in the hallway and ran over to see if I could discover who it was.

"—wake you at eleven," the valet Alastair had been lucky enough to find was saying. "A good night to you, sir."

I waited until there was not a sound to be heard anywhere, chewing my thumbnail and thinking hard. Surely it could only grow more unpleasant if Alastair and I continued at odds. And as time went by, more difficult to regain our former rapport. But if I went to him tonight, tried to explain why I could not confide in him, begged him to understand, well, that might make all the difference. It also occurred to me that I could just pack Lili and myself up and make arrangements to return home with some other travelers as soon as a group was assembled. I had learned last evening that people came and went all the time in Vienna, some staying as little as a week before they returned to England. I would not even require Alastair to accompany us. But that solution I discarded immediately.

I did not even consider my attire as I tapped on the door between our rooms. Without waiting for a response, I opened that door and stepped inside his room. He was standing over beside a desk, looking down at some papers, brandy snifter in hand. As he raised his head and stared at me, I gulped, suddenly aware of what he must think—how this must look—and I wanted to die.

"Yes?" he asked. "There was something you wished to see me about, madam?"

Loosening my fingers, for my nails had been digging half moons in both palms, I nodded and came forward. "Yes. Yes, there is," I told him. I looked at his snifter. "I wonder if I might have some brandy, too?" I asked. "For some reason I am finding this difficult beyond belief."

"And the brandy will ease your way?" he asked over his shoulder as he went to a drinks table against one wall, to do my bidding.

"Probably not, but I think I had better have some anyway."

"There you are. Swirl it around and warm it between your hands before you drink it," he instructed.

I wanted to tell him I knew how to treat fine brandy, but instead I stared down at the amber liqueur as if I had never seen anything half as fascinating.

"Won't you sit down, coz?" Alastair asked, indicating a pair of sofas flanking the empty fireplace. As I obeyed, I thought how unseasonably warm it had been for early October. Winter seemed an age away, yet . . .

Can you believe I was so nervous I was thinking of the *weather*? Scolding myself mentally, I took a small sip of brandy. It warmed me all the way down to my stomach and it did give me the courage to say, "I had to see you, coz." As I spoke, I made myself look at him where he leaned against the mantel. He had not undressed for the night. I had to be grateful for that although it did not make the situation any less fraught with tension. He was wearing a dark green silk dressing gown over his breeches, and his shirt was unbuttoned for ease. His perfectly combed blond hair shone in the candlelight. He looked—sensational.

"I have not been comfortable today," I made myself say. "I have not been comfortable since we parted last night. I knew you were upset with me because I would not confide in you, and I—"

"But it is not my place to be 'upset,' " he interrupted. "Indeed, I was much at fault, for as your hired companion, I must be agreeable to all your wishes."

"Stop it," I said fiercely. "You are not any such thing, and you know it."

"Well, I had not thought so until last evening," he agreed as he strolled over to take the seat beside me.

I took another sip of my drink. "It is just that this secret I have is not mine alone. There are other people involved and I promised on my honor not to reveal it. You do see my dilemma, don't you?"

He nodded and I saw he was studying me carefully. Flustered, I tried to brush my hair back where it had fallen over my shoulder, but it was awkward with the snifter in my hand. To my surprise, Alastair reached out and smoothed it back behind my ear for me.

"Don't you wear a ribbon to tame those curls? Or a nightcap?" he asked, sounding amused.

"I don't like nightcaps and I always lose the ribbon," I said, wondering how we had strayed so far from the subject under discussion.

"You have a problem indeed," he remarked. I did not think he was still talking about an absent hair ribbon.

"I take it this, er, secret you hold concerns the man you saw last evening at the Hofburg ball?" he went on.

"Yes, it does," I admitted, recalling how that man had not even appeared to recognize me. "As I told you, I do not expect to have any contact with him. He won't seek me out and you may be sure I will avoid him like the plague."

"So it is unlikely there will be trouble? Trouble I should be looking out for even though I am not privy to your secret?"

"No, I don't believe so. I reacted as I did last evening because I was startled. It has been a long time."

"Drink up your brandy, 'Nelia," he ordered, using the pet name from my childhood. "Time we both sought our beds."

As I obeyed, he added, "I am sorry you were distressed today. I did not think any poor action of mine could cause you pain or I would have been more careful. Try not to put too damaging an interpretation on my pique, if you please. No doubt it was only the result of my conceit. I meant nothing more by it."

"But we are friends, aren't we?" I asked, peering at him over the rim of my snifter.

Did I imagine he hesitated for a moment? Imagine he appeared to be thinking about it? I felt my spirits plummet. I wanted so badly to remain in Alastair Russell's good graces. I wanted to know he approved of me, liked me, was proud to call me cousin and friend, as I was beginning to be proud of him.

"Yes, if you say so, 'Nelia," he said slowly, and I smiled at him.

He did not return that smile. Instead, he waited patiently until I handed him the empty snifter. As I rose, I tightened the sash of my robe, conscious once again of my unorthodox attire, the flimsy material that was all that hid my nakedness from him. As I started for the door, I stumbled a bit and his arm came around me in support. It felt wonderful and it was all I could do not to lean back against it and turn toward him. I did not understand myself in the slightest, and so I bade him an almost brusque good night and fled into the safety of my own room.

Could it be I was falling in love with Alastair, I wondered? But that was impossible. As I climbed into bed and pulled up the covers, I told myself it was only our close proximity and the length of our association that prompted me to even think such a ridiculous thing.

Alastair Russell was not for me, and I, heaven knows, was most certainly not for him. Or any man, come to think of it.

Chapter Nine

In the days that followed, I did not see the man who had startled me so badly, and you may be sure I was on the lookout for him. Most days Lili and I spent the morning with Mrs. Potter. Alastair, of course, slept late. We either went for a drive around Vienna, ending up at the Hofburg gates, or did some shopping. I was stunned at the things Alva Potter decided she must have. One was a set of sixteen side chairs covered in a hideous brocade, which she chose because the shop owner assured her they had belonged to a cousin of the royal family. I could tell Mrs. Potter was sure the empress must have placed her royal backside on them on more than one occasion. Then there was a set of pearls: ropes of necklaces, ear bobs, a brooch, and several bracelets. She also commissioned a high-perch phaeton as a gift for Alastair, to be done in bright yellow with scarlet wheels. Lili observed her with awe, and it is true the amount of money she could spend in a morning was stupendous.

Once I went to church at dawn with Lili and her maid. As I believe I mentioned, I am not Catholic, but I wished to see if anyone followed the girls, or stared at them during the service. As far as I could tell, the early Mass was attended only by working people, and no one paid us any mind.

Sometimes Alastair joined us in the afternoon when Alva Potter took a customary nap. We went to the royal summer palace, the Schonbrunn, on the River Wien, and to the Vienna Woods on more than one occasion. Lili was enchanted with the tiny villages tucked here and there in the woods, some no more than a few houses at a crossroads. I tried to picture the scene in winter when the snow lay deep. Surely the hearty woodcutters and their families must feel isolated then.

I certainly enjoyed our afternoons more than I did the mornings, and I am sure Lili felt the same. It was obvious Alva Potter considered the girl a nuisance, for she never missed a chance to say something cutting to her, or to point out her youth, her naïveté, her ignorance about wordly matters. I asked her once why she did not like Lili, one time when we were alone, and she appeared flustered for a moment. Then she said, "Well, I've never been one to be mealy-mouthed, so I'll speak right out, Countess. The gel takes advantage of you, and she has no right to do so. Oh, I can see by your resemblance that she was born of your family, but I've heard of these convent misses. Oh yes, I wasn't born yesterday! I'd be willing to wager the gel's a bastard, tucked away there to hide some relative's shame. And now you, so good of you, I'm sure—must take responsibility for the chit. It's a shame, that's what it is—a shame!"

I was stunned by this assessment, and I hastened to say, "I hope you have not wagered any sum on it, however, ma'am, for you would have to forfeit it. Lili is not a bastard, why, what a thing to say! She is the legitimate daughter of Thora and Thomas Martingale. Thora Edson was a second cousin of my mother's. As for our resemblance, it is the widow's peak a great many women in my family have that distinguishes them, and the black curls. I do hope you will be kinder to Lili now you know her background."

Grudgingly, Alva Potter said she would try, but I also heard her mutter she couldn't abide young girls, so I did not put much hope in it. I told Lili she was jealous of her, of her youth especially, and she said she understood and would pray for her.

In the evenings, Alastair and I went to balls and receptions and concerts. We also dined out on occasion with those of Alastair's acquaintance who had come to the Congress, either in their leased apartments or one of Vienna's superior restaurants. One memorable evening we went to Sperl's. The food was excellent, the music and dancing and general aura of good feeling outstanding. I told Alastair I was concerned I must be putting on weight, especially with all the rich desserts the Viennese loved. He only smiled and ordered me some *kirschen strudel* topped with *schlagobers,* which he knew was my favorite.

But when I asked Alastair how the peace settlements were progressing, he shrugged. I gathered little headway was being made for there were so many countries present, all with their own ideas of how Europe should be reapportioned now that Napoleon was exiled. Lili was interested in the Congress as well, although you may be sure I kept her far from any of the festivities, delighted she was only just thirteen and far from out. Never even in London had I seen such a blatant display of immorality as was to be found in Vienna. Courtesans parading as great ladies were normal. One, for instance, the Duchess of Sagan, had been married twice and twice divorced, and she was currently the mistress of Clemens Metternich, the Austrian Foreign Minister. He was one of the most important personages at the Congress, along with Talleyrand and our Robert Castlereagh, who headed the British delegation. It was hard to keep everyone straight, but certainly none of them were suitable companions for a girl only recently released from convent life. Still, Lili seemed to be happy in spite of the circumscribed life she led, and I reminded myself that, compared to the convent, her current routines must seem gay to dissipation. She had no chores to do, no lessons, and this seemed to upset her for she was always asking me if she could do some mending for me, or run an errand. She and the little Austrian maid who waited on her had become very close, chattering away in German on every occasion. I suspected Lili had even visited the girl's family. I did not mind that.

Lili was in no danger from honest Viennese. Besides, whenever she went out, one of the footmen was assigned to accompany her, if the maid was busy and could not do so.

But it was all too good to last, and I suppose I should not have been surprised to see the man I had been searching for at a military review one morning given by the Russians. Alastair and Alva were with us, and Lili was so excited she could hardly sit still.

"I declare you are giving me the fidgits, gel," our sharp-tongued hostess complained as Lili bounced up and down, trying to get a better look at the Russian czar in his form-fitting uniform with the blue sash of St. Andrew on it. "I am sure I don't know why you had to come along, if you can't behave yourself. You're too young, anyway."

I could tell by Lili's rebellious expression she wanted to point out that perhaps Mrs. Potter was too old, but of course she did no such thing.

"Oh, do look at the hat the lady is wearing," she cried instead, nodding at a woman who sat a few rows in front of us. I had to admit I had never seen anything like it, and I was chuckling at the diamond brooch that decorated the wide swooping brim and secured a spray of bright red cherries, when I felt someone's eyes on us. I turned and my breath caught in my throat when I saw that the man I had dreaded was studying Lili with a smile on his face. It was all I could do not to put my arm around her and hug her close to me for protection. He was closer to me than he had been at the ball and I saw there was indeed some gray in his hair. I wondered how old he was now. Thirty-six? Forty? He was staring quite blatantly too, as if he did not care who saw him. No one could blame him. Lili looked quite charming this morning with her black curls tied back with a scarlet satin ribbon under her broad-brimmed sailor hat and her slim, straight figure dressed in a girlish white muslin that ended at mid-calf, as was suitable for a miss her age. Her hose was white as well, and she wore red kid slippers. Her blue eyes were sparkling with her delight, and a gentle color came and went in her cheeks. Silently I vowed she would never come to any harm if I had anything to say about it.

I made myself stare at the man as intently as he was staring at Lili. Eventually, made uncomfortable, he turned in my direction and I glared at him. I know you, I told him silently. I know the evil you are capable of, and there is no way on earth I will allow you anywhere near this child. He peered at me with an arrested expression and I knew it was possible he had identified me.

"That man, Countess," Alva Potter demanded, grasping my arm to get my attention. "Why is he looking at you that way? Do you know him? Is he anyone important? And does he have a title?"

"He is Viscount Melton, Alva," Alastair told her. Startled by his voice, I looked at him and he nodded, as if to say he knew this was the man who had upset me earlier. It was strange, this rapport we had acquired, Alastair Russell and I. I could swear sometimes I knew exactly what he was going to say before he even began.

"Is it a new title? Or one of those trumped-up Irish ones?" Mrs. Potter insisted, shading her eyes to get a better look at Melton. Lili was paying no attention to us for she was busy watching the Russian troops marshall at the end of the field. I was glad.

"He is Gregory Paxton of Dorset. His family has held the title for several generations," Alastair said patiently.

"Aaaah," Alva Potter said in satisfaction as she gave the viscount her most winning smile. He did not see it, for unnerved by the glares I was sending his way, he had turned his back on us.

The review began and we watched as several mounted regiments cantered to the front of the stand, then halted together to salute their czar. Lili exclaimed at the Cossack soldiers on their sturdy ponies who raised their lances in unison and roared their allegiance, and she laughed and clapped when later soldiers performed some Russian dances, squatting on their haunches with their arms crossed over their chests as they threw first one leg, then the other before them. I do not know how they managed the thing, or kept their balance. Surely they were in superb physical condition.

But at no time during the review, fascinating as it was, did I forget Gregory Paxton, and every so often I would glance his way. It was as if I had to be sure I could keep an eye on him, be certain that he hadn't somehow managed to exchange his seat in the stands for one closer to Lili. I ached to hustle her away as soon as the review and demonstrations were over, but of course I couldn't do that. As we were gathering our things preparatory to leaving, she suddenly cried, "Why, look, there's the man who gave me the fare for the carousel! I shall pay him back right now."

I opened my mouth to forbid her to do any such thing, but Alastair was quicker. "I'm closer, Lili," he said easily. "I'll see he gets his money back."

As we made our slow way from the stands, I saw the two men meet. Alastair handed him a coin and exchanged a few words with him. Melton appeared to be asking a question. No doubt he wanted to know Lili's name and direction. I prayed my cousin would be able to withhold that information. When Alastair returned, I had no chance to question him for Alva Potter was close by. She seemed to sense there were undercurrents in the air, and she was determined not to be left out of whatever scandalbroth was brewing. Gossip about the *ton* was her bread and butter. I knew I should not look down on her for her preoccupation, but I could not help it. What difference could it make to her, after all, if she discovered who had discarded one mistress for another, or which wife had taken a lover right under her husband's nose? It was not as if she had anyone to discuss it with.

When she would have lingered, even moved in the viscount's direction, I grasped her arm and led her away. "Come along now, do, ma'am," I said. "It is bad *ton* to tarry. Lili, step smartly."

The girl turned almost reluctantly. I think she had hoped to have a few words with the viscount herself, and I shuddered and resolved to speak to her. On the drive back to the house I let the others talk while I thought of the situation we had just escaped. It was unfortunate Melton was here in Vienna; no, it was actually a disaster, especially since Lili had managed to capture his eye. Could I keep them apart? Keep him from talking to her, entrancing her as he was so capable of doing and with such little effort, too? A picture of his pleasant face, those sleepy eyes and the artless grin he had—his easy, funny conversation and childlike sense of the ridiculous—came to mind. Well, I would try. If necessary I would take Lili and leave Vienna for home. We had been here for some time now, and while I would be the first to admit it had been a pleasant experience, especially with Alastair Russell as my escort, I could survive without it. True, I would be sorry to miss the Peace Ball that Metternich and his wife were giving this coming week—I had heard it was to be an outstanding evening—but I could survive the loss of it. And if Alastair did not care to leave, well, Lili and I could travel with some other English people making their way home.

I ached to ask Alastair what he had said to the viscount, and Melton replied, but when we reached the house, he announced he had another appointment and would not join us until later at dinner. We were to attend a reception that evening, the two of us, and I knew we would have time to talk then. With that I had to be content.

I made a point of following Lili up to her room, where she went to remove her hat. I could tell that her little maid was sorry when I dismissed her. No doubt she had been waiting to hear all about the review.

"Lili, do sit down here with me a moment," I said,

patting the space beside me as I perched on the side of her bed.

"There is something I must tell you," I added as she obeyed. "That man—the one who gave you the money for the carousel?—he is not a good person."

"How do you know?" she demanded, looking at me straightly. I could tell I was going to have trouble. I suspected she would not be persuaded to shun him unless I gave her a good reason. I wondered if the nuns had ever wished, as I did, the girl was not quite so stubborn and strong-willed.

"I met him once long ago. Trust me. He is a bad man. Very bad."

"Why do you say so? What did he do?" she asked, her blue eyes dark with feeling.

"I cannot tell you. It is another's secret. But you may believe I am speaking truthfully, from my concern for you."

"I think it is too bad that you can't forgive and forget, ma'am," she lectured me, and I wanted to shake her. "The Lord asks us to pray for forgiveness of our sins as we pray for those who sin against us. It appears you have not forgiven the viscount. How do you know he has not changed? You said this all happened a long time ago. Perhaps he has reformed, or is trying to."

I could tell she was picturing herself leading him into the light, and I stiffened. "He has not reformed, Lili. Men like him never do. Kindly forget your charming scheme to convert him. You must believe me. I have lived in the world a great deal longer than you have. Melton is an evil man, and all his smiles and soft talk and little jests are only a means to lure you into his confidence, make you complacent and careless. You must promise me you will never, ever, have anything to do with him again, and if he should try and talk to you, you will run away as fast as you can."

She hung her head, seemingly intent on tracing a pattern on the silk coverlet on her bed. "I—I can't do that," she said in a little voice. "It would be too cruel when all he did was try to be kind to me and see I had a good time."

My hand itched to slap her now, but I could tell by the tilt of that stubborn little chin that she was imagining going to the rack before she would promise any such thing. Had I ever really been thirteen? Like this? It was hard to believe.

Taking a deep breath, I said, "Then you will promise me something else or I shall forbid you to leave the house until we set off for England. You must promise me you will never go out without both your maid and a footman in attendance. There, now that is not so hard to do, is it?"

She thought for a moment before she nodded. Reluctantly, it was true, but she did nod and say, "Very well, ma'am. You have my word on it."

There didn't seem to be anything else to say, for she stared at me out of big tragic eyes that regretted my harshness and inhumanity. I made myself pat her cheek and smile before I left her. It had not ended as I had hoped, but I had gained a concession that I thought would keep her safe, and that was what mattered.

Later that day I was surprised to receive a call from Lady Florence Manning, the daughter of the Marquess of Kildeer. Lady Florence came with her companion, a pale quiet lady whose name I never did catch. I did not congratulate myself that I was the real purpose of the call; indeed, how could I when Lady Florence pouted so noticeably when informed that not only was Mr. Alastair Russell not at home, he was not expected either.

Today the young lady was dressed in an afternoon gown of palest lilac. It was nowhere near as revealing as her ballgown had been, yet somehow it appeared about to fall off one shoulder and expose a breast before landing in a flimsy heap at her feet. I decided the lady had a very talented dressmaker. With this creation she wore a soft-brimmed bonnet and carried a beaded reticule and a white cashmere stole.

"You are enjoying Vienna, Countess?" she asked. I hid a smile at the petulance in her voice which she did not bother to conceal.

We discussed the capital at some length before Lady Florence asked about my relationship to Alastair Russell. She was leaning forward, her mouth ajar, when Alva Potter threw open the door and rustled in, her afternoon nap concluded. I suspected she had learned yet another titled lady was adorning her drawing room and had made haste to join us. I could not help but look forward to the coming confrontation. I know, I know. It was very bad of me. Still . . .

Lady Florence looked stunned when I introduced my hostess. Alva had on one of her elaborate at-home gowns, all silk and lace and ribbons and flounces. This one had been chosen to complement the decor. It was a rich Bishop's blue and mulberry.

"I daresay you weren't expecting to meet me, your ladyship?" Alva said with her most brilliant smile as she edged her chair closer to the visitor's. When Lady Florence seemed disinclined to reply, she went on, "Well, I ain't of society but I've the fortune to make that no-never-mind. My late Adam, he who was Dan Potter, the rag and bottle man as he liked to call himself—all in jest, doncha know—left me well ahead with the world. Very well ahead indeed, ain't that so, Countess? You know, of course the countess is staying with me for the Congress, m'lady. And Mr. Alastair Russell as well."

She sat back, preening herself and peeking at Lady Florence to try and detect the awe she was sure her revelations must have inspired. When the visitor only stared at her, she colored up and said, all in a rush to me, "Did I interrupt some private meeting, ma'am? I would not have done so for the world, but Cranston told me it was just an afternoon call. Well! I'll part his hair for him, just see if I don't, and him what was the butler of the Duke of Harfield, too!"

Angry now at the blonde's arrogance, I assured Mrs. Potter she was most welcome to stay. But when she would have ordered a tea tray with pastries she told our guests would have them licking their fingers, Lady Florence rose and beat a hasty retreat.

I am afraid she had barely left the house before I excused myself as well and hurried up to my room. Once there, I am ashamed to admit, I flung myself on the bed and buried my face in a pillow to stifle the peals of laughter I could no longer contain. The look on the limpid blonde's face! I do not think she could have been more horrified if a tiger had sauntered in and settled down on the rug between us. And Mrs. Potter's description of her late husband—priceless! Still, when I eventually began to wipe my streaming eyes, I had to commend Alva Potter for her honesty. She had not tried to pretend to be anyone she was not, and I admired her directness.

I tried to shake out my crushed muslin, feeling better than I had for a long time. That is, I did until I remembered everyone in Vienna would learn about Alva Potter, probably by nightfall. That sobered me and not because of any snobbery on my part. No, it was because with our direction common knowledge, Gregory Paxton, Lord Melton, would know exactly where Lili could be found.

Chapter Ten

The reception Alastair and I attended that evening was held in a villa where a Lord and Lady Glendening had taken up residence. It was located a short distance from Vienna. Lady Glendening especially seemed to feel this a great hardship for her guests, and greeted everyone with her regrets they had had to travel so far. Since the drive had taken less than fifteen minutes, I thought her absurd. I could not tell what Alastair was thinking for he seemed preoccupied with some problem of his own. Since I had every intention of questioning him about his encounter with Viscount Melton, I hoped his mood would change.

For a while we strolled through the rooms, greeting other guests and every so often stopping to chat. When Alastair took two glasses of wine from a footman's tray and handed one to me, I said, "What a charming home this is. I cannot see why Lady Glendening dislikes it."

"She does not, of course. It was only something to say," he told me. "She would consider a journey of several hours appropriate if it afforded an opportunity to visit *her*.

"But I agree with you. These rooms are pleasant, so open and light with their cream and gold colors. Such a refreshing change from royal blue and heavy gold and scarlet."

"You are remembering Mrs. Potter's decor, sir?" I could not help asking, smiling at him as I did so.

But I would never know, for an unknown gentleman

interrupted then, asking Alastair for an introduction. I could see he was a man in his late twenties, and his warm smile and open admiration were reassuring. It soon became obvious he and Alastair had known each other since childhood, although Mr. Beaton told me they had since gone separate ways. "I inherited an estate in Oxfordshire," he confided, "and I can't get Alastair into the country. No one can. Still, I did hear today you spent most of last winter in Scotland, old fellow, visiting a great-aunt or somesuch person? An inheritance, I suppose. There couldn't be any other reason you would travel such a distance to what had to be a wretched location."

"Yes, I was in Scotland," Alastair admitted. He was standing beside me, and as much as I wanted to, I could not turn and look at him without being obvious. But his voice had been so stiff, so constrained. I wondered what had happened on that visit to his great-aunt that had affected him so.

"And you didn't become the heir," Beaton said. "I can tell that from your voice. Don't fret, old fellow. No one who didn't know you well and love you would guess.

"Whom did she name? Anyone I know?"

"A Robert Douglas and his sister, Lila."

"I say, isn't she the one who married the Earl of Byford last spring?" Beaton persisted. I wished I might change the subject for it was plain Alastair was not enjoying this interrogation, but I did not know how to go about it without being obvious.

"Yes, she did," Alastair admitted before he adroitly turned the conversation to the Congress and the people who had come to Vienna to observe it. He gave me a lesson in social grace as well.

"The whole world is here, from what I can tell," Beaton agreed. "Had to put up in a hovel. It was all that was left.

"You are enjoying the festivities, m'lady?" he asked.

"Very much so," I said, smiling at him.

"Good! Now the next time we meet at a ball, I want you to spare me a dance. One of the country ones, if you please, for I've no skill at all."

"And you tell her so and still expect her to dance with you, Charles?" Alastair drawled. He had recovered his usual dispassion and I was glad.

Lady Florence drifted up to join us then. With her came a very tall, pallid young man she introduced as her cousin. Mr. Flemming was distinguished by a lack of chin, poor man. He had little to say for himself, although he laughed often and loudly.

Charles Beaton was introduced, and while Lady Florence was charming and polite, it did not take very many minutes to discern her preference for Alastair Russell to the exclusion of everyone else.

One of the first things she mentioned was meeting Alva Potter. "It was so droll, Mr. Russell, why, I cannot tell you how startled I was to learn *you* were staying with such a person. However did a paragon like you become acquainted with her? But stay! Perhaps she is a relation of yours, Countess?"

I caught my breath in indignation as Alastair said, "No, she is not. I seem to remember 'Nelia had much the same reaction when she first met her. Now, of course, she is much taken with her, she is such an original. Aren't you, dear 'Nelia?"

Before I could reply, he went on, "It is so crowded in Vienna I was delighted Alva had come and taken that huge, luxurious house. She is an acquaintance of mine in London."

"But she is so excessively vulgar," Lady Florence persisted. "And you, sir, are the epitome of handsome elegance; a man who sets fashion."

"And as such is allowed to associate with as many vulgar people as he chooses," I could not refrain from saying. Mr. Flemming brayed a laugh until he saw his cousin's angry face.

"I would, however, suggest you stay far from the

lady," an imp prompted me to continue. "I do not think your reputation illustrious enough for you to turn the trick without ensuring censure.

"But do not repine, m'lady," I hastened to add. "I myself would not dare to acknowledge Mrs. Potter without Mr. Russell by my side, and I am the Countess of Wyckend, you know."

I smiled sweetly, careful not to look at Alastair. Before Lady Florence could think of a cutting enough remark to slay me, Alastair excused us and took me away.

"I suppose I should thank you for as icy a set-down as I am capable of myself," he began when we were safely in another room. "However, I do assure you, coz, I am in no need of rescuing, especially from the likes of Lady Florence. I took her measure two years ago when she drifted into society trailing her title as her only attribute. And her gowns!"

"What is wrong with them?" I couldn't help asking innocently.

"They never look as if she had put them on. Rather, they appear to have settled on her. Like dust, you know."

I chuckled as he added, "Tiresome woman!"

"She is, isn't she? I was delighted when Mrs. Potter sailed into the drawing room intent on adding her to her list of notables. And I had to laugh later till I cried, remembering how m'lady looked when Mrs. Potter decribed her late husband as a "rag and bottle man."

"She did? And I wasn't there?" Alastair said, so indignant at this missed opportunity, he forgot his usual drawl.

"I was glad Lili wasn't there either, for although she does manage very well most of the time, somehow I am sure that would have been beyond her capabilities for self-control."

Alastair looked down at me and smiled. It was truly amazing how that smile warmed me right down to the tips of my toes. It was even better than the precious old brandy I had had the evening I invaded his room.

"Tell me, Alastair, what did you say to Viscount Melton this morning when you gave him the coin to repay him?"

He did not look around as he said for my ears alone, "This is not the place to discuss it. There are too many people here."

Then he introduced me to yet other guests who had stopped to exchange pleasantries and I was forced to be content with the further delay.

It was sometime later that I found myself face to face with Gregory Paxton. Not from design, of course, but by chance. I had been to the room set aside for the ladies and I was admiring an oil painting that hung in the hall as I was returning to the company when I stepped back and literally bumped right into him. I am sure I paled when I turned and saw who it was. I know it made me feel nauseated to be so close to him, and without thinking I retreated a few steps although I never took my eyes from that pleasant, innocuous face.

"Well, well met, my dear. I understand you are now the Countess of Wyckend," he purred as he bowed. "My congratulations. Late to be sure, and perhaps not entirely appropriate since I also understand you have been widowed for some time. In that case, my condolences. Do feel free to select the correct sentiment, won't you?"

I could not speak. I could only stare at him as I would have stared, frozen into immobility, at a snake.

"By the way, who is that charming child you have in tow?" he continued, rocking back and forth on his heels, completely at his ease. "She looks something like you. Is she a relative?"

"She is a second cousin," I managed to tell him. My voice sounded rusty to my ears, harsh. "I warn you, stay away from her!" I added.

His bushy, reddish brows rose in surprise. "But how vehement you are, my dear Cornelia. And how can you say such a thing to me, who loves children so?"

If I had had my pistol with me, I swear I would have shot him right there and then and damn the consequences. Perhaps it was fortunate for my continued existence that I did not carry it to evening parties.

"I will not warn you again," I made myself say slowly and with as much quiet menace as I could muster. "You are not dealing with a child now, sir. And you should be aware I am an excellent shot."

"What a singular accomplishment for a gentlewoman," he said, a laugh lurking deep in his eyes. Why? I screamed silently. Why did he have to come here? Why did I have to meet him?

"Have you found many opportunities to make use of such a talent, ma'am?" he asked innocently.

I swallowed the bile that threatened to disgrace me, and pushed past him. He stood back immediately to give me passage and I could hear his quiet chuckle all the way down the hall as I hurried back to the ladies' room. Safely there, I proceeded to lose my dinner.

When I was a little recovered, I wrote Alastair a note telling him I was feeling ill and wished to leave. Somehow I found myself in the carriage shortly thereafter. I leaned back on the velvet squabs and closed my eyes.

"I have ordered the coachman to stop at the ramparts when we reach town," Alastair told me. "It is a pleasant night and a walk there will be good for you. Until then, rest, coz."

I nodded, and I was almost asleep when the carriage came to a halt. Alastair helped me down, instructing the servants to wait for us.

As he led me up the steps to the top, he said, "It is so early I am afraid Alva might still be up. We can be private here. Now then, what happened to make you feel ill?"

"Viscount Melton was at the reception. I met him in the hall," I told him as we came out on the top of the ramparts. There was some light from a half moon that slipped in and out of the clouds. When Alastair saw me shiver, he put his arm around me. I did not tell him it was the horror I had endured that made me shudder for his arm felt so good. I told myself I had to be careful now in what I said. Very careful indeed.

"Did you exchange words?" he asked as soon as we were out of earshot of an amorous couple wrapped in each other's arms. The woman's gown was above her waist. It was obvious what they were doing, but I was too distraught to care.

"Yes, he remembered me," I said, staring straight ahead, secure in the comfort of his strong arm. For a moment I wished I could unburden myself, let Alastair handle the problem even though I knew such a thing was impossible. This was one problem I had to take care of myself.

"What did you two talk about this morning when you gave him the coin?" I asked.

"I thanked him after introducing myself. For some reason, I had never met the man. I do not know his friends, either. I gave him the coin, over his protests I might add. He seems innocuous enough. Pleasant. Ordinary."

"Did he ask who Lili was?"

"Yes. He appeared to be very taken with her. He said he loved children and she was a delightful girl."

"But what did you tell him about her?" I persisted, my empty stomach churning. I was glad I had nothing left to lose.

Alastair turned me to face him then and searched my face. I was glad when the moon slipped behind a cloud. "Nothing. Not her name, not her direction. Of course you realize that now that Lady Florence has met Alva, she will spread the tale throughout the *ton* here in Vienna. I expect the viscount already knows Lili's direction."

I nodded. "I am aware of that," I said shortly. I began to walk again, restless and uneasy. Alastair fell in step beside me.

"I have been thinking perhaps it would be best if I returned home," I said, almost to myself. "With Lili, of course."

"Give up the field so easily?" he drawled. "I never thought you a coward, coz."

"Nor am I one," I retorted.

"What can the man do here in Vienna? Or anywhere else for that matter, now you are on your guard?" he persisted. "And why withdraw just because he is here and you don't like him. It seems an inadequate reason to me. But of course, if you prefer, we will leave. I understand there is a group returning to England early next week. We can travel with them, if you like."

I could tell he was disappointed although I could hear nothing in his voice. That was as cool and contained as ever. Now, however, I found myself taking a deep breath and saying, "Perhaps you are right, coz. It is silly to leave, isn't it, just because a man I hate has come? Just consider old Mrs. Parmeter, my mother-in-law's bosom-bow. I am not fond of her, but she has not driven me away."

"And by remaining you will not have to miss the Peace Ball. That will be a once-in-a-lifetime experience, one you may dine out on for months."

I smiled and nodded, but deep inside I was still nervous about this decision I had made only to please Alastair. Yes, I admit that was why I had decided to stay. A picture of Lili's pretty face, all aglow with her innocent joy in living, came to my mind, and I resolved that nothing—nothing!—must happen to mar that joy. And to be sure nothing did, from now on I would always have my pistol close to hand, loaded and ready.

We passed another amorous couple half-hidden in the shadows and I said, "This place appears to be well-known, coz, but not for walking."

I looked over in time to see his little smile. "No. It is, as you have correctly assumed, Vienna's favorite spot for lovers' trysts. I did not think of that. I only wanted someplace we could talk without being overheard."

"We have certainly found that," I said as another couple came into view. The man had the woman pressed against the stone wall of the ramparts and she was moaning, although I could tell it was not from pain. "No one here would pay a bit of attention if we suddenly began to shout, 'God Save the King!' "

He chuckled and his arm came around me again. I was suddenly speechless, for every bit of me was concentrated on that arm—how it felt where it touched me, how his fingers were clasping my waist, and where. I was glad I had no stole to interfere with the sensation. As we strolled on, silent now, I wondered what I would do if he suddenly turned to me and took me in his arms to kiss me. I did not think I would protest if he pressed me against the ramparts and began to make love to me. It even seemed like an excellent idea, here in the moonlight on this soft October night so far from home.

"It is warm for October," I made myself say, knowing I was flushed from these wayward thoughts, and very glad of the dark. "Yet I believe Austria has fearsome winters."

"Winter will come soon enough.

"Shall we return to the carriage, 'Nelia? I think Alva must be safely in bed by now."

As I nodded, I sensed his eyes on me, and when he released my waist, I reached out and took his hand, marveling at my boldness.

"You need not worry about Melton any longer, my dear," he said in a soft voice as he pressed my hand warmly. "I shall not let anything happen to either you or Lili. My word on it."

I could tell he thought I had taken his hand because I was afraid, and I knew I should say nothing to enlighten him. This—this attraction I was beginning to feel strongly was one-sided and I did have my pride. It was something I had always been able to depend on all my life, pride. I did not intend to let it fail me now.

Chapter Eleven

I found it difficult to get to sleep later. I must have changed position a hundred times, and I ended up pounding my pillows in frustration. I could not seem to stop thinking of Alastair—his handsome face, his elegant form, even the half-smile he sported when I said something amusing, were all taken out of memory to be explored.

Earlier, we had parted at the foot of the stairs under the carefully indifferent gaze of the butler and his attendant footmen. But once undressed with my hair brushed and my maid dismissed, I could not seem to stop thinking of Alastair, only a few steps and a single door away. It was almost dawn before I fell asleep at last.

I had taken to having my breakfast in bed to avoid Alva Potter. She was an early riser and she enjoyed talking to me first thing, something I had always disliked. This morning I found I had some correspondence on my tray. One was a letter from my mother-in-law, which I did not open at once. The other was a note from Alastair.

He had written only a few scribbled lines to tell me he had ordered the landau for one so we might take Lili into the country for an al fresco picnic such as we used to enjoy while traveling. I wrote a hasty acceptance and, feeling happier just knowing I would see him soon again, broke the seal on the dowager countess's letter.

She had written in a tiny crabbed hand and crossed her lines, making it difficult to decipher, but there was no mistaking her intent. She demanded first to know what I was doing in Austria with that good-for-nothing beau, Alastair Russell. She reminded me of my position as the other widowed Countess of Wyckend, and the necessity of maintaining a spotless reputation since, as she wrote, "it is all you are able to provide for a title that goes back for illustrious generations." I stiffened when I read that, for it was a barbed reference to my childless state. Ogden and I had not had children, despite his mother's constant harassment. Once when she reminded me that of the direct line, Ogden was all that remained, I had retorted it had been most unwise of her then to produce only a single heir. I shuddered even now remembering how she had exploded with fury at my boldness and defiance; how she had fallen gravely ill for over a week. I was careful not to annoy her again, for dislike her as much as I did, I did not want her death on my hands. And so I followed my husband's lead in dealing with his mother, and allowed her to feel she was in charge while ignoring each and every order she gave me.

I read on quickly. Come home at once . . . without Russell . . . expected at Wyckend within the month . . .

Mrs. Parmeter had been busy. I wondered how she had managed to get a letter to the countess so quickly, until I realized she had probably bullied someone she knew at the British delegation to include it in the diplomatic pouch that was sent home so often. No doubt the countess had used the same method for her letter. Despite her insistence on remaining at Wyckend, she knew almost everyone of importance—or at least their fathers and grandfathers.

As I rose and dressed for the picnic, I wondered how I was to reply to her. I had never allowed the countess to dictate to me. There was no need for it, for Ogden had left me a fortune, much to her annoyance. If I had wanted to, I could have carried on one torrid affair after another and there would have been nothing she could do about it. And I had no intention of returning to Wyckend. Not now, I didn't. I decided to discuss the problem with Alastair and put the letter in my reticule.

Earlier, I had placed my pistol there. I did not expect to see Melton today since we were going out of town with Lili, but I meant to begin as I intended to go on. Besides, I felt safer just knowing the pistol, loaded and ready, was within reach.

I went down well before the hour appointed to speak to the butler. Cranston, he of the Duke of Harfield's late employ, was warmer to me than to his common mistress, whom he treated with complete disdain, still, you would not have called him friendly. But when I explained the necessity of having a footman attend Lili every time she left the house, he nodded ponderously.

"I fear Vienna is an immoral city, Cranston," I said, and he nodded again, even going so far as to roll his eyes to indicate his complete agreement. "I do not care to put Miss Martingale in danger," I went on. "If the footmen should both be busy, please send a message to the stables so one of my grooms can serve as escort."

When I left him, I went back to the stables and spoke to our coachman. The grooms were in his charge, and he told me he would speak to them. "There'll be no harm come to the little missy, m'lady," he assured me. "We'll see to that. Foreigners! Bah!"

I thanked him, glad there was no need to tell him the danger came from an Englishman.

Lili was waiting in the hall long before one, humming a tune to the porter's delight and admiring her broad-brimmed straw hat in the hall mirror. I smiled at her happiness and smiled again when my cousin came down pulling on his kid gloves and she called him Al-as-tair.

This afternoon we did to go to the Vienna Woods but along another road that followed the River Wien. It was a lovely day again, warm and sunny, and I was glad I had thought to bring a parasol. Lili amused us by telling us about her shopping expedition that morning. She was not a greedy child, but probably because of her early life, she was fascinated by all the things in the shops. I was glad I had thought to give her some pin money, not that she spent much of it, and then only on others. She had given her maid a pretty scarf, and she had embroidered a handkerchief for me. She had also embroidered one for Alastair. He used it one evening at dinner, to please her I knew, for I could not see him brandishing it in company. It had a border of forget-me-nots in a vivid blue. Not his style at all.

The spot Alastair chose for our outing was a small meadow on the bank of the river. After the grooms unloaded the basket of food and a rug for our use, as well as some fishing gear, he sent the carriage on to the nearest village, ordering its return in two hours' time.

"I didn't know you cared for fishing, coz," I teased him as I settled down on the rug.

"I don't, but I think Lili will. Until she catches something and has to watch it die anyway," he explained before he called to her where she was exploring the riverbank.

We ate our picnic first, bread and cheese, fruit and cake and wine, then Alastair took Lili to the river and gave her some basic instruction. I saw she was fascinated by this new activity, and when Alastair returned to me, she settled down quietly on the bank, intent on her pole.

"This is delightful. Thank you for thinking of it," I told him as he poured us both another glass of wine.

"I thought it might make you easier, to be away from town for even a little while," he said, busy putting away the remains of our picnic.

We fell silent then, but it was not an uncomfortable silence. Rather it was the kind often shared by two good friends who do not have to chatter constantly when in each other's company.

I felt sleepy and I lay back on the rug, tipping my straw hat over my face to shade it. It was then I remembered Alastair's friend, Charles Beaton, and his remarks last evening at the reception. I had meant to ask Alastair about them, but once we were alone on the ramparts, I had forgotten completely.

"What happened during your stay in Scotland last winter, coz?" I asked idly.

"Why do you think something happened?" he said, but I noted his lazy tone of voice had disappeared.

"I suspected you were uneasy last evening when Mr. Beaton mentioned it and I wondered why. Of course, it is none of my concern. Please forgive me."

"No, that's all right," he said, still in that stiff voice. "I made rather a fool of myself is all, and it has continued to bother me,"

"You? Making a fool of yourself? I cannot conceive such a thing."

"I am not infallible, 'Nelia," he said, plucking a blade of grass and concentrating on it. So he would not have to look at me, I wondered? "Occasionally, oh, very occasionally to be sure, I do falter, as lesser men are so wont to do."

He stared off into the distance then. We could see a barge on the other side of the river making its slow way to Vienna, but we could not hear the men on it, nor the sounds the oxen made as they plodded along the barge path. I saw Lili was still intent on her fishing and marveled she could keep so still.

"I went too far, trying to gain the inheritance," Alastair admitted, much to my surprise. I had thought the subject closed. "I needed the money and I saw no reason why my great-aunt should not choose me for her heir. There were some peculiar things happening in that castle; someone trying to do away with the heirs. So I arranged for my valet to fire a shot at me, hoping the old lady would think I had been threatened and thus feel more kindly toward me."

He threw the blade of grass away with a disgusted gesture and I held my breath, trying to picture what he was describing. This was a side of Alastair I had not known before, and I was not sure I wanted to hear anything that would destroy the image of him I had come to believe was true.

"Unfortunately, although a deft man with a cravat, he was not a good shot and instead of hitting the wall behind me as I had instructed, he managed to hit me. Fortunately it was only a flesh wound, and after my initial fury, I came to see the accident enhanced my chances. Still, I was discovered in the end and sent away in disgrace, an outcast from the family. And now you know what a terrible person I am."

His eyes searched my face, for I had sat up and removed my hat to stare at him. "To be sure, it was not a good thing you did," I said finally. "Still, I can understand why you were tempted. And as you said yourself, no one is perfect. No, not even you, Alastair, so do not be so hard on yourself."

He looked easier then and I added, "I should think the pain you suffered would have been punishment enough, but perhaps the family will forgive you someday."

He shrugged. "Most of them can go to the devil for all I care. But I did grow fond of Lila Douglas. I was not invited to her wedding, though."

"I am sure that set you to brooding for at least a month," I said. "I know how you men just adore weddings."

What he would have had to say to this sally went unspoken for Lili cried out then. "Al-as-tair, come quickly!" she called. "I have caught something, oooh, it is so strong!"

I went with him to the bank to see a large fish thrashing about trying to escape the hook. With Alastair's help, Lili reeled him in to the bank so Alastair could slip the net under him. I watched my cousin with dreamy eyes. He had removed his coat and the muscles in his back that moved so smoothly were easily seen under his fine cambric shirt. I swallowed. Hard.

Our fisherwoman would not think of keeping her prize to eat at dinner, and so we threw the fish back.

I was glad it was able to swim away. Lili decided she had had enough fishing and wandered off to pick wildflowers. Alastair and I returned to the rug and settled down again.

"You are not the only one with difficult relatives," I said to him as I spotted the countess's letter in my reticule when I searched for my handkerchief. "I received this this morning from the dowager," I added as I gave it to him.

"Old Mrs. Parmeter's doing, no doubt," he said as he took it.

I could not see a single reaction cross his face as he read it, and it was not until he threw it down and wiped his hands on the rug that I could tell how disgusted he was.

"I assume you are forced to obey this summons?" he asked. "She holds the purse strings?"

"No, not at all. Ogden knew his mother would make my life miserable, so he left me a separate fortune as well as Wyckend. I do not live there because his mother rules that roost. I don't care if she does. My time will come."

"She cannot live forever, coz," he said lightly.

"I think she is determined to try. She has such dread of what will happen when I take her place, you see, I, who could not even give Wyckend an heir."

"That happens, sometimes," he remarked, stretching out beside me, his hands under his head as he studied the sky. "What confuses me is why you are so concerned about this summons, if, as you say, you are independent."

"The dowager is given to rages when she doesn't get her way. And she has a heart condition. No, no," I added when I saw his sneer, "it is not something she holds over me. She is very ill. Both the earl and I always treated her with care and let her think she was in charge."

" 'Nelia, listen to me," he said, taking my hand for emphasis. "The woman is in her *eighties*. She is going to die soon."

"All the more reason not to upset her," I told him. "I don't want to be the one responsible for her death. I do owe her that, even if I could never respect her, never mind love her. She has cared for Wyckend faithfully ever since her husband's early death, and she raised Ogden as best she could. I try to remember that whenever I get impatient with her."

"And so you will obey her? Leave Austria for England and hurry down to Wyckend, the obedient daughter?"

I smiled at him. "No such thing. I shall write and tell her how sorry I am she is upset. I shall promise to see her as soon as I can. I will ask for news of Wyckend and tell her about the Congress, but I will not obey her. I never do. It is all pretend, to spare her sensibility."

To my regret, Alastair let go of my hand and settled back on the rug.

"You are a nicer person than I am, coz," he said lightly.

"No, I think it's because I am a woman."

"So I have noticed," he drawled, and then he shut his eyes and went to sleep. At least I think he did. I sat there, hardly daring to breathe, and watched him. He looked like a Greek god in repose—that perfect profile, the high cheekbones, his straight nose and firmly set jaw, and especially his beautifully shaped lips. I wished I could bend and kiss those lips. I wished I could feel his arms come around me to pull me close. I could not help myself. I reached out and softly touched his hair.

Alastair opened his eyes. "There is something wrong?" he asked.

"I thought I saw an ant crawling in your hair, but I was mistaken," I said as carelessly as I could, although my heart was pounding in my chest. "Go back to sleep, coz. I'm going for a walk with Lili."

Fortunately, Lili was full of conversation when I reached her. She had an armload of wildflowers, most of which were drooping already. As we walked, I smiled and nodded, and occasionally asked a question, but my mind was back with Alastair.

At last we settled down on the riverbank and fell silent as we watched the boats and the water flowing by. The humming of the insects in the tall grass behind us seemed very loud and the warm sun beat down on our heads.

Idly I wondered why Alastair had told me of the dire consequences of his stay in Scotland. He had not had to do it. He could have refused, or changed the subject, even told me in effect, to mind my own business. But he had told me, he, who had always been so intent on presenting a perfect image to the world. Why, I wondered? Because we were related? Because we had grown closer on this journey? Because he wanted me to know what kind of man he was?

I could not approve either his actions or his motives. They had been deplorable. He must be deeply in debt to have risked the exposure that eventually came. Perhaps that was why it had been so easy to persuade him to travel to France with me, because he needed the money, or hoped to escape his creditors, or simply because he wanted to get as far away from Scotland and his disapproving relatives as he could. I realized I might never know the answer. It was not something I could ask him, for he was a proud man. As proud as I was.

Yet he had told me a secret about himself that no one, outside his family, knew. I felt a tide of happiness flow through me that he had chosen to share a confidence with me. Because he *trusted* me. It was as simple, and as heartwarming, as that.

Chapter Twelve

To my astonishment, and surely to Alastair's secret amusement, Alva Potter became something of a celebrity in Vienna. Lady Florence's tale of her vulgarity, her showy gowns and overdecorated mansion, made people long to see for themselves. Long, in fact, to have a Potterism of their very own to report to the *ton*. There was also the added incentive of knowing Alastair Russell had taken her up, even going so far as to reside in her mansion, along with his cousin, the mysterious Countess of Wyckend. I had, by some strange device, become "mysterious." Probably, Alastair told me, because I had always shunned society until now.

At first, the callers were only a trickle, but only a few days passed before they became a flood. Cranston began to earn his keep, for the knocker was seldom still. Alva was perfect. She would only see those who were titled, and she treated everyone from a knight to a duke exactly the same. She had little patience with diplomats or foreign princes, and even less with untitled members of the *ton*. "For," she told me one morning when the footman brought her a bouquet from a mere Mr. Edwards, "I ain't impressed."

I told her he was the son of an earl, and therefore the Honourable Mr. Edwards, although, I was quick to caution her, the "honourable" was never used in address.

"What good is it, then, if it's not used?" she demanded.

"It is used for addressing letters," I explained.

Alva snorted, for she was riding very high. "Ha!" she said, "Poor stuff, I say. I won't encourage 'im."

When I pointed out Alastair did not have a title either, she stared. Her look seemed to say that as Alastair Russell, he didn't need one, for wasn't he as fine as the King?

She confided in me that she was quite excited by her sudden notoriety. I knew it would be short-lived. Most of society's crazes were. But for now, at least, she was a happy woman, and perhaps, when she returned to her mansion on Park Lane in London, she would be content with her memories.

I became used to finding the front hall full of servants bustling about taking wraps and calling cards, or carrying yet another tray of pastries and scones into the drawing room. And I became used to the billows of laughter that issued from that room, and to hearing Alva's pronouncements repeated at parties.

"Would you believe she said the Regent was a disappointment? That she'd seen costermongers who'd make better royalty?"

"Yes, and she told me she thought he had a weak chin. Her Adam, as she calls her husband, told her you could always tell how clever a man was by the size of his chin."

"That isn't all her husband told her. Did you hear she claims the length of a man's nose reveals how large . . . oh, I cannot say it!"

"She refused to receive Marshall Edwards today. Told her butler to send him off with a flea in his ear. Whatever do you suppose she meant by that?"

No one seemed to know. The general consensus was that Alva Potter was an eccentric and an original, as well as a delight.

I kept a close eye on Lili now, and I often found myself pulling aside the draperies in my room to stare down into the street, to see if there was any sign of Gregory Paxton. I never saw him, but I told myself that did not mean he had not been there. Lili had been different ever since I had told her Viscount Melton was not a good man, and made her promise not to go out without her maid and a footman. Oh, she was still pleasant, she still smiled and chatted, but I could sense a wall between us that had not been there before. I was sorry for it. But then I would remember the secret that only I and a few others knew, remember my sister Phillipa's tearstained face and breathless pleas, and I would stiffen my resolve. It was too bad Lili felt me a turnkey but it hardly mattered. What mattered was her safety.

Then one day I came downstairs to discover Melton had not only joined the throngs who called on Alva Potter, but had lingered in the hall to exchange pleasantries with Lili, who had just come home from a shopping expedition. I knew she had been accompanied by the servants I insisted on, but both of them had long since returned to their household duties.

I heard his voice first, telling her a funny story about a horse race and I stood frozen at the top of the flight, clutching the newel post for support. When I heard Lili's giggle, I picked up my skirts and ran down the stairs. Lili flushed when she saw me, but Gregory Paxton was all urbane courtesy as he bowed and wished me good afternoon. I curtsied only because Lili was there watching me. I longed to go to her and put my arm around her, but I knew he would see that as the defensive move it was and he would find it amusing.

"You have been calling on Alva, sir?" I asked, wondering if my voice sounded as strange to them as it did to me.

"Indeed. Your hostess has become the queen of Vienna. She is so droll, is she not?"

I inclined my head slightly. "As you say. But we will not keep you. No doubt your family awaits you . . . oh, you are married, aren't you, m'lord?"

"Yes, I have two sons and a little daughter," he told me, and his smile grew at the horror I could not quite keep from my face.

"Unfortunately, they are in England. I am sure Lili

would have enjoyed meeting Mary. They are almost the same age and I miss her very much."

He sighed and I could tell Lili was touched. She would not have been if she knew him as well as I did.

"I was about to ask Lili to come and have an ice with me," Melton went on. "I do so enjoy talking to her."

"How kind of you," I said quickly before she could think of accepting. "I am sorry. Lili has something else she must do right now."

"Perhaps another time?" he asked as he set his top hat at a jaunty angle. "Your servant, ma'am. *Au revoir,* Lili!"

We both stood silent until the door closed behind him.

"I would not have gone, ma'am," Lili said, her voice stiff. "You did not have to answer for me."

I could not speak. I was shaking inside and I was not at all sure I could get the words out. How brazen he had been! How impudent! And then to dare to mention his daughter, just thirteen! I told myself I must stop thinking about it or I would become ill.

"There isn't anything you want me to do right now, is there, ma'am?" Lili asked. When I shook my head, she turned and went up the stairs. I could sense the jut of her little jaw, her scornful eyes, hear the righteousness and indignation in every footstep, but I was not tempted to smile. Instead, I sat down abruptly on one of the hall chairs, and it was several minutes before I was able to return to my room, all memory of what had brought me downstairs in the first place gone from my mind.

Later that evening, after Lili had gone to bed, I asked Alva to forbid Melton the house. Alastair was not with us. He was spending the evening playing cards with friends.

"Forbid him? Whatever for?" she demanded. "He's a lord, ain't he?"

"Yes, he is titled," I agreed. "But he is an evil man. I can say no more, for I am pledged to secrecy."

I saw she was looking rebellious, loath to give up even one of her lordly callers, and I stretched out my hand to her and said, "Please, ma'am? As a favor to me?" I did not dare mention any danger to Lili, for I knew that would not sway her.

"Very well, if you wish it, Countess," she said at last. "I'd like to know what's wrong with the man, but never mind. I've known enough proper bad 'uns in my time not to question your judgment. He's a funny man, though, ain't he? Always has a smile and a jest. Whoever would have thought . . .

"I'll speak to Cranston and the porter first thing tomorrow. He'll not cross this threshold again."

I smiled and thanked her, then I asked about her day's callers. She was delighted to tell me everything, including the momentous fact she had been invited to drive with the Marquess and Marchioness of Wendover the following morning. We discussed gowns she might wear, and I managed to convince her a plumed tiara would not do for morning wear.

I discovered the next day my caution was all to no avail, for Alastair had assured her it would be the perfect accessory. When I scolded him later, asking him how he could have encouraged something that would only make her look ridiculous, he told me that the *ton* wanted outrageous behavior from her. If it stopped, he said, they would drop her. I did not like it, but I could see the truth in what he said.

The day of the Peace Ball dawned fair, something all Vienna was grateful for. Some eighteen hundred guests had been invited, and the success of the evening depended on the guests being able to dance in the pavilion that had been especially built in the garden. The ball was being given to commemorate the first anniversary of the Battle of Leipzip, and all the ladies had been asked to wear gowns of silver or blue. Fortunately I had a blue ball gown. We were also asked to wear olive leaves in our hair, and that was a problem, for when I began to look for some, I discovered there were none left in the entire city. Alastair brought me a wreath late in the afternoon on the day of the ball. It was not made of olive leaves, to be sure, but he told me that tucked among my black curls, no one would notice.

"I'm sure the servants will still admit us," he said as we were being driven to the ball. He was seated across from me facing back, for Alva had been invited as well, and her hoops took up most of the seat. My gown was in the current fashion with narrow skirts, so I was not too crowded. She had made no attempt to find olive leaves, scorning them as shabby. Instead, she wore her plumed diamond tiara, the plumes dyed a bright green as a concession. It was certainly a memorable outfit, for her bright silver gown had a long train, which I hoped she would be able to manage without tripping over. She had told me she had been practicing in the privacy of her room.

The ball was an occasion I am sure no one there ever forgot. Besides the dancing and the various musicians tucked away in the gardens to entertain, there was a *tableau vivant* and a ballet presented as well. Charles Beaton was among the gentlemen I danced with. He was not as bad a partner as he had told me, still, I was always delighted to return to Alastair's side. He looked stunning this evening in understated black with a silver waistcoat and a diamond in his cravat. I know many women were envying me as we waltzed together, and I made the mistake of mentioning this to him as the dance concluded and we left the floor.

I was surprised to see his face darken. "But what is this?" I asked lightly. "You look offended, and here I have just given you a compliment, not an insult. Surely you enjoy being lionized and copied by the men, and sighed over by the ladies. What man wouldn't?"

"This one," he said. "Oh, I did enjoy it when I was younger. I was impossible then, so conceited and puffed up with my own importance. But one does grow up. Eventually."

"And you began to dislike admiration?" I asked, not at all sure he could be telling the truth.

He nodded as he collected two stems of champagne and led me deeper into the gardens to a bench some distance away from the crowd. It was cooler there, and quieter, although somewhere to our left a string trio was playing softly. Alastair took a sip of champagne before he said, "Tell me, 'Nelia, how would you like it if all you were admired for was your looks?"

"I cannot even conceive of such a thing," I said tartly.

"Don't demean yourself. You are a handsome woman. But think for a moment about how it would be if all people saw or thought of when they met you was how beautiful you were. Then imagine this had been going on since you were a small child."

He sighed and shook his head, his mouth twisted in a grimace. "It did not help that my mother doted on me. At first she was terribly disappointed I was not a girl, but when she discovered what a beautiful child I was, how handsome a young man I promised to become, she was reconciled. I am told she wept for days when my father insisted she take me out of my dresses and have my long curls cut off. She always placed my beauty first. It was the most impressive thing about me to her. And so, of course, I grew up agreeing with her that it must be so.

"Oh, of course my father was revolted by her adulation and insisted I learn to ride and hunt and shoot; defend myself as well, but he was not proof against her hysteria when he suggested sending me to Eton. I was educated at home."

"I am sorry," I managed to say, my mind full of the unfortunate boyhood he described. "I never thought of it like that."

"No one does. Why should they? I am considered lucky beyond belief. I once had a friend who told me he would sell his soul to the devil to look like me. Sickening, don't you agree?"

"Of course I do. But still, I can't help but think of

all the people who have had joy just looking at you, admiring you, trying to emulate your style and manner of dress."

He nodded. "Yes, I have learned my part well. You have never thought of me except as a fop. Don't be concerned. You are only one of a vast number. So, since that is what people wanted from me, I became one. The finest one ever. I have no estate to manage, no work to do except that. And now all I am good for is to be held up as an example of how a proper gentleman of the *ton* should dress and behave and look and converse. And I hate it."

"You do?" I asked, astonished in spite of myself. "I always thought you considered yourself above the rest of us poor mortals."

"I told you I learned my role well, did I not? But I do have a mind—I even think—I have opinions. I would like to be asked for those opinions, looked up to for my knowledge. Not that I will be, of course. My tutors were hardly great scholars. But just once, to have someone think of the *man,* not the god, would be refreshing."

"I will try to from now on, Alastair," I told him, putting down my champagne to take his hand. "There is much more to you than just your looks, your sarcasm, your wit. I know that."

He raised my hand and kissed it, his lips lingering, but for once I did not feel thrilled. Instead I felt sorry for him in a way I never would have thought possible.

"Enough of this brooding," he said, rising and pulling me to my feet. "This is a gala occasion. Come and dance with me, 'Nelia.

"Besides, you know," he said as we moved back to the pavilion, "I suspect I would hate to be ugly. No, I don't suspect it, I am sure of it."

Later, after a lavish supper had been served, the guests returned to the gardens to see the special fireworks display Prince Metternich had arranged. Balloons were sent up, the fireworks released from those balloons when they reached a certain height. You may imagine the guests' surprise when they saw the fireworks had been made to display the flags of the countries present at the Congress. I had never seen anything so impressive, and from the exclamations I heard around me, neither had anyone else. I even had to wipe away a tear when the British flag burst into brilliant red, white, and blue. When I saw a burly Russian soldier weeping openly at the sight of his country's banner shortly after that, I felt better.

The fireworks were barely over before a footman came to tell us Mrs. Potter was in dire need of our assistance.

"The train," Alastair muttered as we followed the servant back to the mansion. "It has to be that train."

He was right. When I saw Alva in one of the rooms set aside for the ladies, I discovered she had not only missed the fireworks, but was not fit to go anywhere. Not only had the train of her gown been trodden on, it had been ripped away, taking with it most of the back of her gown. Standing, her whalebone hoops were plainly visible, as were her thin, bowed legs.

"Whatever am I to do?" she demanded. "Oh, if I could just get my hands on that nasty Prussian animal, in such a hurry to get a good place for the fireworks he did not care who he trampled. Bah! Foreigners!"

I tried to hush her. The room was occupied by many foreigners, whose early concern for the elderly lady was becoming very tepid.

"I am sure we can find something, a tablecloth, for example, so you can leave in modesty, ma'am," I told her. "Wait here. I will get something, and have Alastair order our carriage brought forward."

Alastair chuckled when I told him her predicament. "There is no need for us to leave, coz," he drawled. "We can see her safely to the carriage and her servants can take care of her from there, if you prefer it."

I considered this for only a moment. True, it was not quite three and the ball was scheduled to continue till dawn, but for some reason I felt uneasy and glad of the opportunity to go home. Alastair was more than agreeable, for what was another ball in the life of a man who had spent years attending them?

Mrs. Potter fussed and fretted all the way back to the Johannesgasse, more like a small child deprived of a treat than an elderly lady who should have been in bed anyway at this hour. She did not stop until Alastair told her she was becoming a dead bore, and then she subsided into wounded silence.

Her maid was summoned and she was escorted to her room. I saw Alastair go into the library as I followed her up the stairs. Going down the hall to my room, I noticed the door to Lili's room was slightly ajar, and smiling, I went in. Perhaps she was waiting up to hear about the ball. She had been very excited about it, as I remembered.

But when I held my candle high, I discovered that not only was she not in the room, but her bed had not been slept in. I stared at the smooth counterpane, my hand going to my throat in my distress. Where was she? Where could she be at this hour? It occurred to me then I had not seen Viscount Melton at the ball and I am sure I would have remembered him if he had been there.

Whirling, I ran down the stairs and across the hall, startling Cranston, who was locking the front door for the night. I did not stop, but hurried into the library.

Chapter Thirteen

Alastair took one look at me and came to take my hands in his. "Lili?" he asked.

"She is not in her room. Her bed has not been slept in. Oh, Alastair, I am so afraid something has—"

"Not now," he ordered. "Come with me."

Back in the hall he asked Cranston if he knew anything about Miss Martingale's whereabouts. The butler's supercilious look was replaced with one of confusion.

"Why, sir," he said, "I saw her go up to bed hours ago."

"Get her maid down here!"

We waited in uneasy silence until a footman came to tell us the maid was missing as well.

At that, the white line around Alastair's mouth eased, but I was not reassured until he said, "There now, we know she had company when she left the house. She was not abducted, 'Nelia. You don't take a maid along when you're kidnapping someone."

"But—but Melton was not at the ball," I whispered.

"How could you possibly tell when there were almost two thousand people there?"

I supposed he was right, but my heart was still in my throat. Lili, I cried to myself. Where are you?

Alastair leaned against the center table, the butler and footmen staring at him as they waited for orders. I stared at him too, for I had no idea what we could do now.

"Get all the other servants down here," he said, and when they appeared, still buttoning their gowns—

and in one man's case, minus his shoes—Alastair questioned them all. None of them knew where Lili and Brigitte had gone, or if they did, they were not saying. By this time, the formidable housekeeper had arrived, and she questioned the maids with more success.

Yes, Brigitte had talked about the fireworks, they all had, one young girl volunteered. "Real excited about them, she was," she added. "We all planned to stay up and look out the attic windows to see if we could catch a glimpse, but I fell asleep."

As the other maids nodded, I felt a glimmer of hope.

I looked at Alastair. Everyone else was looking at him as well. He stroked his jaw for a moment before he said, "They knew they had to have a way to get back into the house. I assume it is locked up tight after the last of us comes in?"

"Yes, sir," Cranston told him. "Every door. Every window. I see to it myself."

"But I doubt they are all locked tonight. I want you and one of the men to go through the ground floor, and the cellars, and check every latch. If you find one open, lock it."

I heard a stifled gasp, but when I looked at the maids, I could not tell which one had made the sound.

"Yes, they had to have had an accomplice for someone had to creep down and unlock a window after the house was secured for the night."

"I want you to know, m'lord, that as soon as I discover the culprit—and I will—she will find herself unemployed without a character or her yearly wage," the housekeeper said in an awful voice. "Such things do not happen with *my* maids."

"Well, it appears they have, this time," Alastair said mildly. "Ah, Cranston, back so soon? Which window was it?"

"One in the dining room, sir. I looked out and there is a box placed beneath it."

"One can only applaud Lili's foresight. Or perhaps

it was her maid's idea? From what I understand, Miss Martingale never tried to escape the convent."

"Brigitte goes as well," the housekeeper muttered.

"Please, let's not make any decisions until the girls return safely," I said. I was amazed at how calm I sounded, almost detached if you can believe it. Of course, inside I was as taut as the E string on a violin.

"Very well. You are all dismissed," Alastair said. As the servants looked at each other, confused, and in some cases, disappointed not to be in on the ending, he added, "Off to bed with you. Oh, Cranston, please have one of the footmen relight the flambeaux at the front door."

Not waiting to see if his orders were obeyed, Alastair took my arm and, once back in the library, pushed me gently into one of the leather wing chairs there. As he poured us both some brandy, I said impatiently, "Now what are you about, coz? Shouldn't we be doing more? Setting the servants to searching the streets? Notifying the authorities?"

"I expect our wandering girl to return within the half hour, 'Nelia. If she does not, well, then it will be time to think of search parties and the authorities."

I took the snifter he handed me and, without observing any of the niceties, took a healthy swallow. I had to wait a moment for the burning sensation to go away before I could say, "But why did you have the window locked?"

"So they will have to come to the front door and knock, of course. Lili is clever enough to know, when she discovers the locked window, that she has been discovered. Do sip that brandy slowly, my dear. It is priceless stuff."

I was about to tell him I didn't care, when we heard the front door knocker.

"And here they are now," Alastair said in satisfaction. "Just as I predicted. Coming, 'Nelia?"

I was at the door before him, but I let him open it. Please let it be Lili, God, I prayed. Please don't let it be someone telling us she is injured or dead.

I gasped in relief when I saw her standing there in the flickering light of the flambeaux. Her maid stood a little to one side, and behind both girls were two sturdy young men.

I felt my brows rise as I inspected the party. The young men looked both resolute and uncomfortable. Brigitte hung her head. Only Lili looked perfectly at ease. I did not know whether I wanted to hug her or spank her.

"Did you enjoy the fireworks, Lili?" Alastair asked, his voice courteous as he waved them all inside.

"How did you ever guess?" she demanded. "We had it planned so carefully so no one would worry about us!"

"I saw your door was not quite closed when we came home," I told her. "I decided to look in on you to tell you about the ball, if you were awake."

Lili and her maid exchanged rueful glances. The possibility that I might do such a thing had obviously not occurred to them.

"I think we may assume this is your maid?" Alastair interrupted. "And who are these two strapping youths?"

"Oh, this is Hans and Werner," Lili said, and the boys bowed. "They are Brigitte's brothers. You see, I didn't break my word to you, ma'am. I didn't go out alone, or even just with Brigitte. But I couldn't ask a footman. He might have tried to stop me, or tell on me, and I did want to see the fireworks so badly.

"So Brigitte got Hans and Werner to come with us, and I am very glad she did. We saw everything so clearly. The boys knew the best place on the ramparts to go and watch."

I closed my eyes for a moment, wondering what else Lili had seen up there besides fireworks. Something educational, I was sure.

"You have our thanks, gentlemen," Alastair said. "And I must say it was brave of you to come to the door with the girls."

Brigitte murmured a translation, and Hans—or was

it Werner?—spoke up in German, which neither Alastair nor I understood. I gathered, however, from his gestures and the hand he put on his sister's shoulder, he was telling us they had had to make sure the girls were safe.

Alastair thanked them and sent them on their way. Brigitte was sent to bed. Lili trailed us to the library.

"You still haven't told us how you liked the fireworks," Alastair said as she sat down on the edge of a chair, looking slightly apprehensive now.

"They were wonderful, weren't they? I cannot imagine how they are made, or how they got up so high. But what are you doing home?" she added. "I did not expect to see you 'til morning."

"How unfortunate our hostess had an accident with her gown then," Alastair drawled.

I sipped my brandy slowly. I was thankful Alva had slept through the excitement. She did not like Lili. This escapade would do nothing to change that. I could almost hear her telling me the "gel" was spoiled.

"I don't think you realize how this adventure of yours caused the countess undue worry and concern," Alastair told her. His voice was gentle, but I found myself shivering. I saw Lili also looked perturbed. I suppose she had still been excited about her daring romp, and since it had ended so well, she felt there could be no consequences. Alastair's words showed her how wrong she was.

"I am sorry, ma'am," she said, coming to kneel at my feet. "I did not think you would find out."

"That does not make it right. I was frightened for you. Very frightened."

She hung her head, and when she looked up, her eyes were filled with tears. All very well to cry, I thought. That does not make it better, either.

"I will pay any penance you wish, ma'am," she said in a choked voice. "I am very, very sorry."

I could not speak. Over her head, I looked helplessly at Alastair.

"A penance will certainly be required, but it has

not been decided just yet," he told her. "Do get up and stop dramatizing yourself, Lili. You look like an actress in a bad play."

As she struggled to her feet, her face flushed, he added, "Off you go to bed. We will speak to you later."

She paused at the door. "About Brigitte," she said tentatively. "I made her do it. She did not want to. I hope she will not be punished, too."

"We will try and see she keeps her place here. It is not our decision," Alastair said, and she had to be content with that.

After she had gone, I leaned back in my chair, exhausted. It was over. Lili was safe. Why did I still feel so unsettled, so tense?

"I think it is time you seek your bed as well, coz," Alastair told her, taking my empty snifter and helping me to my feet.

As we went to the stairs together, I said, "I can never thank you enough. I don't know what I would have done without you, gone all to pieces, probably. And made such a stir, it would have been all over Vienna by noontime."

"You're wrong, there," he objected. "You forget the ball is not over yet. No one who is anyone will even wake until midafternoon.

"Go to bed, coz. I must extinguish the torches and lock up. Now why do you suppose I sent Cranston to bed?"

"So he wouldn't listen to what happened to Lili?"

He grinned up at me for I had begun to climb the stairs. "Hardly. You know how servants always find out what is going on. You can't keep a thing from them. I've stopped trying."

I smiled, but I was too tired suddenly to say another word. How strange it was, then, that after the maid had undressed me, I was unable even to think of sleeping. Instead, in nightrail and slippers, I went to the windows. The street below was quiet. There was no one about, although flambeaux still burned before other mansions, a sure sign the ball was not yet over.

I sensed he was there although I had not heard a sound, so I was not startled when I felt his hands on my shoulders, the back of my neck, massaging the tension away.

"This won't do, 'Nelia," he said. "You need sleep."

I sighed and leaned back, and he put his arms around me. The top of my curls came just to his jaw line. It was a moment before he lowered his head to put his cheek against mine. We stood like that for a long time, or so it seemed to me. I had closed my eyes, and I could smell the lotion he used and, beneath that, the man himself. It had been a long time since I had been in a man's embrace, but I did not feel awkward. It seemed right that Alastair hold me close to him; that we were together like this. Why, I love him, I thought wonderingly. I love him.

I turned then in his arms and reached up to draw his head down to mine so I could kiss him. He did not hesitate. Instead, he took possession of my mouth, and once again, his arms tightened. It was as if we were one person. Almost one person. I stopped thinking then, to revel in sensation.

"Now I should apologize for kissing you," he murmured later, between additional little kisses he left on my cheek, my brow, my hair. "I find I can't."

He stepped back, holding me at arm's length. I was glad, for I was sure I would collapse if he let me go. "I have wanted to do that for a long time," he told me. "And I am not made of iron, my sweet."

Stunned by the love I felt for him, I could not reply. He smiled before he turned me about and gave me a little push.

"Go to bed, 'Nelia. Sleep now."

And then he was gone, the door clicking shut behind him. I stood indecisive for a moment before I climbed into bed. I moved slowly as if in a dream, and I fell asleep with my hand against my cheek where his lips had been.

* * *

It was after twelve when I finally awoke and rang for the maid, and I blushed when I saw the large bouquet of flowers on the tray she brought me. There was a note with it, and I sent her to the dressing room before I broke the seal. But my little smile of delight faded abruptly as I read that note, then reread it as if I could not believe my eyes.

"Please forgive me, ma'am. I forgot myself," it began. "Although my impetuous behavior gave me a memory I will always cherish, you have my word it will not happen again."

I tried to tell myself there must be some mistake. Alastair could not mean what he had written. Why, hadn't he called me "sweet"? And surely he had meant that kiss. It had been deep and consuming and overwhelming . . .

. . . to me. Alastair Russell was a complex man, a cosmopolitan. I knew he had had many mistresses.

But why hadn't he gone on, then, I wondered? Why did he leave me when he must have known all he had to do was carry me off to bed?

And what had possessed him to write this note and send these flowers? It made what had happened insignificant. Trivial.

Of course, I thought as I sank back on the pillows. Of course. It was only a kiss, not the momentous event I had been making it out to be. And the flowers, the note, had been sent because Alastair knew I was not as sophisticated as he.

I saw I had crushed the note in my hand, and now I tore it into pieces before I rose and went to the dressing room, my breakfast forgotten.

When I went downstairs later, I found myself beset with other problems. Alastair had gone out, but he had left orders Lili's maid was not to be dismissed. When Mrs. Deevers, the housekeeper, came and begged a word with me, she was full of righteous anger that her authority had been taken from her.

"She's no better than she should be, that Brigitte,

m'lady," she told me, her hands folded over her comfortable stomach. She was clad as always in neat black, her graying hair tucked up under a white cap. "She's just a Viennese girl we hired as extra help when we arrived and I think it most unwise for the other maids to see her escape punishment. Give them ideas, mayhap.

"Besides, she will not tell me the name of the maid who helped them by unlocking that window." She snorted. "I don't know what the world is coming to, when common maids act so saucy, m'lady. Not a bit sorry, she isn't from what I can see. And now Mr. Russell, telling me she must be kept on—well! How am I to explain this to Mrs. Potter?"

"I will speak to Mrs. Potter. And you know, it is not Brigitte's fault, not a bit of it. I am afraid Miss Lili must take all the blame. It was all her idea."

Mrs. Deevers sniffed, not a bit mollified. "That may be, ma'am. But even if it 'twere so, that Brigitte should have come and told me about it, so I could have put a stop to it. To think of Miss jauntering about the streets in a foreign city late at night, and her only just thirteen and fresh from a convent! It makes my blood run cold, it does, just thinking about what might have happened to her. For you and I know what *foreigners* are like, ma'am."

"Indeed," I agreed before I dismissed her, hoping she never found out Lili had been up on the ramparts.

I did worry about Alva's reaction, but to my relief and great surprise, she barely heard me out before she began to chuckle. The handy box under the dining room window and Brigitte's two strapping brothers especially seemed to amuse her. It was almost as if this escapade of Lili's touched a sympathetic chord in her, and it made me wonder what deviltry a young Alva must have got up to when she was Lili's age. Perhaps remembering those days made a bond between them. Or perhaps knowing Lili could be naughty made her less a saintly convent girl, too good to be true, and therefore much more likable.

But to be honest, I paid very little heed to these petty problems, and when Lili dared to ask her punishment, I told her I must discuss it with Alastair. Then I set her to searching her Bible for ten passages to memorize that had to do with willfulness, and I went away to a small parlor to sit with my needlework forgotten on my knee while I tried to forget the note he had written to me and the reason he had done so.

Chapter Fourteen

I did not see Alastair until dinnertime. As always, he was dressed impeccably, his blond hair gleaming in the candlelight. He had a smile for me, but it was no warmer than the smile he gave Alva as he discussed the Peace Ball with her, and he ignored Lili, who ate her dinner without a word. I was hurt. He was making it so plain that any affection I might feel for him was not returned. It was all I could do to swallow the food set before me.

I wished we were not going to the opera that night, the three of us. Alva had been invited to join the Wendovers in their box, and she had asked that Alastair and I be included. Looking forward to the treat, she was resplendent in a gown of brilliant red, her gray hair done up in side curls and a youthful fringe that was not at all becoming. Still, I told myself as I accepted the cloak Alastair put over my shoulders, I supposed I should be glad she was there, for her inadvertent chaperonage would make it unnecessary for me to speak to Alastair alone. And since we had nothing to say to each other, what could be better?

I had the headache when we returned home at last. The opera had been a brilliant spectacle, the singing superb, or so everyone assured me, for I barely heard a note of it. Alastair had sat beside me and there in the dark I had been too conscious of the tall, handsome length of him to concentrate on anything else. It reminded me too poignantly of how he had held me close only a few short hours before.

But in the privacy of my room, knowing he was not

in the house, but gone on to a party with friends, I took myself severely to task. I was not some little ingenue, made helpless by her first love, I told myself. I was the Countess of Wyckend, an heiress with one of England's most impressive estates and a luxurious house on Upper Brook Street in Mayfair. I had any number of compatible friends and a very comfortable life to enjoy. And I had my pride. That pride I had always used as a shield. I was determined it would not fail me now. What had happened between me and Alastair after the Peace Ball had been only the impulse of a moment, because, as he had told me, he had forgot himself and he was not made of iron.

It should have been obvious to me he had no desire for any entanglements or for marriage, for hadn't he reached the age of thirty-something still single? In a way it was ludicrous to think of Alastair Russell and marriage in the same breath. They did not go together. I remembered something else then, how Alva had said he would never marry because he was already wed—to himself. I should have thought of that sooner. It would have saved me a lot of pain.

Perhaps I could tease him into an affair, but I was not interested in a lover. I never had been since my husband's death five years ago in a riding accident.

I loved Alastair Russell. I could not help it, and I could not change it. But I wanted more than a few weeks or so, I wanted him forever, and since I could not have him that way, I wanted nothing to do with him. Or so I told myself. It really is amazing what women will think of late at night, pacing their bedchambers and trying to be sensible, isn't it?

The days went on, one after the other, filled with balls and parties and the theater—all the activities of a Congress that still seemed a long way from resolution.

Lili had been punished by being confined to the house. She was not even allowed to go to church every morning for a week, and this was the hardest of all for her, for she was used to attending daily Mass. I had decided on this punishment for two reasons. First as a penance, and second because it kept her away from Melton. But of course I could not keep her indoors forever, which was why she was able to drive out with Alastair and me one crisp afternoon in the new phaeton Alva had commissioned for him. I told myself I was glad she sat gooseberry between us.

Alastair had not come to my room at night again, although I had endured some sleepless nights hoping he would do so. He spent much more time away from the house on the Johannessgasse these days, so much so that Alva commented on it one rainy afternoon when he left us to visit a friend at the British delegation.

I told her I had no idea why he was absent so often, and looked up to see her studying me and looked so sympathetic, I stiffened. Had I been that obviously disappointed? Pray not!

"Now I know why Alastair was so anxious to come on to Vienna, ma'am," I told her, forcing a smile. "He was missing the stimulation a city provides. And, of course, the adulation of his admirers. Did you hear Mrs. Harrison has declared she will have him? There are a good many wagers on the outcome."

"The woman's a fool," Alva said tartly, diverted as I had hoped she would be. "She'll end up a mockery, for he don't want her, not even for a night, he don't."

I managed to change the subject then by asking her if she was to see the Marchioness of Wendover on the morrow. She had become very cozy with the Wendovers, to the point she was allowed to address the very proper lady as Beatrice. If I had not been so full of my own problems, I would have worried more about her future, when she was no longer the darling of the *ton*.

But I was missing Alastair so! More than I would have if he had left Vienna and gone home, if that makes any sense. It was a constant ache under my heart, and to have to see him and pretend nothing had happened between us, that there had been no kiss, no embrace, no soft words of his calling me his "sweet 'Nelia," was sheer torture.

The next afternoon, Brigitte asked if she might speak to me. Lili had gone out with Alastair. I suspected she wanted to beg to try the reins, not that that scheme had any hope of succeeding. I had cried off, claiming I had letters to write.

I studied the maid as she made her curtsey. She was taller than Lili, older too, of course, and a pretty girl with her long blond braids and fresh complexion, her bright blue eyes. She was plump and always dressed very neatly. Today I thought she looked worried about something and I felt a stab of apprehension.

"What is it, Brigitte?" I asked.

"I didn't want to tell you this, but you've been good to me, m'lady, seeing I didn't get turned off after the fireworks. So no matter how Miss Lili would dislike it, I feel I have to. I know from things she's said, you don't like that Viscount Melton. I—I don't like him either, ma'am."

"He has been bothering Lili?" I demanded, not even trying to hide my concern.

She nodded. "Yes, I think so, although she doesn't. I'm always with her, and the footman Herr Cranston assigned to her, though. She doesn't see him alone."

I was relieved to hear that. For one frightening moment I had thought Lili might be meeting him in secret. From Brigitte's account it appeared he was very often there when they came out of church in the morning. He claimed to enjoy a brisk early walk before the crowds gathered. And somehow or other, he managed to find them when they went to the shops.

"What does he say to her? Can you hear?"

"Oh, he talks of this and that, m'lady. Tells her jokes, he does. He's funny, I'll give him that. The footman has trouble not laughing. He asks Miss Lili about her family, the convent even. He walks along with us, you see, wherever we're going. Mentions his little girl, too. He says he hopes Miss Lili will have a chance to meet her when you all go back to England."

She paused then and thought for a moment. "Maybe I'm wrong, ma'am, but I have a feeling about him, for all he's a lord. I don't like him. There's something about him that makes me nervous and wishing I could get away from him. And I feel Miss Lili is in danger, though I don't know why."

She blushed and clasped her hands tightly before her as she added, "I hope you don't think I'm silly, m'lady, or that I've forgot my place. It's just that Miss Lili likes him so! And when I tell her you would want her to stay away from him, and you must have a good reason for saying so, she just tosses her head and says you don't understand him.

"He gave her a note once, in a box of candy he bought her. I saw it, oh, not to read. I can't read English. I think he must have told her some story about you, though, and why you don't like him, because right after that she said she was sorry for you that you could be so unforgiving, and about such a little thing, too."

I felt the hatred inside grow until it threatened to overwhelm me. He was clever, this Gregory Paxton. Very clever as well as evil. I would have to be clever, too. But first I had to think.

I thanked the maid, told her she had done well to come to me. Then I reminded her she must say nothing of our conversation to Lili. Neither should she try to keep Lili from seeing the viscount. Just before I dismissed her, I assured Brigitte this would all soon be over.

When she left, I began to make plans. I knew the only possible course open to me now was to take Lili to England. Yes, take her home and get her settled with a suitable family somewhere in the country where Melton could not find her. For if he could not find her, he would forget her. I knew he would forget her—in time.

I was reminded of all the English parties traveling back and forth and how easy it would be to go with one of them, until it occurred to me that to do so would be to court disaster. Surely Melton would expect it. Furthermore, Lili would tell him just as soon as she learned we were leaving.

I would have to talk to Alastair whether I wanted to or not. This whole situation was full of pitfalls and I was not sure I could manage it safely. I was too involved, too intense, to think coldly and clearly. Alastair, on the other hand, never thought any other way. His advice, and his escort, would be invaluable.

I chanced to see him then from the window, helping Lili down from the phaeton. A moment later, I heard her chattering away as they climbed the stairs, even heard her door close when she left him. He looked surprised when I opened my own door and beckoned to him, but he asked no questions as he joined me.

Breathlessly, I told him what the maid had revealed—how desperate I was to get Lili safely away.

He studied me for a long moment before he nodded. "Yes, I can see you are worried, coz. To be sure, the situation is troublesome. Whoever would have thought the tiresome child would decide to champion the man? Whatever did you say to her?"

"I only told her the truth, as much of it as I could," I retorted. "I said he was a horrid man, that he had done something unforgivable some years ago."

"Which of course instantly intrigued her and set her off on a noble quest to save him from his own iniquity. 'Nelia, 'Nelia! And you were her age once yourself."

I bit back a hasty reply. I did not like this mood Alastair was in, nor his sneering words, but I needed his help too badly to risk losing it. "I thought to travel with a party," I told him instead. "But Melton would certainly find out, in fact he'd probably arrange to be one of the same group."

"You wouldn't enjoy travel en masse. I never do," Alastair said absently. "No, we will not go that way."

To my surprise and disappointment he added, "I must have more time to consider this. Do you have an engagement this evening? No? We will dine at Sperl's then, just the two of us. Not the best place for a tête-à-tête, but it will take us away from Alva's eager ears. And perhaps by then, I will have thought of something."

When I was dressing later, Lili came to tell me all about her drive with Al-as-stair. I watched her in the mirror as the maid arranged my hair. She was perched on the side of my bed, her ankles crossed as demurely as the nuns had taught her, but she gestured wildly as she described my cousin's prowess. She was such a contradiction, Lili, half child, half young woman. But she was all beauty with those black curls tumbling artlessly over her head and the color coming and going in her round cheeks. Her eyes sparkled with fun, and when she laughed, she put her head back and closed her eyes in complete enjoyment. She was wearing a white muslin dress, its flat bodice decorated with narrow tucks of lace. As I watched her and listened, I vowed I would never let anything or anyone destroy her love of life, and I wanted to kill Gregory Paxton for even breathing the same air she did.

Sperl's was one of Vienna's finest restaurants, and it attracted crowds for its music and dancing as well as its excellent food. Somehow Alastair had acquired a table apart from others in a small alcove. There were similar alcoves set around the room, and from what I could see, most of them were filled with couples more intent on each other than their dinners. For a stabbing moment, I wished Alastair and I might be counted among them, instead of being here to plot our escape from the devil.

Alastair waited until the soup plates had been removed before he said, "I hope you did not have a tiring day, coz."

When I looked a question, he went on, "We are leaving tomorrow at dawn. I have set my man to packing only such essentials as I will need for a few days. You should do the same. Lili's clothes can be packed when she is awakened in the morning."

"Tomorrow?" I echoed as the waiter served us some blue trout. "As soon as that?"

"Of course. It is by far the easiest thing to do. We'll take my new phaeton. The old carriage can follow with the rest of our baggage. I am delighted you insisted on keeping our English coachman and grooms. They will travel a more direct route to Antwerp, where we will find a ship for England. I have already sent notes to our acquaintance here that you have received an urgent message from the dowager Countess of Wyckend calling you home. I implied she was very ill."

"But Mrs. Parmeter! She will be distraught to hear such a thing," I protested, although to tell the truth the elderly lady's well-being had never been one of my prime concerns. And now, of course, I was perfectly prepared to sacrifice her for Lili.

"She'll only think you have finally decided to obey the countess's summons to Wyckend, and about time, too. And she'll preen herself for being instrumental in your recall. Old ladies can be so self-centered, don't you agree?"

"Melton will discover we are gone very quickly," I reminded him, putting down my fork, my appetite gone.

"Of course he will, but there won't be anything he can do about it. Do eat your trout, 'Nelia. It is delicious."

"He will follow us, even find us, perhaps," I whispered.

"I doubt he will try. There are so many routes we could take. No, I expect the viscount will make his own way home and wait for us to arrive in London. That is another problem we must solve.

"You cannot take Lili to your home there. It is the first place he will look for her."

The waiter poured more wine for us and it was a moment before I could say, "Yes, that's true enough. I thought, perhaps, to my sister, at least temporarily. She and her husband live outside Bath. It is not an ideal situation for Franklin is very ill, and Phillipa is not strong herself, but I could think of no one else."

"Melton will find her there," Alastair said before he took the last bite of his trout. The attentive waiter hurried forward to take our plates. "It is the next place he will look.

"Fortunately, I've another solution. A dear friend of mine is married to a retired Army captain. He was wounded in the Peninsula Wars and they live quietly in the country. They always wanted children. I am sure they would welcome Lili."

"Is your dear friend a suitable chaperone for a young girl?" I asked. My voice must have betrayed what I was thinking, for a tiny smile curled one corner of his handsome mouth.

"She is the daughter of a vicar. We played together as children. Is that suitable enough for you?"

The veal we were being served now smelled delicious and I managed a bite before I said, "She is not in society? I do not have to fear she will bring Lili to London?"

"Hardly. But she is gentry. I'll write to her tonight."

He took a sip of wine and said, "May I tell you what I have surmised of this precious secret of yours? I believe it might simplify matters between us."

When I nodded, he went on, "Gregory Paxton is not a normal man for all he is married with three children. He is attracted sexually to young girls, as are other men like him. You know this, for someone you are close to was abused by him many years ago. It is why you were so horrified when you discovered he was here, why you became so frantic when he began to pursue Lili."

Not wishing to meet his eyes, I listened to him with my head bent over my plate. "Am I right?" he asked quietly.

"Yes," I managed to say, before I dared to look up at him. He was very close, for he was leaning over the table, his clear green eyes intent on my face.

I felt crowded, almost cornered, and I pressed back in my chair. He did not retreat, although he must have known my feelings.

"There is a much simpler solution, you know," he said in an ordinary, conversational tone. "I know you've considered it yourself, for you carry that pistol of yours so constantly. You even have it tonight. Don't you?"

I could only stare, my dinner forgotten.

"Yes, I do mean arranging his death, and please spare me any exclamations of false horror. It would be a simple matter to kill the man. Simpler here than at home, certainly. Vienna is crowded, and as well as the high and mighty of every nation, you may be sure there are just as many criminals who came here to prey on them. No one would be at all surprised if the viscount were to meet an untimely end, stabbed or shot, and robbed, returning late from an evening party."

He paused for me to comment. After a moment I whispered, "Yes, I've thought of killing him a number of times. I know I could do it if he even touched Lili, and heaven knows that is reason enough. But *you*? You have no quarrel with the man. I would never ask it of you."

"As your kin I would consider it my duty," he said stiffly. "Besides, the man must be killed, the sooner the better. Even if you save Lili from him, you cannot want him to go on abusing little girls. He is a monster.

"To speak of more mundane matters, we need not concern ourselves with his title. He has two sons to carry it on, not that it matters. England is littered with viscounts. What is one less?

"Some dessert? No? Then I suggest we take a short stroll on the ramparts while we perfect our plans."

After we had left the restaurant, I looked back for a moment. My mind was full of what he had just told me. It was ugly and I wanted to forget it. So I tried to memorize the gay scene before me—the whirling dancers, the music, the hum of conversation—even the wonderful aroma of Viennese cooking. I would miss Sperl's. As we went down the steps, I realized I would miss Vienna. It was a delightful city and I had been happy here until Melton had come and destroyed all my peace. Alastair, too, was guilty of that, for kissing me then telling me it had all been a mistake.

The ramparts were crowded, but still there were stretches where we were alone, and able to speak freely. I agreed to leave at dawn, and I was mentally selecting clothing to take with me when I recalled our hostess.

"But what of Alva, coz? She won't be pleased we are deserting her. What can we tell her?"

"It is early. She is still at her evening party. When she comes in, we will tell her about that urgent message you received from the dowager countess. And you can make your good-byes. After you go to bed, I'll have to tell her something more, for I want her to keep our departure a secret as long as possible."

"Why will that matter? The servants will gossip . . ."

"With any luck, Melton will not think to question them for a day or two. He may be disappointed but he will not be surprised if Lili does not attend church tomorrow early. By the next day he will begin to get suspicious, but by then we will be beyond his reach.

"I almost wish he would come after us. It would be easy to kill him, then. I could say I thought he was intent on robbing us. I've heard a number of travelers have been plagued by thieves."

"I pray he doesn't," I said quickly. "Imagine Lili having to see such a thing, coz! It would be beyond terrible."

I shuddered then, picturing Alastair standing over Melton's body, while Lili had hysterics. Immediately, Alastair put his arm around me, saying, "You are cold. There is a chill in the air tonight. I'm afraid winter is coming at last."

We had turned to walk back to the steps where the carriage waited, and I heard a couple moaning somewhere ahead in the dark.

"Where do the lovers go, I wonder, when winter comes?" I asked.

He did not answer. Instead he said, "Did Lili ever

mention anything else to you that she saw up here? Besides the fireworks, I mean?"

"Not a word. Do you suppose she was afraid she might shock me if she did?"

For a brief second his arm tightened, then he let me go. "You are a gallant woman, 'Nelia," he said, his voice somber. "The more I know you, the more I have come to admire you. You are not to worry. We'll get Lili safe away, home, too. Melton will never have her, my word on that."

Chapter Fifteen

I set a maid to packing the clothes I had selected as soon as we reached the house on the Johannesgasse, and I had a word with Brigitte as well. At first she was upset Lili was leaving, but she promised she would not say anything about it, and do her best to keep the other maids from gossiping. She was grateful for the money I gave her. We both knew it was unlikely Mrs. Deevers would keep her on once we had left.

Alva Potter was home by eleven. I was thankful elderly ladies did not normally keep late hours. She protested our departure as I had predicated, and was only slightly mollified to learn a dowager countess had called us away.

"I shall come and see you in London, m'lady," she told me. She looked militant, as if she expected to be rebuffed.

"I shall be looking forward to it, ma'am," I replied with a smile. She smiled in return, and Alastair gave me a mock salute.

I do not know what he told her when I left them, but when he knocked on my door later, he said it was all arranged and we could leave without fear of immediate pursuit.

Once again he sounded disappointed, and I was quick to grasp his hand. On the drive back to the house, I had made him promise he would not kill Melton unless the man was threatening Lili. "I know," I whispered, although there was no one to hear us in the vast empty hall. "I am even sorry. But I wouldn't feel right about you destroying the man in cold blood."

"You are thinking like a woman, coz," he drawled. "Deep inside, you know his destruction, as you put it, is the best thing that could happen. Someone must rid the world of this beast who preys on little girls. I would consider it an honor to be the one to do it."

He shrugged. "But then, you have made me promise not to, and I do keep my promises."

We stared at each other, and aware I still held his hand, I tried to release it. He was having none of that, and he kept possession of it as he raised it to his lips and kissed it. Startled—my breathing erratic—not at all sure what I might do or say next, I managed to pull away.

"The maids know when to call us," Alastair said, all business again. "Sleep well. It will be a long day."

We were fortunate it was fine the next morning. I had not even considered how uncomfortable it would be in an open carriage if it was raining. Our small amount of baggage was strapped on behind, and Mrs. Deevers had given us a package of food for the journey. Lili sulked. She had been amazed when I woke her and told her to hurry into her clothes as a silent, red-eyed Brigitte packed a few necessities.

"I don't see why we have to rush off like this," she complained as I brushed her hair and tied it back with a ribbon. "Why can't we go tomorrow? Or even the next day? And what about your friends? Won't they be hurt when you leave without saying good-bye?"

"Alastair has sent word to everyone. I told you this is an emergency. There now, say your good-byes to Brigitte and come down as soon as you can. I believe the carriage is already at the door."

I left the two girls weeping in each other's arms, and it was several minutes before Lili joined us where we waited by the front door. I saw her maid at the top of the flight. She was signaling to me, and I said, "Oh, I almost forgot! Go ahead, both of you. I will be with you shortly."

As Brigitte handed me a folded sheet of paper, she whispered, "She just wrote this, ma'am. She told me to give it to that viscount when I saw him today after church."

I scanned the few short lines. She was sorry she had to leave like this. She thanked him for his kindness. And she said she looked forward to seeing him in England. Repulsed, I tore up the note and told Brigitte to burn it.

As we set off in the gray light of dawn, Lili sitting between us, she said, "Could we drive by the Stephansdom, Al-as-tair? It is such a beautiful church. I would like to see it one last time."

Since it was only five in the morning, I hardly thought Melton would be hanging about, still, I was delighted when Alastair refused her request.

"We must make haste, Lili," he said after we had exchanged a quick, knowing glance over her head. "Aren't you excited to be traveling again? There will be so many new things to see. Just think, soon you will be sailing across the North Sea to England."

Lili didn't answer. She was staring straight ahead, her brow knit in a frown. I knew she was thinking of Melton. But by the time the sun was up and we were trotting along a country road that followed the Danube north, she had regained her spirits. The delicious scones Mrs. Deever had packed, filled with butter and strawberry jam, helped. We stopped an hour later for a more substantial breakfast. Lili paid no attention as Alastair and I examined a map. She was down on the floor, playing with the inn's kitten, and completely engrossed.

"It would be quicker if we went this way," Alastair said, tracing a route very near the border with France. "Still, I think it best we employ some subterfuge here. The two of us and a young girl in that handsome phaeton are sure to be remembered. Let us head northeast for a while, stop for the night in some nondescript little village."

"So you do think he will follow us!" I whispered.

"Not really. But since you have forbidden me to kill him, we must take the safest way."

"Will you ever forgive me for it?" I asked. "You have mentioned it several times now."

"I would forgive you anything, 'Nelia. Anything at all," he said before he excused himself to see to the horses, for of course we did not have a groom.

I stared after him. As usual, this morning he was dressed to a nicety, his linen dazzling white, his cravat crisp. He wore gray. Perhaps to discourage the road dust from marring his appearance? I had my doubts Lili and I would be remembered. I was sure Alastair would be.

We made good time that first day. The light phaeton, while uncomfortably crowded with three abreast, covered the miles easily, and we did not have to rest the team so often. We even found a respectable inn, complete with feather beds that almost swallowed Lili and I up, to her delight. I was glad to see her sunny spirits had returned, and I was sure Gregory Paxton would soon be only a distant memory.

The following days continued much the same. Going an unusual route as we did, we saw no English travelers. One day when it rained hard, we spent the day at an inn where we had stopped. Lili wrote some letters to her friends at the convent. As I had suspected, she also wrote to Viscount Melton, but Alastair was able to intercept that letter after she gave it to the innkeeper to post. I hated this deception we were forced to employ. It seemed so hateful to trick her like this, even if it was for her own good. But when I considered what the alternative would be, my resolve was stiffened.

At last we arrived in Antwerp. It was a much larger city than Vienna, and a bustling port. Lili's eyes were wide as she took in the sights, and she wrinkled her nose when she discovered how strange salt water, tar, and a low tide could smell.

We put up at an inn on the outskirts of town, and Alastair went off to look for a ship. Much later, after

Lili had gone yawning to bed, we sat in our private parlor and discussed the matter.

"There are no ships sailing to England for three days, ma'am," he told me as he poured us a glass of wine. "However, I've booked passage on the best. It can even take the phaeton lashed down on the deck. I would have hated to have to sell Alva's extravagant present.

"I also wrote to Nancy Moorland this afternoon, apprising her of our arrival. The ship we take goes to London. We will drive from there to Oxfordshire. It is not too tiresome a journey, and then our travels with Lili will be over."

I rose and went to the window. I could see nothing of the dark street, nothing at all except the reflection of Alastair's handsome blond head, that distinctive profile as he turned when a log snapped in the fireplace.

"Yes, it will be over," I agreed, resting my forehead on the cold pane. "I pray Lili will like Mrs. Moorland and her husband."

"She's a good 'un, is Nancy," Alastair said. "She used to follow my lead in every kind of prank."

"Hardly an attribute one looks for in a chaperone, is it, sir?" I asked as I came back to the table.

He looked amazed, but I saw the light in his eye. "Oh, surely you are wrong, ma'am," he drawled. "Just consider. Knowing the young's capacity for deviltry, she will be able to forestall any of Lili's antics before she even gets up to them."

I smiled, but my heart wasn't in it. Indeed, I was feeling blue-deviled this evening, my heart heavy when I thought of the impending separation. And to be honest, it was not my separation from Lili that made me sad. No, indeed.

We had been together for so long, Alastair and I, what with the traveling and the weeks spent in Vienna. I would miss him dreadfully after he delivered me safely to my door on Upper Brook Street in Mayfair. And he? Glancing at his serene face as he studied the red wine in his glass, I was sure he would be relieved. This had all taken so much more time than I had told him it would when I first proposed the expedition. Then I had contemplated a dash across France to collect Lili, the same dash back, a short sail across the Channel, then home to London. It should have taken no more than a couple of weeks all told, yet here it was late October. The cold wind off the North Sea I had felt on arrival here told me we would be lucky to escape the first snow.

No doubt Alastair would be glad to return to his own comfortable rooms on Jermyn Street and the services of his longtime valet, to say nothing of his usual routine—his clubs, his friends, his tailor and vintner, all his amusements. I studied him again, marveling at how my opinion of him had changed. When we had set out, I considered him a fop, with little fortitude and resolve. I had even regretted having to ask him to serve as my companion, regretted there had been no one else more masculine and assertive, someone skilled with weapons or their fists, in case the need should arrive. But I had learned a careful attention to detail in one's dress and person was not everything. That it was only a part of the strong, decisive man Alastair Russell was. I would trust him with my life now.

Besides, I love him, I reminded myself, although the thought was never far from my mind. I looked down at my clasped hands where they rested on the table. How shall I manage without him, I wondered. How could I stand not seeing him every day, not being able to talk to him in the evenings like this, before a fire and over a glass of wine? How tiresome my life would seem not to attend balls and receptions and the theater on his arm, knowing how I was envied, secure in his escort. How was I to bear not being able to look up at him to share some secret amusement, or to know we were even thinking identical thoughts?

I looked up now to see him regarding me, his eyes intent and his face serious. For a moment I could only stare back at him, hungry to commit every one of his features to memory. "Yes?" I asked when the silence between us had gone on too long. "There was something you wanted to say, coz?"

He shook his head. As I sipped my wine, I wondered if I had only imagined the regret I thought I saw in his eyes. There were currents in the room tonight, vague stirrings that made me uneasy. I was glad when he began to talk about what we could do to keep Lili amused until the ship sailed. When I mentioned it might be wise to practice caution, he only shook his head.

"He'll not come here, 'Nelia. He will go directly to Calais for the shorter voyage across the Channel. Besides, you yourself remarked how quickly we were able to travel, rid of that cumbersome carriage. No, we need not skulk about Antwerp. Let us enjoy our stay."

And so we did. We inspected all the wharfs, admired the fleet of boats in the harbor, and exclaimed over the fishermen's catch. We ate in various inns and restaurants, saw all the shops, and walked everywhere, to Lili's delight. It had been hard for her to be cooped up on the crowded seat of the phaeton, for she was young and active. Often, in our rambles, she skipped ahead, only returning to tell us of something she had admired. I knew she looked untidy, for I was not a lady's maid, but she didn't care about her appearance yet. I am sure I did not look all that well myself, unlike Alastair, who put us both to shame. I remarked it one morning when he came down from his room, and he laughed.

"I told you I had learned well how to be an exquisite, since that is the role I am assigned in society," he said as Lili set off ahead, and he offered me his arm.

"Don't say that! You're *not* a fop, far from it in fact!"

"How fierce you sound, 'Nelia. But I'm glad you think so. It has become important to me, your good opinion. Very important."

I felt my heartbeat quicken, but before he could

elaborate, Lili was back insisting we hurry. There was an old sailor ahead with a darling little monkey to sell, and please, couldn't she have him? She was sure he wouldn't be any trouble, and he had a scarlet coat with brass buttons and a dear little hat . . .

"The monkey or the sailor?" Alastair inquired. "And no, Lili, you can't have either one," he added, and the moment was gone.

I loved Lili very much by this time, but I must admit I did not love her interruptions. Far from it.

We boarded the ship in the morning of the day appointed. She had been brought in to one of the wharfs, to take on the phaeton and team. Lili and I both laughed till we ached to see that elegant gentleman's vehicle, all shiny yellow and scarlet, lashed securely to heavy metal rings set in the deck of the vessel. It looked for all the world like a spectacular insect, come to light for a moment on a piece of prosaic wood, and astonished to find itself there.

The passage was uneventful and, thanks to a brisk wind out of the north, swift as well. Lili stayed on deck with Alastair while I sought refuge below. She was warm enough in her cherry red cloak with its fur hood.

While the phaeton was being unloaded, Lili and I waited at a nearby inn. Alastair took a hackney to his rooms to retrieve his post. He had decided it would be best if Lili were not seen in London.

"There's a tidy inn I know of where we can spend the night," he told me when he returned from his errand. "Tomorrow, we can drive to Oxfordshire. I've had a letter from Nancy. She tells me they are looking forward to meeting Lili and having her stay with them. For as long as you like, ma'am."

I nodded but I could not speak just then. I seemed to have acquired a large, uncomfortable lump in my throat.

Lili seemed aware of our impending separation as well for she became very quiet. The inn where we spent the night was very nice. Yes, the bed was comfortable. No, she didn't care for any more chicken, thank you. How strange it was everyone spoke English. Why, she had heard no French, no German, since we landed.

My heart went out to her. I wished I might hug her close, but I knew it would be better to pretend everything was as it should be. Lili had known from the beginning she was not to live with me, that I was only a relative sent to bring her to England.

When we reached it, we saw that the village of Holford was small and quiet. It had a common surrounded by a church, a grist mill, and some cottages. To me, the familiar English scenery meant home, and it was lovely even in late autumn. I wondered what Lili thought of the distant hills, the stubbled fields and empty pastures. We rumbled over a wide stream and I admired the tidy farms we passed, with their hayricks and barns filled for winter.

The Moorlands owned an extensive property several miles from the village. The house was reached by a winding drive. It was built of gray stone and had a slate roof. As we went up the path to the front door, Lili reached for my hand, and I held it tightly. The pretty woman who opened the door for us had one of the kindest faces I had ever seen. I felt better immediately, and even Lili was able to summon a smile when she curtsied.

We were shown into a cozy parlor and introduced to Captain Moorland. I learned he was blind when he told Lili he would expect her to tell him exactly what she looked like—and no cheating, mind!—so he could picture her. And he said he had been looking forward to conversing in French again. The room had a great many books. I caught Lili looking at them and I knew she was already planning how she could read them to him. A friendly sheepdog at the captain's feet was begging for her attention, its tail wagging, and I was able to relax. By the time we all had a cup of tea, we were much easier together, talking and laughing.

Alastair and I were to stay overnight, leaving early in the morning.

I went up with Lili at bedtime. The room that was to be hers looked out over the fields to the woods beyond. It had pretty blue and white curtains and a soft rag rug as well as a dainty rocker set near the window. Resting on the bed was a doll with a porcelain face and blond hair. She was dressed in a pink satin gown, and her bonnet had a feather to match.

"She used to be mine," Nancy Moorland told Lili. "I hope you are not too old for dolls."

"I never had one," Lili told her. "I shall call her Clarissa."

She smiled then, and the lump in my throat I had been afraid was becoming a permanent fixture seemed smaller. I knew it would be all right. Lili would be happy here, and her happiness was just as important to me as her safety.

When Lili fell asleep, Nancy Moorland and I went down to join the gentlemen again. Alastair was telling the captain of one of his wife's more exciting adventures as a child, to that man's great delight. For a while we talked of times past, but eventually Alastair brought the conversation around to Lili. I was glad to sit back and let him tell the Moorlands about Viscount Melton and the threat he presented.

"I am sure there is no need to worry about the man now," Alastair concluded. "There is no way he can discover where Lili is, for only 'Nelia and I know. I mention it only as a precaution."

"What a horrible man!" Nancy Moorland whispered, hand to her throat. "You may be sure we will be alert for any strangers."

"You said you had told the child to address all her letters to you," the captain said. He wore a frown now. I suspected he was cursing his blindness, wishing he might be able to sight down a pistol barrel if ever Melton showed his face here. "Didn't that make her wonder?"

"No, for I told her I would be traveling about for

some time," I contributed. "The supposed emergency that called me home was the elder Countess of Wyckend's illness. But I told Lili I did not know how long I would be visiting her, nor when I might go to stay with my sister, and that it was easier all around to send any letters to me to Alastair, in London, for he would know where to find me.

"I hope you will write to me the same way," I added, almost shyly. "I will be anxious to hear how Lili is coming along. And I must thank you for taking her in. She is a dear child, although she is not without faults, of course."

"Much better to let the Moorlands discover those on their own, don't you think, 'Nelia?" Alastair drawled, and we all smiled.

We had a sad farewell the next morning, and I shed as many tears as Lili did. But at last we were rumbling down the drive. I blew my nose and told myself I would not look back.

"I am so sorry, Alastair," I said as we reached the road and the gray stone house could be seen no more. "I am not in general a watering pot. But I have come to love Lili. Really, I never expected to, for I am not generally fond of children."

"But it would be strange if you were not attached to her, after all our adventures," he told me, looking straight ahead. "I, myself, have grown very fond of her. And I have *never* liked children."

Chapter Sixteen

We were forced to spend another night on the road. I found it awkward to be alone with Alastair, for some reason. I told myself it was only that I missed Lili between us, chattering away and calling our attention to something interesting she saw. Alastair, too, seemed different. He was quiet, preoccupied even, and he looked stern. I wondered what he was thinking. Was he glad this whole experience was almost over? Was he looking forward to returning to his carefree bachelor ways, unencumbered by a thirteen-year-old child or a distant female relative?

It was almost a relief when we stopped before my home on Upper Brook Street early in the afternoon the next day. After Alastair lifted me down from the phaeton and set me on my feet, he continued to hold my waist with both hands. "So this is how it ends, m'lady," he said, his eyes steady on mine.

"Yes, I suppose so. It is hard to believe." Then, loath to let him go, I added, "Would you care to join me for dinner later? I must give you those addresses where I can be reached."

"I would like that very much indeed," he said as he let me go at last to unstrap my portmanteau and carry it up the steps for me.

"It won't be a fancy repast," I warned him. "There is no need to dress."

"There is every need to dress," he contradicted me, his voice tart. "Into something other than this grubby gray coat. And I would be pleased if you never wore that navy gown again, coz. Too tiresome!"

I was smiling as I left him. Smiling as I greeted my dear old butler, who seemed so glad to see me. But I stopped smiling when I saw the card that sat on the foyer table beside the early-afternoon post. I knew whose card it was, and I felt a chill even before I picked it up and read Melton's name in elegant, etched script.

"The gentleman has been here these past three days, m'lady," Goodson informed me. "He seems very anxious to see you."

For a moment I toyed with the idea of asking Goodson to deny me to Melton when he came again. For he would come again, I could wager anything you liked on that. And heaven knows I had no desire to see the man. Ever. But then reason prevailed. I would have to see Melton sometime. Surely it would be better to get it over with as soon as possible. Besides, Alastair was coming tonight, I reminded myself, my spirits lifting. I could ask his advice on how I should handle the man.

There was nothing to worry about. Lili was safe in Oxfordshire and there was no way on earth Melton could find her. No one knew where she was but Alastair and myself. And his caution in making sure she had no direct contact with me made it certain Melton could not find out her whereabouts from a careless servant. Lili was safe. She would certainly forget Melton, and in time, while he might not forget her, he would cease to want her, for she would be a woman grown and of no interest to him anymore. I shuddered as I went upstairs to my room.

I could hear the bustle of well-trained servants seeing to my bath and clean clothes, and preparing to entertain that premier beau, Mr. Alastair Russell. And I wondered why, now I was home and all was well with my world, I felt so blue-deviled again. It was only when I slid down in the hot, scented bath water that I realized tonight would be the first one since the night in the convent that Alastair and I would not be sleeping under the same roof. And although in one way it was no great distance from Upper Brook Street to Jermyn Street, where Alastair kept rooms, in another way we might as well have been an ocean apart. And this would only be the first of many such nights. All the rest of my life, in fact. No wonder I had a fit of the dismals!

Alastair came at eight and I received him in the drawing room. A welcoming fire burned on the hearth, for the November evening was damp and chill. I was wearing one of the nicer gowns I had left here. Somehow I was sure it would not meet with the particular Mr. Russell's approval. I was right. He barely waited until my butler served us sherry and bowed himself away before he said, "Whatever possessed you to order that gown, 'Nelia? And in that insipid lilac shade, too? It doesn't even fit well. You look like a dowager."

"I am as good as a dowager," I reminded him. Holding up my glass, I added, "Thank you so much for your kind words, sir."

"You'll get no false compliments from me, my girl," he said, abandoning his pose by the mantel to sit down across from me. "This is excellent sherry. Part of the earl's cellar?"

"No, I purchased it. But I do use Ogden's vintner, and I follow his recommendations."

"I wish you would follow mine when you shop for gowns," he said. "You don't seem to have the slightest idea what becomes you. And you are nowhere near particular enough about the fit. You have a stunning figure. No one would suspect it, however, from the way you dress."

I raised my brows and tried to look shocked, but he ignored me as we were called to the table.

I had arranged for us to serve ourselves, old-fashioned though it might be. I wanted no stilted conversation, no untimely interruptions by servants bringing yet another dish or a different bottle of wine. And I had

had us placed across from each other at the table so we could see each other easily.

"The quail looks delicious," Alastair remarked as he took one of the little birds. "Shall I serve you?"

I nodded as I helped myself to salad. I had very little appetite tonight.

"Now perhaps you will tell me what is bothering you," he added as he filled his plate. "And don't bother to deny it. I know you well enough by this time to sense when something is wrong."

"Melton is here. In London," I told him, not a bit surprised he could sense my uneasiness.

"And . . . ?"

"He has called here for the last three days and left his card," I said, trying not to sound as apprehensive as I felt.

"Of course he has. The sole is excellent, coz."

"Alastair! What am I to do?" I demanded, putting down my fork.

"To start, eat your dinner," he said, promptly setting a good example. Eventually, he went on, "Come now, you knew he would follow us home. You know, I find it amazing he is so persistent. There are many little girls. What is there about Lili that captivates him so? Or is it that he cannot bear to be thwarted, and once his fancy lights on a particular child, he must have her and none other?"

"Please do not talk about it," I said stiffly. "It makes me sick."

"As you wish. The story is told anyway, for Lili is safe from him."

"Are you sure there is no way he can discover her whereabouts?"

He sipped his wine before he said, "Well, you and I know, but we won't tell him. The Moorlands, too, of course, but they don't know Melton and we have alerted them to the danger he presents. Lili might tell him herself, if she knew how to reach him. If by some strange chance she should find out, the captain is ready to intercept any letter she might write. As for our servants, the men bringing our trunks have orders to deliver everything to my rooms. I will have yours brought here. Lili's trunk can be sent on by carter. My man will see to it. He is invaluable to me."

"Is he the one who shot you in Scotland?" I could not help asking. "I would not say he was *invaluable.*"

"Ah, but he is," he assured me with a devilish grin. "He is so distraught at what he did to me, not to mention ruining one of my better coats, he cannot do enough for me. I never had a coat that fit me better. I'll not let him forget it. No, King is the least of our worries. Melton will not learn anything from him.

"As for your servants, I am sure you did not assemble them this afternoon and tell them all your adventures."

"No, of course not. They do not know why I went to France. They do not even know Lili exists."

"There you are," he said as he poured another glass of wine. I saw him frown when he observed I had barely touched my glass or my dinner, and sure I was about to be treated to one of his sarcastic lectures, I began to eat.

After dinner and a heady trifle I knew cook had made especially for the famous Mr. Russell, we sat on at the table over our port.

"How comfortable this is," Alastair said, looking over the cozy dining room and the crackling fire that burned in the hearth at one end of the room. "How pleasant it is not to have to make interesting conversation with people on either side who are not interesting at all. Take care, ma'am, lest I begin hinting for invitations to dine alone with you at every turn."

I was not required to answer this sally, for he went on, "Tell me of your family, if you please. In all the time we have been together, I do not recall you mentioning them except in passing. And I know little of them for I tend to shun family occasions whenever I can."

I sipped my port to give myself time to think. "There is nothing much to tell," I said finally. "My background is ordinary. You would find it all tedious, I'm sure."

"Try me."

"Well, as you know, the family home is in Berkshire. Near Sutton Courtenay. You look confused, sir. You are not familiar with the area? The nearest town of any size is Abingdon.

"I have only the one brother, George, and one sister, Phillipa. They are both older than I, George by twelve years, Phillipa by seven. I suspect I was not too welcome a surprise addition."

"As the baby by so many years, were you spoiled?"

"I don't remember being so. My father was strict, not given to indulging anyone. My mother was a dear, however. I loved her very much. She died a few years ago."

As I paused, he said, "I understand your father has married again?"

I grimaced. "Yes, to a widowed and wealthy neighbor. He is a man who has his eye firmly on his main objective—acquiring as much land and wealth as he can."

"You do not care for him. I can understand why," Alastair murmured, leaning back in his chair. His fingers rested lightly on the stem of his glass. He had an elegant hand, white and long-fingered with perfectly manicured nails. He wore no rings. His hand looked effete, much as he himself did, but I could attest to its strength. And its gentleness, on occasion.

" 'Nelia?"

I hoped I did not flush as I looked up at him. Hoped he could not divine my thoughts now.

"You have told me all I care to know of George and his brood of children. But what of Phillipa? Your voice warms when you speak of her. You love her, as you loved your mother?"

"Oh, yes, Phil is grand. We were not close when I was a child, for then she seemed just another grown-up to me. But as I grew older, the age difference mattered less."

"Whom did she marry?"

"Sir Franklin Wheelock. She married late, at twenty-five. He is much older than she, and he is ill now. Phil, too, is not in good health. I worry about her, for Sir Franklin depends on her so. They live near Bath, so he may have the benefit of the waters."

"Do you visit often? Any of your family?"

I sipped my port before I answered, "I see Phil as often as I can, George and his family rarely, and my father, never. We are estranged."

"And, I gather from your militant tone, that is a closed subject. Don't fret. I've no intention of prying.

"How did you meet the earl?"

I wondered what Alastair would consider prying, but I did not hesitate. "He was an acquaintance of my brother's. He came to Berks to visit once, he and a friend of his, for the hunting season."

"And he fell in love with you," Alastair supplied. "He must have been much older if he was a friend of your brother."

"Yes, Ogden would have been forty-two this year."

"Did you love him?"

I stared across the table at my handsome cousin. No, I thought. Not as I love you. "Shall we go to the drawing room?" I said instead.

As we took our seats there, I said, "We will not discuss the earl, if you please. My marriage is personal."

"But you have given me an answer already, my dear," he told me. "Now I am free to indulge in all sorts of fantasies. Did your father perhaps force you into this advantageous alliance with an earl? You were young so it could not be you accepted him because you were at your last prayers. Or could it be you were compromised? No, I doubt that. You are too clever a puss to allow that to happen."

"Fantasize all you wish, sir. I shall not be tricked into saying aye or nay to you, clever puss that I am."

"Very well. Tell me instead if you plan to go and

visit your sister, travel to Wyckend and the wicked dowager?"

"I must see Phil soon. I have to give her news of Lili."

"I am sure she especially will be anxious to hear."

I wondered at his tone of voice, the way he stressed some words.

"May I suggest you keep Lili's whereabouts a secret? The fewer people who know, the safer she will be. For when Melton can gain no information in London, he may well cast his net further."

"I hadn't thought of that. I must also see my agent, tell him to discontinue the search for any distant relatives Lili might have. Oh, I cannot thank you enough for the Moorlands."

He held up both hands and I chuckled. "Very well, sir," I said. "Tell me what I should do when Melton calls tomorrow. My first impulse was to forbid him the house."

"You can, of course, do that. But you will have to see him sooner or later. Would you prefer to meet him at a crowded party where anyone might overhear you? Or perhaps in Hyde Park where your meeting will be commented on?

"If I were you, I would see him here. You have nothing to say to him, so it will not last long. Later, tell your butler you will not receive him again, and it's done."

I nodded and we talked of this and that for some time. Alva Potter and her unexpected captivation of the *ton,* the Peace Congress and Napoleon, the current fashions and whether I needed a lady's maid, town gossip Alastair had gleaned at his club. I was surprised when I heard the hall clock strike twelve. It had not seemed that late to me.

As I walked him to the door, we made arrangements to meet at a modiste Alastair favored, so I might have his help selecting new clothes. We were observed by a carefully expressionless Mr. Goodson. I wished I might have seen his face when Alastair bent and kissed me good-bye. As he straightened, he murmured, "It is quite all right, dear 'Nelia. We are cousins. You might remind your faithful old retainer of that if he takes umbrage at my taking liberties. Besides, it was a cousinly kiss. Unfortunately."

Melton came at two the following afternoon. I had just received a visit from my agent. There had been several pressing matters to do with Wyckend to be decided, investments to be discussed, and household funds to be arranged. I was tired, but I did not hesitate when Goodson brought Melton's card to the library.

I did not rise from my place behind my desk when he came in, nor did I speak as he bowed. He smiled at me, that warm, deceptive confiding smile of his that made him look so trustworthy. I made myself think of Alastair. I would get through this. It would take only a few minutes.

"How kind of you to see me, Countess," he began. "I hope you had a good journey home?"

"What do you want?" I said baldly, playing with the pen I had been using.

His brows rose. "May I sit down?" he asked, sounding amused.

As he looked around for a chair, I said, "I don't think it necessary. You will not be here that long."

"How very ungracious of you, my dear," he said, looking less pleasant now. "Very well, if it is to be business, let's get to it, shall we?"

"I have no business with you, nor you with me."

"True. You have some information I require, however. I think you know what I am referring to, ma'am."

I nodded. "You will never get that information from me. That is all I have to say to you. Do not come here again. I intend to give my staff orders I will not receive you."

"How haughty we are! Becoming Ogden's countess has made you arrogant. But I wonder how arrogant you will be if word gets out about your marriage to that gentleman, ma'am. The true nature of it, I mean."

I stared at his triumphant face, hoping I looked calmer than I felt.

"Oh, yes, it would be too bad if it became common gossip, wouldn't it? It would probably kill the dowager to learn about her beloved son. Do you want that on your conscience? Come now, tell me where Lili is and I'll bother you no more. And no one will find out about the earl. My word on it."

"I can't tell you just like that," I said, stalling for time. "I will send you word—"

"No, we will settle the matter today. I've waited long enough. I'll have the child's address and I'll have it now. Where have you put her?"

I reached into the desk drawer and pulled out my pistol, glad I had placed it there earlier in anticipation of any trouble.

"I will not tell you. I will never tell you," I said through gritted teeth as I rose and faced him. "And if one word about Ogden gets bruited about, I will have you killed. I am tempted to do it right now myself, but I am rather fond of the carpet and I don't want it to get bloodstained. Go away, Melton. You are the most despicable, ugly, unclean specimen of a human being I have ever had the misfortune to know. Your death would be a blessing so do not tempt me."

"You are making a mistake, ma'am. A big mistake. And there are others who will be hurt if I choose to talk about your past. Have you forgotten them? Your beloved sister Phillipa, for example."

I know I paled. I could feel the blood leaving my head and I took a deep breath to steady myself. My heart was beating as fast as a drum calling men to battle. Fiercely I concentrated on aiming the pistol directly at his heart.

"If you are not out of this room in three seconds, sir, you will never leave it alive. One . . . two . . ."

He must have seen something in my face that told him I meant every word I said, for he turned and left quickly. As I heard the front door close behind him, I put the pistol down carefully to rub my hands. They were tight with cramp where I had clutched the gun so tightly in my determination. For I meant it, you know. I would have killed him. Part of me was sorry I had not.

I sat down abruptly, my breathing shallow and a cold, damp sweat beading my brow. What was I to do? What *could* I do to keep him from destroying so many lives? On the other hand, I could not give Lili up to him. Oh, no, there was no way I was going to do that.

Chapter Seventeen

I do not keep a stable in London. When necessary I use a livery nearby, and it was to this establishment I sent a message only a short time after Melton had left me.

I had decided there was only one course open to me. I must go to Bath and see Phillipa and I must do it now. I was of two minds about telling her of Melton's threat. I would have to see if she were strong enough to bear the consequences if he made the story common knowledge. What my father and brother would think of it, I neither knew nor cared. I had obeyed their dictates for quite long enough, and now I would act as I saw fit. For I had discovered I was so tired of subterfuge, I really did not care what happened. I did, of course, regret that Sarah, the Dowager Countess of Wyckend, must learn the truth about Ogden. But it might be possible to keep the news from her. She never came to London and at her age had few friends and acquaintances to tell her "for her own good." I would have to enlist Mrs. Parmeter's aid, dislike the woman though I might. But all of this was for the future.

I did not think Melton would make any sudden moves. No, surely Alastair was right. He would try again to find Lili's whereabouts by guile, now he had not been successful in cowing me into revealing them. I must warn Phillipa of that. Prepare her. Besides, he could not reveal his part in all this. To do so would destroy him, and his family. He would have to be very careful what he said, and how he said it. For a moment

I toyed with the idea of contacting his wife, enlisting her aid to procure his silence. But I shrank from imposing such pain. If she discovered she was married to a monster, it would have to be by some other method.

Alastair. Oh, how I wanted to send the footman running to his rooms to summon him to help me! But I knew this problem was mine alone to solve. The elegant Mr. Russell would not find himself tainted with this sordid story.

And so I issued a number of crisp orders to my staff, and wrote a number of notes. To my sister, apprising her of my arrival, to my agent, to some friends, and of course to Alastair. I had to tell him, for I would not be able to keep the appointment we had made to clothe me to his meticulous standards. I kept his note short, however, saying only that I had decided it best to visit my sister immediately. As I signed it, I remembered he would be expecting to hear how my visit from Melton had gone and in a post script I said the gentleman had come and gone no wiser than before. And then I sat and stared at the note and wished I might tell him I loved him.

I left London at eight the following morning. My note to Alastair would be delivered at noon, for I could not be sure he might not volunteer to accompany me.

As I sat and stared at the London streets we were making a slow way through, I hoped my journey would be successful. Perhaps I could get Phillipa to agree the time for secrecy was past. That nothing would come of any gossip Melton might set about. For he had no proof. He could only start rumors, and rumors about long-ago events rarely stirred any interest today. Except, I realized with a sinking heart, when they were about such lurid, unbelievably evil events. Such were my depressing thoughts as we reached the Great West Road and the horses lengthened their stride.

I was tired of traveling. Tired of sitting in a carriage suffering the drafts, the bumpy road, the smells, and the constant swaying motion. Tired of posting inns with suspicious beds, plain food, and noisy company. Beside me, my maid slept with her head back, snoring gently. She had been very busy getting my clothes ready on such short notice. I smiled a little. My dear Phil would not care my gowns were dowdy and did not fit me well.

But of course, all things come to an end, and it was with a great deal of relief that I stepped down before the Wheelock home in the tiny village of Limpley Stoke. This location had been chosen because Sir Franklin's nerves could not support the noise and commotion of Bath itself. I had often wondered how he would have fared in London, for to me Bath was so quiet it was almost moribund.

The butler who admitted me welcomed me in a whisper before he hurried away to warn the groom to set my portmanteaus down quietly.

I found my sister in the front parlor with her needlework. The door that led to Sir Franklin's bedchamber adjoining was slightly ajar, and before I could say a word, she put her finger to her lips and hurried to close it gently.

"He is sleeping," she breathed as she took me in her arms and kissed me. "How are you, dearest Cornelia? Oh, I am so happy you are home safely!"

I hugged her carefully, for she was very thin. Much thinner than the last time I had seen her. As I stepped away, I studied her face. It looked worn and pale, and the black curls so like my own were streaked with gray, that prominent widow's peak entirely white. Her hand, too, I noticed as it clasped mine, seemed almost translucent.

"I am well," I said softly, taking the seat beside her on the sofa she indicated. "You do not look well, however. Tell me, Phil, do you *ever* get outside? Get some fresh air? You are so white, my dear!"

She flushed a little, her eyes straying to the connecting door. I knew Franklin kept that room because the stairs made his heart flutter. Or so he said. I had long considered my brother-in-law a petty tyrant who delighted in keeping Phil constantly on call for the smallest thing. I had once heard him summon her from three rooms away (by bell, for raising his voice gave him the headache) because he had dropped his handkerchief. In vain I had begged her to hire a male nurse. She had refused even to consider it, for she said Sir Franklin preferred her ministrations to any others. He did not like his doctors, either, and changed them with great regularity. Those who agreed with his own diagnosis of his health tended to be summoned more often than those who said they could find nothing wrong with him. One had even told him brusquely it would do him a world of good to rise at an early hour and go for a bracing walk every day. Just the suggestion of such a thing had been enough to keep him tied to his bed for a week. Yes, you are right. I did not like Sir Franklin. I had never understood why Phillipa loved him so.

"I do go out in the garden, but not in November, goose," Phillipa was saying now, and I scolded myself mentally for starting our time together with a belligerent question. My sister had lived this way for many years. No doubt she would continue to do so until her husband died, or she did. I was sure the man would outlive all of us. He took such care of himself, how could it be otherwise? I told myself I was going to be pleasant. I would not have to see much of him, he was so often napping, or feeling indisposed for company. And that was a blessing.

And so I smiled and asked for news of him before I began to speak of my journey abroad, and of Lili, and the dear girl she was. It was not until we had finished a cup of tea that I cautiously mentioned Melton. Phillipa's eyes grew round with fright and she caught her breath. I was putting out my hand to steady her when a bell rang in the next room.

"Oh, there is Sir Franklin calling for me," she said, rising quickly. I thought she sounded almost relieved. "I will be back as soon as I can, dearest. Perhaps you might care to rest? . . . the same room . . . later . . ."

These words she said over her shoulder as she hurried from the room. I sighed and shook my head. This was not going to be easy. Not that I had thought it would be, I reminded myself as I went upstairs to my room.

I had a difficult time getting Phillipa alone long enough to put my proposition to her. I suspected she was avoiding me. Whenever I began a dialogue, she would declare the invalid needed her or there were household matters she must see to. The weather was depressing as well, for it was wet and windy the first days of my stay. I did not have to see Sir Franklin. He was laid low by the drafts only he could feel, and the noise of the wind. I did not miss him, you may be sure.

The fourth day of my visit, however, dawned fair and mild for November, and Sir Franklin decided to risk a journey to Bath to take the waters. This was an undertaking of monumental proportions, and I was hard put not to laugh several times during the lengthy preparations. But at last the master of the house tottered out supported not only by two canes but by my frail sister and a footman as well, to take his seat in the carriage. He was swaddled from head to toe in blankets and a hot brick was put reverently at his feet. Phillipa sat across from him clutching a large portmanteau containing such medicines and comforts as he might need on the short journey.

The carriage proceeded at a funereal pace. So his head would not be jolted, I presume. It was followed by a cart containing his wheeled chair tied securely in place.

I had to turn away lest they see me laughing at the whole, ridiculous parade. And then I was reminded of Alastair's elegant perch phaeton lashed to the ship's deck, and my smile disappeared.

I had been invited to go to Bath with the invalid, but I had refused gravely, saying there were letters I must write. How many times, do you suppose, had people claimed such a task, to escape some unwanted activity? Thousands? Millions, perhaps?

I walked around the dormant garden for a while. I would have liked to ride out, but I had not brought my habit with me. Instead, I decided on a long, brisk hike. The house, so dark and quiet and smelling of various herbs and potions, smothered me. Besides, such continual preoccupation with illness made me want to do something—run or jump or climb.

I asked cook to put some food and drink in a small parcel for me, and set off in the direction of Freshford.

It was a lovely day for a walk, and I strode along, breathing deeply and swinging my arms. I passed few cottages or farms, and I saw no one to speak to until much later in the day. I was tired by then, and my strides had become mere steps, and slow ones at that. When I saw a carriage approaching from the opposite direction, I wished it were going my way so I might beg a ride to Limpley Stoke.

You may imagine my surprise when the carriage came closer and I saw it was a shiny yellow high-perch phaeton driven by my cousin Alastair. Smiling, I waved to him as he pulled to a stop.

"Have you come to astound the rustics, sir?" I asked, for he did look out of place on the dusty country road. "I doubt high-perch vehicles are seen much in the neighborhood."

"I am sure they are not. Nothing much is seen here, from what I can tell. Can you manage to climb up yourself? I can't leave the team to its own devices. They're hired and frisky."

I looked around to make sure I was not observed before I hiked up my skirt and scrambled up beside him. I saw he had transferred the reins to his left hand, and I had no sooner settled down on the seat than he put his free arm around me, pulled me close, and kissed me. I did not protest. I did not make the smallest effort to escape him. Instead, amazed and grateful, I put my arms around him and kissed him back with all my heart, reveling in his nearness, his warm, demanding lips.

"Don't you ever do that again," he growled when he raised his head an inch or so later.

"Do what?" I asked. I realize it was hardly the epitome of sophisticated conversation, but it was all I was capable of in my weakened condition. I could not even open my eyes.

"Leave London without telling me. Go anywhere without telling me," he said, giving me a little shake.

"But I did tell you," I protested. "I sent you a note . . ."

"Yes, after you had scurried away all by yourself," he said swiftly. "Sit up, 'Nelia. There's a farm lad about to cross the road with a herd of cows. And straighten that awful hat you're wearing. Why are you wearing such an atrocity, by the way?"

As I did as he told me, ignoring the lad's cheeky grin as he opened a gate and herded his cows across to another pasture, I said, "I had to wear a hat. I was out for a walk. But never mind that. Why did you kiss me?"

It was quiet for a moment and I dared to peek at him. I gasped when I saw the light in his green eyes, the intense, passionate expression he had. And he was looking at me. *Me!*

"Because I had to," he said, serious now. "Because no matter how I tell myself I don't love you, I find I do. I know that you don't trust me with this family secret you have, but even that doesn't matter. I've never felt this way before, 'Nelia, and it's not at all comfortable. I think of you constantly, want you, long to be with you . . .

"You must think I'm insane."

"No," I managed to say. "I think you're lovely."

At that, he laughed. The cows near us stopped to turn their huge heads and stare at us. "I'm not lovely at all," he protested. "The very idea! I'm not worthy of you, is what I am. And you will think I want you for your wealth, but it is not that. Truly, it is not that. Just think, I'm proposing even knowing you will eventually have to live in the country at Wyckend, and I hate the country."

"You are proposing? I did not hear any proposal," I said primly.

"If you are in the habit of kissing men as you just did and not expecting a proposal immediately after, you are a bold piece indeed," he scolded. Then he happened to glance at the cows and he added, "What on earth is that cow doing?"

I looked and saw the bossy nearest us had stopped and raised her tail. A rich aroma wafted our way and my handsome lover wrinkled his patrician nose and said, "Never mind. To think we will have to drive through it and get it all over the wheels and the horses' hooves . . ."

"You are in the country, sir. No one will pay the slightest heed," I soothed him, trying to contain the bubble of laughter that threatened to overcome me.

"But I will, you also. How can we ignore it?" he complained.

The cows crossed at last, the gate was shut behind them, and the herd boy went away whistling. It was only then, amid the rich odors of the country on a dusty road, that Alastair said, "Will you marry me, dearest Cornelia?"

His voice was humble, humbler than I had ever heard, and any laughter of mine died unborn. As I stared up at him in wonder and delight, I realized there was no way on earth I could marry him. Oh, not because of Wyckend and the money, never that. But because of this awful secret I kept. For a dark moment I told myself he did not *have* to know, that I could keep it from him and he would never guess what had happened. But then I realized I could not live with it between us. I would have to tell him, and when I did, he would not want me anymore. And that would break my heart. I was sure of it. It was breaking already.

"I can't," I managed to say. "I can't, and oh, Alastair, you will never know how much I regret it! For I *do* trust you and I do love you! So much. But . . ."

He did not seem to want to hear any more, for he began to kiss me again. It was terrible. Just awful to be shown bliss, all the time knowing it could never be mine. I began to cry, even as I kissed him back as fervently as I could, hungry for memories if nothing more.

When my tears touched his face, his lips, he leaned back.

"Don't cry, sweet," he murmured. "I can't bear it when you cry."

I swallowed and reached in my pocket for my handkerchief as I tried hard to obey him.

"You do understand you must now tell me about this thing you keep hidden, don't you? I assure you there is nothing—*nothing*—that will stop me from loving you, and I promise that secret will be safe with me. But you must tell me, 'Nelia."

I nodded. He could say that, but he would change his mind. Any man would.

"Is there someplace we can go? Someplace private?" he asked.

Remembering a small woodlot a little distance back, and the rough lane where we might turn in, I nodded and pointed ahead. We did not speak as we drove there. I was glad of that, for I was trying to find some words that would make what I had to tell him less horrible. I was not successful.

I took the reins he handed me while he tied the team to a branch. When he lifted me down, he held me close to him for a moment, my feet dangling above the ground. I closed my eyes and put my arms around his neck, wishing the moment might last forever.

He took me to a fallen tree trunk and sat down beside me, his arm tight around me. And he waited patiently until I said, "This is all so difficult. I—I don't know where to begin."

"Shall I tell you what I think, and you can either agree or correct me?"

He waited until I nodded, before he went on, "I don't believe what has made you hate Melton happened to some other girl, as you would like me to believe. I think it happened to you."

He waited, but I had no reply. Instead, I stared fixedly at the dead leaves around my feet. After a moment, Alastair went on, "That was the reason you reacted so strongly at the Prater that day when Lili confessed a stranger had given her money for the carousel. Why, when you found out Melton was interested in her, you became so upset. I wondered at your strong reaction at the time. Most people would think his attentions only a kindness to a little girl, and commend him for it. You knew better because he had once treated you the same way."

Again he paused, and when I did not speak, he said gently, "Your silence tells me I am right, 'Nelia."

"Yes, you are," I managed to say, and then the words came tumbling out for he had not seemed disgusted. Not yet, anyway.

"I was twelve when he came to visit a friend in the neighborhood. He saw me first in church. He made a special effort to talk to me, then seek me out. And he brought me things, a pretty ribbon, a book he thought I might like. I loved his stories and jests. I liked the attention. He made me feel important, something no one in my family did. They were all so much older and busy with grown-up matters. I was just a—a nuisance. But Paxton, for he was not a viscount then, made me feel special. And when he said we must keep our friendship a secret, I agreed.

"Then one day after I met him in the woods as he had arranged, saying he had a surprise for me, he kissed me and touched me. I was frightened and I fought him, tried to run away. But he was too strong for me. Later, when it was over and before he went away, he told me I must never tell anyone what had happened. That he would deny everything, and because he was an adult, he would be believed. I was confused—mortified—and I didn't know what to do. I went home, determined to remain silent, oh, not to spare him any embarrassment, never that! I did it because I believed him and I was so ashamed I didn't want anyone to know."

"Did your family find out anyway?"

"Yes. Phillipa chanced to come to my room almost as soon as I reached home and, seeing my tears, soon had the whole story. I remember I could not seem to stop crying. She told my mother, who told my father . . ." I shrugged.

"What happened? Obviously there was no scandal. If there had been, Melton would not be received as he is."

I could not keep the bitterness from my voice as I said, "Of course there was no scandal. He left the area the next day. He need not have hurried away. He was not accused of anything, he faced no recriminations. You see, my father claimed what happened was all my fault. That I had made Paxton lose his head. Yes, that is what he said. Paxton had lost control because I flirted with him, teased him. He wanted to beat me for it, but my mother intervened. But he could hardly bear to look at me after that. I had become a wanton in his sight."

"Feeling as he did, how did he arrange a marriage for you with the Earl of Wyckend?"

"He had nothing to do with that," I said, then I paused to bite my lower lip. I did not have to tell Alastair this part. I did not have to say another word. But he had not sounded horrified by my awful tale, only calm and measured, so I dared to continue, "I managed that very nicely on my own. Ogden came for the hunting season with my brother George when I was eighteen. I had not had a Season. My father refused to consider it, so I had remained at home. I was sure I was going to be a spinster. I didn't mind that, not after my experience with Paxton. In fact, I preferred it."

I paused for a moment and I turned to look at him. I could tell he was furious, and my heart sank even as I said, "What I am about to tell you must remain a secret as well. Do you promise?"

"On my honor."

"Very well. I suspect my brother let something slip about my fall from grace one night when he was in his cups. Ogden sought me out afterward, which surprised me for he had all but ignored me up to then. When he asked me to marry him, I told him I could not do such a thing. And when he pressed me, I told him why. He said that was the reason he wanted me to wife.

"Do you remember when I told you how he came to Berkshire with a friend? His name was Perry Randall. He was a handsome young man a few years younger than Ogden. They were inseparable. Ogden confessed he loved Perry, that he could never love a woman that way. But his mother, the dowager countess, kept after him to wed and provide an heir for the title and for Wyckend. Ogden had no interest in heirs. He thought entailment archaic and was glad Wyckend was his to bequeath. The estate was only a place to him, not the religion it is to his mother. He wanted to marry only to make her happy. He explained it would be a marriage in name only. Perry would live with us. Ogden had no intention of—of . . ."

"I understand," Alastair said calmly. "He took a chance, telling you. Homosexuality is punishable by death. Many men of that persuasion have had to flee England for their lives."

"He said I was the first to know, that Perry was in agony about how I would receive the news. But although I was surprised, having no inkling such behavior existed, I was not shocked. And the business arrangement he suggested seemed immensely suitable. It would provide me with a secure future and remove me from my father's house. I could hardly wait for that.

"A marriage based on love could never be, and I knew it. I accepted his proposal and told him to assure Perry there was nothing to fear from me."

"I know he believed you. You are such a gallant woman. And even though you were only eighteen, he must have seen that in you."

It was his turn to pause now and I waited, my hands clenched in the folds of my skirt where he could not see them. I knew what was going to happen. He would thank me for confiding in him, promise me again of his silence, and then he would take me back to Phillipa's house and I would never see him again. I could not blame him, not a bit, but that did not make the words he was about to say any easier to swallow.

Chapter Eighteen

"I am sure this all must have seemed ghastly as well as unfair when you were a child," he began. "But why does it continue to haunt you and dictate your behavior? You should have come to terms with it, put it behind you, by now. Your family as well.

"And what has it to say about your marriage to me? Why can't you marry me? Because you fear marriage physically? But you do not shrink from my embrace, in fact I would swear you enjoy it. I am afraid I do not understand."

I did not understand him. Was he taunting me? But no, Alastair would not do that. Besides, he had sounded distinctly puzzled.

"No man could ever want me after what happened to me," I said stiffly. "My father said it was so, and George agreed with him."

"If he was correct, how did he explain the earl's suit?"

"He said he was probably not right in the head, but I should get down on my knees every night of my life and thank God it was so."

"I find I dislike your father more with everything you tell me about him," Alastair drawled. "He sounds a dreadful man. I suppose your brother is just like him?"

"Yes. Perhaps worse."

"Then we will most decidedly cease friendly relations. In fact, my first act as a husband will be to forbid you to have anything to do with your family again. With the exception of your sister Phillipa, of course."

I turned to stare at him and he took my hands in his. "I am most displeased with you, 'Nelia," he said sternly, the smile playing at the corners of his mouth betraying him. "To think you considered me such a shallow fellow—such a bigot. I really must do something to change my image. Perhaps marriage to you will mellow me."

"You mean it?" I whispered. "You mean you still want me?"

His embrace and his fervent kiss were my answer, and never had I received one I welcomed more. It was a very long time before I could stop kissing him long enough for him to say, "This is all very well, sweet, but there are other things I must know, if you please."

He put me firmly away from him, even moved down the log a little. I could not seem to stop smiling.

"Anything," I said airily. "Anything in the world."

"Then tell me, you much too tempting female, what did Melton say to you when he called the other day that sent you haring out of town as fast as you could go?"

His question brought me back to the real world in a hurry. "He threatened to tell the *ton* of my background. Yes, that was probably an idle threat, for how could he do so without hurting his own reputation? But he also knew about Ogden and Perry, and he said he would make sure everyone found out what kind of marriage I had had. Ogden is dead, he cannot hurt him, and Perry has gone abroad to live. But it would kill the dowager, learning her son was homosexual. I am not fond of the woman, but I could never let that happen."

"So you ran to Phillipa, rather than to me."

The comment was made gently, but I could tell he was hurt. "I had to see her first. You see, she became betrothed just a few months before I was attacked. She felt she had to tell her fiancé lest it all come out later and he think she had deceived him. He broke the engagement. Phil was devastated. I remember how quiet she became, how she wept, and I remember how my father ranted at me for being the cause of her unhappiness, the entire family's shame."

"Personally, I think she was well rid of the fellow."

"I agree. But it was five long years before Franklin proposed and she accepted. This time she did not say anything about me. Age brings wisdom, I guess. And although I myself would have preferred spinsterhood to serving as his slave the way she does, he is her choice and she loves him. I could not ruin her marriage."

"But what does the Earl of Wyckend's sexual preferences have to do with your sister and her husband?"

"I am not sure. Franklin is such a conventional man. I thought to ask Phil what I should do, get her advice. Besides, you did not know anything about the situation then, and I did not know if I could tell you."

"You were afraid I would be disgusted and abandon you as your sister's unworthy suitor did, am I right? For shame, 'Nelia!"

I was flustered and I am sure it showed as I said, "Well, you are the great Alastair Russell, premier beau of the premier beaux, are you not, sir? How could I tell what you would do? And you have always been so proud, so quick to cut the unworthy, the pretentious, the unadmired. I think I was justified in assuming you would cut me off, too."

He moved closer on the log and showed me only too clearly he would do nothing of the sort. I was quivering when he stopped, and feeling a sudden urge I had never known before. It enveloped me from my toes to the top of my head, a warm, luscious wave of yearning. It was all I could do to concentrate when he said, "We should think of something else now, before I disgrace myself. As my future wife, you deserve homage, and homage you shall have, although I warn you I intend to press for early nuptials."

"Oh, yes, please do," I breathed.

"The trunks arrived just before I left London," he said, setting me firmly away once more. "I had yours sent on to Upper Brook Street. Lili's is on its way to Moorland Farm by carter. I cannot wait to get you out of your terrible clothes and . . ."

"Yes? And?"

". . . and into your French gowns, minx!"

I laughed, but for some reason I was suddenly feeling uneasy. Then a mental picture of Lili's trunk came to mind, and I caught my breath. Alastair had bought it for her in Salzburg. Most trunks are black with plain straps. Only the locks and hinges are colorful, being made of brass. But Lili's trunk was distinctive. It was painted scarlet and it had a playful design of brass on the top and shiny black straps. Lili loved it.

A sense of horror crept over me and I reached out to grasp Alastair's coat.

"How did Lili's trunk travel? By mail coach?"

"King took it to a well-known carter. I gave him orders to do so when I left for Bath. What is it, 'Nelia? Why are you so concerned?"

"It is such an unusual trunk," I said slowly. "Anyone would know it for a child's from its bright color. I wonder if Melton had your rooms watched after I would not tell him anything? Is your man a familiar figure? Would people know he was your valet?"

"Yes," Alastair said, sounding grim now. "I have had him for years, and there have been those who have tried to entice him away from me. In his own way, King is famous. And the trunk was clearly marked with Lili's name and its destination—the nearest regular stop, probably Oxford."

"Then all Melton had to do was go there, ask a few questions, and he would find Lili," I said, all the horror I had ever felt before, returning. "Oh, what are we to do, Alastair?" I begged him, clutching his arms hard. "What can we do?"

"First, you can stop ruining this coat," he told me easily. "Second, you can calm yourself. There is no reason Melton would be so astute." He held up a hand when he saw I was about to burst into speech, "Granted, it is a distinct possibility he had King followed, and one I fear we cannot ignore. We must travel to Oxfordshire once again and make sure she is safe. Try and remember this is only a precaution. We do not know for a certainty that Melton has discovered her."

"We will be too late," I said in despair, ignoring his rallying words. "It has been days since you and I left London. He has probably found her by now, and oh, Alastair, if he has done anything to Lili, I shall die!"

"No, you won't. But he will," Alastair said grimly and I knew he meant it.

"Come, we had better get you back to your sister's. Can you be ready to travel tomorrow at dawn? The November days grow short and we must make what miles we can in the daylight."

He sighed as he drew me to my feet. "All these dawn journeys will be the death of me. They are not at all what I am used to."

"I must tell Phil what has happened," I said as we went to the phaeton.

"As you wish. Do not let her convince you you must stay with her," he warned.

As he backed the phaeton expertly, he said, "Do you know, at one time I thought Lili was your sister's child. Then after I learned she would have been too old to capture Melton's interest, I was sure you must be her mother, young though you were."

I stared at him, the problem of Lili's safety forgotten for a moment.

"I? Good gracious, no. Thora Martingale was real. I even remember meeting her when I was a small child. She had the most infectious laugh, like a collection of small bells ringing. I can still hear it in my mind."

"Now why do I have the distinct feeling I would not find her laugh anything but irritating?" he asked no one at all. As we turned out into the road and he gave the team the office to trot, he said, "Why did you say your sister was as good as a slave to her husband? Is he so demanding?"

I knew Alastair was trying to take my mind from Lili's problem, and the possibility I was reliving my own experience at Melton's hands, and I was grateful although distracted when I said, "He has become a chronic invalid and no one will do to wait on him but Phil. I wish you could have seen the procession when they went to Bath this morning. I had the hardest time not to laugh. The wheeled chair sitting bolt upright in the bed of a cart that followed the carriage, the measured pace, was so funny."

"He is very ill?"

"Most doctors do not think so, but he is sure he is only a step from death's door. He is a tyrant. The entire household functions in almost perfect silence lest he be upset."

"Perhaps we should also scratch Sir Franklin from the list of people we will know," Alastair suggested. "He sounds dreary.

"Tell me, love, did you come here with a trunk? You can't bring it with you in the phaeton if you did."

"Yes, a trunk and a maid. I'll see she takes it back to London, for I'm used to phaeton travel by now. I'm sure Phil will loan me a small portmanteau."

We reached Limpley Stoke a short time later. Alastair had told me he was putting up at Bath's premier hostelry, York House. He would go on there after I got down.

He did not kiss me good-bye for there were people in the street, all of whom were staring at the unique carriage. I am sure nothing so dashing had ever been seen here before. But somehow Alastair managed to convey a kiss with the expression in his beautiful green eyes, and the slightest movement of his lips, and I blushed.

" 'Til dawn, ma'am," he said.

" 'Til dawn, sir," I echoed. "It will seem an age 'til then, I do assure you."

* * *

I found the Bath party returned and the household all aflutter, for Sir Franklin had had a difficult day. He claimed he was in great pain, or so the butler informed me in his usual whisper. As I went up to my room, I could hear him moaning for myself, and I knew there was no hope of my seeing Phil now. Not until she had her husband settled in bed, thoroughly dosed, and hopefully, fast asleep. Instead I told my maid of my plans and set about selecting what I would take on the dash to Oxfordshire.

My hands shook as I took clean shifts from the wardrobe, and I ordered a cup of tea. I had no time for nerves now. And since I knew that dwelling on Melton's possible whereabouts, and Lili's danger from him, could do nothing but agitate my spirits, I forced myself to put those thoughts aside.

I was calmer after I drank my tea, and able to think more clearly. I would need my warm cloak, of course, and the heavy wool gloves, and never mind they were not as stylish as kid. Perhaps I could borrow a woolen scarf from Phil? Another pair of warm stockings? I remembered the pistol I had brought with me simply because I was used to carrying it now, and I tucked it in my reticule along with extra shot and powder.

As I worked, I thought of Alastair and everything that had happened this afternoon. I still had the greatest difficulty believing he loved me, in spite of his pledge and his kisses. Alastair Russell and Cornelia, Countess of Wyckend, were such an unlikely pair. The *ton* would be all abuzz when it learned.

As I reminded my maid to be sure and pack my books and needlework, I wondered how this kind of married life would agree with me. I had no fear of the physical side of marriage, in spite of what had happened to me as a child. Not now after I had experienced that wave of yearning this afternoon.

But I had been alone for eight long years with no loving contact but the occasional pat on the shoulder from Ogden, or an even rarer kiss if the dowager clearly expected one. How would it be to live with someone else, someone, moreover, who had very demanding tastes and opinions? How would he like my friends, and I, his? And what were we to do about his antipathy to the country? Perhaps when Wyckend was his, he would develop more of an interest?

I sighed. It did not matter. I loved him and that was all that was important. We would work the other things out eventually.

I refused to think of the dowager's reaction to my remarriage. She would hate it, of course, for Wyckend would pass from her hands. Perhaps we could keep the news of it from her? I scolded myself when I wondered how much longer she could live. Such a thought might be all too human, but that did not make it right.

I did not see Phillipa until dinner, which we ate alone as was our custom. I let her talk about the day she had spent, Sir Franklin's woes, and what his new doctor had told him.

"He said he believes Franklin has a wasting disease," she said earnestly, shaking her head when I would have given her a larger piece of game pie. I was about to protest when she went on, "Oh, dearest, you cannot imagine how my heart sank when he said that! It is all as Franklin suspected, and indeed, he has been growing weaker every day."

"But not thinner," I remarked, for I had seen his bulk that morning. He was quite stout. "Wouldn't a wasting disease mean loss of weight? Perhaps the doctor was wrong."

She brightened for a moment, then her face returned to its sad lines. Poor Phil, I thought. It is such a shame she must live like this.

At last we repaired to the small parlor that adjoined Sir Franklin's room. Phil went in to him at once, returning after a moment to say he was sleeping soundly.

"I am delighted to hear it," I whispered. "Please shut that door, Phil. I have something I must tell you and I do not want to disturb him."

"Oh, I cannot! What if he needs me and I do not hear him?" she protested.

"You can hear that bell of his all over the house. Do as I say," I ordered. No doubt she was stunned by my determination, for she obeyed at once.

When she sat down again, I told her of Vienna and Lili and Melton's attraction for her, and when she would have fled the hearing, I made her stay. And I told her of Alastair and our approaching marriage as well. That drew a smile. It did not last long, however, for I had to tell her of Melton's threat to reveal my past. Even though I reassured her he would not dare, lest his own part in my downfall become known, she could not be calmed.

"Oh, 'Nelia, do consider the shame if it becomes generally known," she pleaded. "How will I hold my head up? And what of Father and George and his family? Of course I am sorry for Lili but you have done all you can, and you said the Moorlands know of the danger. Why do you have to go there? Let Mr. Russell do it. It is a man's task. And for you to be jauntering about with him now you are more to each other than distant cousins is a disgrace! Why, what will Franklin say? It will upset him so!"

I looked at my sister's distraught face, her pleading tear-filled eyes, and I felt great sorrow. But it was not enough to stop me and I said, "This time I will not listen to you, Phil. Still, I pray you can forgive me. I love you very much. You are all I have left to me of family. As for Father and George, they cast me off years ago. I find I have not the smallest bit of concern for their feelings.

"I don't care what Franklin thinks, either. I have been unhappy for most of my life, it seems, and now I have a chance to change that. What difference will it make if Alastair and I travel together? We are to be married as soon as possible."

"But some terrible gossip will see you, I know it," she protested, "and then it will become common knowledge. And if it gets into the papers, Franklin is sure to find out. Have pity on him, 'Nelia. He is so ill!"

"Didn't you tell me you often read the papers to him because holding them tires his arms so? Goose! All you have to do is skip that part if it should chance to appear, which I do not at all expect.

"Come now, Phil. Kiss me and pray we are successful, Alastair and I. Oh, and lend me a woolen scarf and a small portmanteau, if you please. All I have with me is a trunk, and we cannot take it since we travel by perch phaeton."

The minute I uttered the words, I cursed the inadvertent slip. Phillipa looked horrified and stunned as she said, "Really, Cornelia, are you determined to bring down shame on us? To say nothing of the danger, why . . ."

But I had run to her to hug her tight and kiss her. Perhaps it was the happiness she saw in my eyes that stilled all her protests at last. I hoped so.

Chapter Nineteen

The next morning at dawn, the euphoria that I had wrapped tightly around me had disappeared, and when I climbed into the phaeton unseen by even the earliest riser in Limpley Stoke, I was feeling almost blue-deviled. Alastair gave me a rug to wrap around my legs, and as I moved close to him for additional warmth, I was reminded of how Lili had sat between us, chattering away, and I knew the source of my depression.

I think Alastair missed her too, for he was very quiet as we set out for Bath, where, he told me, we would pick up the road to Chippenham. He thought we might make Swindon tonight, if we could acquire good teams when we stopped for the change.

It seemed a very long time before the faint gray light was routed by a pale sun. The day warmed slightly, to my relief, for there was an unpleasant bite in the air reminding me we could expect snow at any time. When I mentioned this to Alastair, he grimaced.

"Not for a few days, I pray. I want to be back in London before the first snowfall. I remember all too well the blizzards in Scotland last year. Too tiresome."

"You did not miss much in London, sir," I said. "It was bitter cold. Surely you heard of the Frost Fair that was held on the Thames when it froze solid?"

For a while we talked of such innocuous things, falling silent on occasion. We made good time until the morning progressed and we were slowed by the traffic that began to appear, farm carts and carriages and people walking, as well as villages and crossroads. We stopped about ten at an inn in one of the larger villages. I retired to the private parlor Alastair had procured to enjoy a hot cup of tea and a muffin before a roaring fire while he saw to the changing of the team. It seemed much too short a time before we were on our way again.

The bright yellow phaeton had attracted a lot of attention, and I mentioned this as we left the village behind.

"I know. It is not at all the thing for the country," he said.

"You mean one should have different carriages for different places?"

He spared me a quick sideways glance. "But naturally, dearest 'Nelia," he drawled. "A somber black chaise would be better here, especially in November. Really, this vehicle is only suited to a toodle around the park in summer."

I looked at the sky with a countrywoman's eye. The sun had disappeared behind a high haze and the sky to the west was growing distinctly darker. I shivered a little.

We did not reach Swindon that day. The clouds that amassed throughout the afternoon grew increasingly ominous, and a spitting sleet began to fall. I could tell Alastair was annoyed. His forehead was creased and the set of his mouth was decidedly grim. Why is it that men cannot bear any change in their plans without sulking like little boys?

We sought shelter in a country inn some miles from our destination. Alastair made arrangements for bedchambers and a private parlor before he set out to attend to some business he had. I could not imagine what that might be, but I was tired and only too glad to rest. Travel by perch phaeton is not at all relaxing. You are constantly on the alert lest you be spilled into the road. And you are so high above it, too! I did not like it one bit, and more than once in all our travels I had wished Alva Potter had been content to give Alastair a more conventional rig.

I did not see my companion until dinnertime, for I had fallen asleep in the comfortable bed in my room. Quickly, I washed and tried to run a comb through my tangled curls when the maid called me. I did not bother to change my crumpled gown. I only had one other, equally serviceable, with me. I was not at all fashionable, but that was the last thing on my mind.

The dinner we were served was not fashionable either, but it was plentiful and well-cooked. I was reminded of the poor fare we had received in France, and was very glad to be home.

"Do you think we will reach the farm by tomorrow, Alastair?" I asked as I cut my chicken.

"We should do. I warn you, the weather may not cooperate. But the new horses are sturdy beasts. I wouldn't want anyone in the *ton* to see me driving them, but they will do nobly here. Unless it comes on to snow. But we will be able to reach Oxford at least, and we can start our inquiries there."

"As Melton must plan to do, if he hasn't already," I said, all my appetite suddenly gone.

"Eat your dinner, my sweet. We don't know he has arrived before us. Chances are, he has not. Let us be optimistic."

Fine words, I thought, noting by his expression that he seemed to expect the worst.

"I have a surprise for you," he said, breaking the silence that lengthened between us. I looked an inquiry and he went on, "I have made, er, arrangements to borrow the vicar's curricle. It will be more comfortable and it has the added benefit of having a hood in case of foul weather."

I had not missed his slight hesitation. "Arrangements?" I asked innocently. "Now how were you able to persuade the good man, I wonder?"

"Why, I left him the perch phaeton in its stead," he said, all urbanity.

The picture of a plump parson all in black seated high up in the dashing, unsteady carriage had me giggling. "I do hope there is no parish emergency then,"

I managed to say. "I imagine the fund for the new church roof was much enriched today?"

"I believe it was something to do with dry rot. I was not perfectly attending," Alastair said as he helped himself to another slice of mutton.

After dinner we sat on in the private parlor. The dishes had been cleared away, and Alastair had ordered a bottle of port and two glasses. I am afraid I was becoming quite fond of port, the way things were going.

At first I had been glad to be alone with Alastair. Of course we had been alone all day, but then he had been concerned with driving the team, the speed we were making, the weather. He could hardly play the lover then. But now, somehow, the situation was not a bit comfortable. What conversation we indulged in seemed stilted, and I found it hard to meet his eye, all the time wondering why he did not take me in his arms, kiss me as he had yesterday. I found myself thinking of my four-poster as well, the firelight making leaping shadows on the wall and Alastair beside me under the quilts. I took a sip of port, hoping any blush of mine might be attributed to the warmth of the room.

"This will not do, my sweet," Alastair said finally, and I saw he wore a grim expression where he sat across the hearth from me. "You are feeling awkward, no, do not deny it. I am feeling awkward myself.

"But we will be married shortly. In fact, I'm thinking of going directly to Doctor's Commons when we reach London."

I must have looked as confused as I felt for he went on, "The Archbishop of Canterbury's office is there and that is where I can obtain a special license. We can be married immediately, unless you fear that might give rise to unseemly gossip, love?"

"I think it is an excellent idea," I managed to say.

He nodded, his expression brightening. "However, until that happy day, we will sleep alone," he said. "I told you I would honor you, and so I shall. I will not do anything prematurely."

"Perhaps I wish you would," I was horrified to hear myself saying.

He rose and came to sit beside me then, taking my hands in his and kissing them.

"Do you know how hard it is for me to act the gentleman when I want you so much, my love? Still, I am convinced this union of ours be done correctly and not in the heat of desire, no matter how fervent that desire might be.

"And it is," he added a little grimly, shifting and then rising to take his own seat again.

"Shall we plan on an early start tomorrow?" he asked, and I realized the discussion was over. In a way, I was disappointed, yet in another way, relieved. Strange, that.

I went to bed shortly thereafter. Alone. Still, Alastair did take me in his arms and kiss me, a kiss so warm and fervent I fell asleep with a very silly smile on my face.

The snow held off the following morning, but when I came down to the vicar's curricle, I did not like the look of the sky. And there was that breathless feeling of stillness to the air that to me had always told of snow. The new team looked sturdy, and I gave the folded-back hood of the curricle a little pat as I took my seat. Yes, this was much better, I thought as we turned out of the inn yard.

On we traveled, to Swindon and Faringdon, past farms and villages that looked much like the ones I had seen yesterday. And always, always in my mind no matter how I tried to banish it, was my concern for Lili and the realization that time was passing. And the longer Melton had, the easier it would be for him to find her before we could arrive.

"Do you think Melton will be able to locate Lili by asking questions in Oxford?" I asked at one point.

"It is possible, if he was clever enough to have had

King watched. But even if he knew where she was, he would have difficulty in getting close to her. Remember, Moorland Farm is isolated and the nearest village does not have an inn. He would have to put up in Oxford and travel out there hoping to be able to attract her attention. It is almost winter, too. Lili will not be outdoors for long periods of time, and when she is, she will not wander away from the farm buildings."

"Perhaps Mrs. Moorland will stay with her when she goes out," I said. "After all, she appeared concerned when we told her of Melton."

"Try and remember there is an excellent chance he does not know Lili's location even now, my dear," Alastair told me with a quick smile. "I suspect he is in London, brooding over his disappointment and wondering where on earth you have gone. For there would be no sense in spreading dire rumors if the object of those rumors was not available to feel the result."

"You are making me feel a great deal better," I told him as I sat back and tried to enjoy the scenery. Perhaps this was all a needless excursion. Perhaps Lili was in no danger at all. But reassure myself as much as I did, I could not shake the feeling that Lili was in grave danger.

It was a long day, long and uncomfortable. The snow held off, but that was all that could be said for the weather. The damp nasty wind that blew up not only made us feel the cold, but also made the team skittish. Alastair had his hands full, and I heard some choice curses I chose to ignore. It was almost dusk when we reached Oxford, too late to begin our search for Melton that day, to my great disappointment.

I do not know how he did it, for he told me he was not familiar with the town, but Alastair turned into the yard of the best inn and in a short time had us settled in comfortable rooms with a tasty dinner ordered. We took a short, brisk walk to stretch our legs before we retired to the fireside to make plans.

"I think we should make some inquiries here in Oxford before we go to the farm," Alastair began.

He must have seen the disappointment on my face, for he reached for my hand and pressed it before he said, "I know, love. But we will see Lili soon enough. Best we conclude our business first; try to locate Melton."

"What will you do if we find him?" I asked, almost against my will. I really did not want to know, yet something drove me to ask.

He settled back in his seat, propping up his chin with one hand. His eyes were half closed as he stared into the flames. "If he is here, I think we can assume it is because Lili is, too. That releases me from my vow to you not to kill him, for he can only be here *intending* to hurt her. And best to get rid of him before she even knows he is in England. She will forget him that much faster, don't you agree?"

I nodded, for I did not trust my voice. Never had I thought I would ever sit in a prosaic inn parlor before a blazing fire on a cold November night, discussing murder as calmly as you please.

"But won't it be dangerous?" I asked, suddenly fearful for his safety. "Won't you be brought up before the local justice? Held over for the Assizes even? Murder is serious. You could be hanged for it! I could not bear it if I lost you, my dear!"

I do not think he even heard that last, impassioned plea, for he seemed to be looking at something beyond me, brooding over it. "I must arrange for it to look like an accident somehow. Don't worry. I will not kill him on the busy street at noon. Trust me to be more subtle than that."

"Have you ever killed anyone before?" I whispered. When he frowned, I hastened to say, "I have always maintained I would kill Melton, and indeed, I have my pistol loaded and ready. But I wonder if I could do it if I had the opportunity? I am afraid I would falter, hesitate, and lose the chance, and then hate myself for my weakness."

"You will not have to kill him, sweet. I promised I would do it for you, remember? And yes, I admit to killing before. London is a dangerous place, especially late at night. And there was a footpad there I encountered once. He was intent on slitting my throat for my purse. I shot him."

"I wish Melton had never been born," I muttered.

"I am sure you are only one among many to say so. Hopefully, you will be the last.

"Ah, here is our dinner," he added as a servant knocked and brought in a tray loaded with covered dishes. The discussion was over; indeed, we did not refer to it again that evening.

We were out early the next morning. By now I had discovered Alastair did not care for conversation in the morning until he had had breakfast and a cup of strong tea. Still, he had questioned the inn servants, none of whom remembered the gentleman he described.

Before we sought out other hostelries, we went to the carter's office. It was busy there, for a large shipment of goods had just arrived, and the owner was busy checking over the items against a list the driver had given him.

I wanted to scream with frustration at the delay, but Alastair only shrugged. We found a woman in the office about to send a boy off with a package instead.

"Make sure Mr. Geary gets that safely, Sammy," she ordered. "And whatever you do, don't drop it! It's a china teapot."

"I wonder if I might inquire for a trunk," Alastair said as the boy grinned at me and sidled out the door clutching Mr. Geary's teapot.

The woman stared, then recalled her manners and dropped a hasty curtsy. To Alastair, not to me. I am sure she did not even see me. "Yessir?" she inquired. "What can I do for you, sir?"

"I expect a trunk to be delivered here from London. It is for my daughter, Miss Lili Martingale. I am Farnsworth Martingale. The trunk was to be delivered to

Moorland Farm, near Holford. I thought since my wife and I are going out there today, I could take it to her myself instead of waiting for a delivery."

"Oh, that trunk," the woman said, smiling. "It certainly was a pretty one."

"Yes, the child adores it. It has come then? You have delivered it already?"

"Someone from the farm picked it up, sir. Two days ago."

"What did the man look like?" Alastair drawled. You would not know from his voice how perturbed her answer had made both of us, for it was as calm as ever. "Did you know him?"

"Why, o' course I did. 'Twas Capt'n Moorland's brother Benjamin what took it with him. Say, is there something special about that trunk?"

"Why do you ask?"

"Because another gentleman was in here yesterday inquiring for it, and its destination. Most insistent, he was, and so disappointed it had already gone. I told him he'd have to go to Moorland Farm to find it."

She laughed but neither Alastair nor I could even smile. As we went down the steps, all I could think of was that Melton had come, that he knew where Lili was, and he was a day before us.

"Yes, we will go to the farm now," Alastair said as we hurried back to the inn. "There is no more time to lose."

Chapter Twenty

No journey had ever seemed longer than the short one to Moorland Farm that morning. Alastair and I did not converse, for suddenly there was nothing to say. Instead, we each had our uncomfortable thoughts, and a real sense of dread to keep us company. I found myself picturing one terrible scene after another, and the horror I had known as a child came back to me threefold, until I was sure I was about to be ill. It was only by swallowing hard and telling myself there was no time for it that I was able to control my nausea.

We found the Moorlands in their parlor. There was no sign of Lili and I held my breath until Nancy Moorland told us she was down at the stables with the captain's brother, learning how to saddle her horse.

"She has a horse?" Alastair asked. "I was not aware she could ride."

"She can't," the captain said with a chuckle. "But she is determined to learn, and Ben said he would teach her."

"You need not fear for her," his wife said quickly. "Ben is a good young man. He'll see she comes to no harm."

She looked confused, as if she wondered the reason for our unexpected visit and the tension I am sure she could see on our faces. I was glad when Alastair told them of Melton's arrival in Oxford.

"Sit down, both of you," the captain ordered and I realized I had not even removed my cloak. "Nancy, be so good as to order tea for us, if you please."

"Have any strangers been seen in the neighborhood?" Alastair asked after tea had been served and we were alone again. I sipped gratefully. The hot drink was comforting and it soothed my nerves.

"Not that I know of," the captain said, frowning. "But I am hardly the one to ask. Ben would know, for he's out and about. In fact, he serves as my eyes these days, he and Nancy, that is."

His wife reached for his hand. The look on her face told me the couple shared a very happy marriage. "I've heard nothing from the maids, and our Rose is a regular chatterbox," she said. "Perhaps he has not found the farm yet?"

Alastair shook his head before he told them of what we had learned at the carter's office.

"So he knows she is here," the captain said slowly. "I think it best we apprise Ben of the situation. I did not tell him before, for to tell the truth, I did not think it necessary. But now . . . now we will need his help."

"I agree," Alastair said. "Just as long as all this can be kept from Lili. She is so young. I do not want her scarred by it. In any way," he added darkly.

"Are there any places Melton could stay that are nearer to the farm than Oxford?" I asked, speaking for the first time. "It would be a long drive to and fro every day. I do not think he would dare come onto the property so he will have to wait for a chance meeting. He must suspect we have warned you about him; that you will be on your guard."

"There are some neighboring farms, small ones," Moorland said slowly. "But the farmers would not take in a stranger. The village folk are suspicious of outsiders, too. He'd find no welcome there. Nancy, will you inquire, just to be on the safe side?"

She agreed as our discussion came to an abrupt end. Lili ran into the room, her cheeks glowing with color and her curls crushed from being tucked under a hat. " 'Nelia!" she cried as she saw us. "And Al-as-tair!

Oh, I am so glad to see you! Just wait 'til you hear everything I have been doing . . ."

She hugged me tight before she remembered her curtsy. Somehow it was comforting she had called my name first when I knew how she adored Alastair.

Behind her at the threshold stood a tall young man in his early twenties. He was a good-looking man with the strong body of a countryman. His tan spoke of hours outdoors. Beside him, my dear Alastair looked pale indeed.

Introductions were made and Lili was persuaded to perch on a plump hassock before she began to tell us of her life here at the farm. It was a long, happy story full of all her activities and her riding lessons, and a new kitten she had been given that she had named Rusty. She peeked at Alastair as she said, "She is orange, of course. But she also has a very regal manner. I think it is the way she walks and holds her head. Like Al-as-tair. And Rusty could also be short for Russell."

"You are a minx," Alastair told her sternly and she giggled.

Nancy Moorland took her away then to see to the noon meal after we promised to remain at the farm for a short visit. When she was gone, Alastair told the captain's brother of the danger Lili faced. He was red with indignation and his lips were set hard by the time the unsavory tale was told. I did not envy Melton if he should meet this young man.

That afternoon Alastair went back to Oxford to collect our baggage and to make inquiries there about new faces in the area. Benjamin Moorland accompanied him. Being well-known, he would ease Alastair's way, for country people are apt to be wary of strangers. A more unlikely pair I had never seen, but in some strange way they seemed to respect each other. I admit it. I shall never understand men.

I spent the time with Lili. She showed me around the outbuildings and introduced me to her horse. The mare was elderly and placid so I stopped worrying it might unseat her, or run away with her. And of course, all afternoon I kept my eye out for Melton. I had my pistol in my cloak pocket and I was very conscious of it especially since, for now at least, I was Lili's sole protector.

That evening, after Lili had gone to bed, Alastair admitted he and young Moorland had had no luck discovering where the viscount was staying. Nancy Moorland wondered hopefully if perhaps he might have gone away, but we were quick to tell her of his stubbornness and determination.

"I saw no sign of him either, and you may be sure I was looking for him," I reported. "And Lili and I were out for most of the afternoon. I wish she did not wear that scarlet cloak. It is so distinctive it can be identified from quite a distance."

"Is Lili in the habit of going out alone?" Alastair asked our hosts. "I ask because I don't want her to become suspicious if she is always accompanied now."

"Generally there is someone with her," Ben Moorland said. "And she never leaves the farm alone. Sometimes she does run down to the stables by herself, or visits the henhouse or dairy on an errand for Nancy. Easy enough to send one of the maids instead, and one or the other of us can keep an eye on her when she is outside. There are apt to be some of the farm workers about as well; even in November there are chores to be done. There's no way this chap can get anywhere near her that I can see."

A little comforted by this last remark, we all observed an early bedtime. I had forgotten this aspect of life in the country and wondered what Alastair thought of it, he who so often went to bed at dawn and did not rise until the following afternoon. I was careful not to look at him as I took up my candle lest my laughter betray me.

For the next two days, our lives were a study in contradiction. For Lili's sake, we all went about the usual routine of life on a large farm, pretending we were not on edge, apprehensive. Alastair and I had little time together, and I regretted this for I missed our private conversations and especially his kisses.

The third morning I chanced to meet him in the upstairs hall as I left my room for breakfast. I was astounded when he put his arm around me and swept me back into my bedchamber to shut and lock the door behind us. I was not given the opportunity to ask what he thought he was about, for he began to kiss and caress me until I was quite breathless and incapable of speech. I did not care a whit, it was so glorious to be in his arms again. We only stopped when Lili knocked and rattled the latch to ask if I were coming down. Deprived of my lips, Alastair was kissing the tender spot in my neck just above the collarbone, his hands warm and insistent on my back. It was all I could do to say I would be there in a minute, but not to wait for me.

"We must stop. You are very bad, love," I whispered before he could capture my lips again. "Just suppose if someone should see you leaving my room!"

"And at dawn, too," he grumbled. "Remind me never to take up residence on a working farm. The hours that are kept here are barbaric! In bed at nine—and alone, too. I wouldn't mind at all if you were there with me—and then awake when it is still dark because that accursed fowl begins to crow! I would like to know why he has to make such a fuss about his conquest of a few ugly hens. It is not as if they have any choice in the matter."

By now I was overcome and grasping the bedpost while trying to stifle my laughter with my other hand.

"It is almost enough to make me reconsider our marriage," he continued. "I assume Wyckend also has hens? Roosters?"

"You won't be able to hear them," I said, mopping

my eyes with the end of the sheet. "They are not kept anywhere near Wyckend Court. Oh, do stop, Alastair! I am weak with laughter."

"I am so glad you find this amusing," he told me as he went to check his cravat in the mirror and smooth his hair. "I fail to see any humor in the situation myself."

I straightened my gown while Alastair inspected me with a critical eye. Only when he was satisfied did he unlock the door, and demure as any nun, I went down the stairs, followed by a casual, urbane Mr. Russell.

That afternoon, Alastair and the younger Moorland took the chaise and went out to investigate the neighborhood in a wider circle than they had previously drawn. For as Alastair said, the man had to be staying somewhere. It was only a matter of time before he would run him to earth. Lili was busy practicing the piano in the parlor, Mrs. Moorland beside her to correct her mistakes. The captain was upstairs, taking his usual nap. I had learned that, besides his blindness, he had other injuries that still pained him.

Left alone with only a rather dull book to read, I decided to go for a walk. I donned my hooded cloak as well as my scarf and gloves, for the November day was cold and there was a brisk wind blowing. The sky, too, was full of scudding clouds, sagging close to earth with their burden of snow. None had fallen as yet, but surely it could only be a matter of time. As I shut the front door behind me, thankfully shutting off Lili's wrong notes as well, I felt in my pocket to make sure my pistol was there. I had no expectations of meeting Melton, but it paid to be prepared.

Today I set off down the drive. One of Moorland's farmers tipped his hat to me as I went by, and I smiled at him. He and some others were chopping wood. The tree they were working on must have fallen in a summer storm and been left till now to season. Moorlands boasted an extensive wood lot, which was fortunate since it had to supply the fires of several farm families as well as the manor itself.

Some oak leaves swirled around my feet as I strode briskly around the curve in the drive. In the distance I could see the road to the village and the two gateposts. One of them had a sign proclaiming this was the Moorland Farm. Really, I thought, it could not have been made any easier for Melton if we had flown a banner. Still, he had not appeared and Lili was safe. But I knew we could not continue here indefinitely. Guests are nothing but a nuisance to any household after a certain period, and both Alastair and I were eager to reach London to acquire the special license. I almost wished the man would make a move so we could bring this situation to a conclusion. A successful conclusion, I was quick to add mentally.

I began to dream about my wedding to Alastair then as I walked along, and to wonder what our lives would be like—how I was to tell the dowager countess of it—and what all our friends would think.

I was not paying any attention to my surroundings and so I was startled when I heard hurried footsteps behind me and felt someone grab me from behind with one hand while the other pressed a foul-smelling cloth over my nose and mouth. I tried to escape, fight the assailant off, but it was useless for he was much stronger than I. In a moment there was blackness and I was gone.

I have no idea how long I was unconscious. I woke slowly and kept my eyes closed as I tried to think about what had happened. My parched mouth made me recall the cloth he had used, and it all came back to me in a rush. Well, Melton may not have found Lili, but he had certainly found me. Part of me wondered what on earth he had kidnapped me for, for being a woman grown, I was of no interest to him now.

I could feel gritty rough boards beneath my cheek, and by moving ever so slightly, I discovered my feet were not tied, but my hands were, and behind my back, too.

I could hear Melton pacing nearby, for the floor of this place creaked as it took his weight. How he had found it—whatever it was—and why the Moorlands had not known of it, I did not know. Unless, of course, I had been unconscious for a long time and he had taken me many miles away. Oh, pray not!

I began to wonder what on earth I was to do. Bound as I was, my pistol was no use to me, although I could feel it still in the pocket of my cloak, where it lay under my thigh. How considerate of him to allow me the cloak, I thought bleakly, for lying still as I was forced to do, I could feel the cold seeping up under my skirts from beneath the floorboards, feel its icy finger on the skin that was exposed between my glove and sleeve.

The footsteps approached again and I concentrated on remaining still. The longer I was able to avoid talking to Melton, the better, for it would give me a chance to think. Think about what I could do to escape. I made myself breathe normally, and finally, after what seemed an age, the footsteps moved away again.

The man must be mad, I thought. What good could come of him holding me captive? Did he think to exchange me for Lili? But Alastair would never permit that, I told myself. No matter how he loved me, he would know I was safer with this monster than Lili would have been. And he would know, too, that I would expect him to consent to my remaining with Melton, until he could find me, rescue me. And I knew he would find me, no matter where Melton had me hidden. Strange how only a couple of months ago I would not have believed that, for then I had considered Alastair a simpering fop, intent only on his glorious face and form, his magnificent clothes, and his high standing in society. Now, of course, I knew how much more there was to him, and why he behaved as he did.

Perhaps there was some way I could help myself? Just in case I was somewhere it would take a while to locate? I tried to review the situation calmly and logically.

Surely Melton must have brought me here in a carriage. I could not see him galloping along a country road with an unconscious woman draped across the pommel. Country roads were so often populated when you least wanted them to be. Witness the cowherd the other day when Alastair had proposed to me. That memory almost made me groan, remembering how happy I had been then.

I listened closely. The sound of footsteps was faint and I dared to open my eyes a slit. Wherever I was was dimly lit, but after a moment I was able to make out the interior of what seemed to be an old barn. Not a shed. It was too large for that. I could not see Melton, but I could hear his footsteps approaching again and I closed my eyes.

This time when he stopped beside me, he remained. I felt a foot nudge my hip, and afraid he would discover the pistol if he tried to roll me over on my back, I moaned.

"Ah, so you are awake, my dear Countess," he said in his light, jovial voice. I felt despair, for just hearing it made my situation seem so much worse.

"Come now, open your eyes, sit up," he commanded, kneeling beside me to assist me. As he raised me to a sitting position and dragged me back to lean against a post, my head spun and for a moment I was sure I was about to be ill.

"What—what did you use on me?" I managed to ask. "Oh, I feel so dizzy. So sick!"

He chuckled as if I had just told him an amusing bit of gossip. "Do try not to be sick, ma'am. I have no idea how long you will have to wear those clothes."

"Why did you kidnap me?" I asked, staring hard at him. I wished I had the nerve to kick him as hard as I could.

He backed away as if he had read my mind, and

leaned against another post across from me. I could see the shape of a stall behind him. Looking up, I saw the hay loft above us. Nearby I could make out some old boxes and a broken barrel. A pitchfork missing all but one of its tines leaned drunkenly against the wall.

"At one time this was a stable," Melton said. "It ceased to be one long ago, however. It is nowhere near the new manor house and so of no use to those Moorlands who acquired the property early in the last century."

I tried to hide the elation I felt. So, I was still on Moorland grounds, was I? Not that far from the manor? But why hadn't the Moorlands remembered this barn? Why hadn't it been checked for Melton?

"I found a bill of sale for a saddle from 1734. It was in an old tin box," he went on, almost as if he were hungry for someone to talk to. "The box preserved it from the rats. Oh, yes, dear ma'am, the place is infested with 'em. You can hear them anytime, not only at night. Hush. Just listen," he ordered, cupping his ear.

To my horror, I could hear animals scrabbling about beneath the floorboards, even in the wall behind me, and I could not conceal a shudder. I didn't like mice, but I hated rats.

"So loathsome, rats, aren't they?" he said, folding his arms across his chest and putting one leg over the other, quite at his ease. "Let us hope you do not have to remain here long. It could become quite, er, unpleasant, shall we say? They are such hungry little beasts, especially now winter is coming on. And you are so helpless, aren't you? And when it gets dark, as it does quite early these November days, you will not even be able to see them creeping closer and closer. It won't do any good to scream. There is no one to hear you. We are miles from any habitation, at the far reaches of the Moorland property. It was fortunate for me, wasn't it, their holdings are so extensive. I daresay they have quite forgotten this old ramshackle place. Of course I do not stay here at night. It would be much too uncomfortable, don't you agree?"

I stared at him in horror. Surely he was not going to leave me here alone, was he? In the dark? With the rats?

Chapter Twenty-one

Melton chuckled again, thoroughly amused. "It is too bad of me to tease you and try to frighten you, isn't it? It is just to pay you back for being so unpleasant to me. Why, I was certain you must have put our first encounter from your mind, and long ago, too. After all, it was bound to happen sooner or later, wasn't it? I just made sure it was sooner, that's all."

I felt hatred rising in my chest like a red-hot stream of lava, and it was a moment before I could say, "I was only twelve! A child!"

"A very delicious child, as I remember," he said, still smiling. "Such perfect unblemished skin you had! Such a sweet mouth! You were my little friend. Much as the adorable Lili has become my little friend."

"You will never have her," I said through gritted teeth. "If you kidnapped me, hoping to trade me for her, you have been foolish indeed. Alastair will not give her up for me."

"I had no such intention. I shall use you in quite a different way, and one that is much more clever. You see, Lili shall get a note from me tomorrow morning. By that time your hosts, and Mr. Russell, will be thoroughly alarmed by your continued absence. Ah, the scurrying about, the bustle of search parties sent out, the alarms given. I wish I could see it. But I digress. You must forgive me. I have spent so much time alone these past several days, with no one to talk to, it has made me garrulous.

"Now, where was I? Oh, yes, the note to Lili. In it, I shall tell her I am visiting in Limpley Stoke and I have discovered your abductors. Only I know your whereabouts, and only she can save you. I shall give her directions to slip away from the house and meet me on the road where I will have a carriage waiting. She will be told she must not breathe a word of this to anyone and she will mind me. She knows how much you and Mr. Russell dislike me; how he would keep her away from me. I will end by saying if she does not come, you may well die. Your life will be in her hands.

"There now. Do you think she will even hesitate before she rushes to your rescue like one of the knights of old? If you do, you do not know fanciful young girls as I do. And I do assure you, ma'am, I have made quite a study of this particular young miss, her whims and dreams. She does have the most vivid imagination! Haven't you found it so yourself?"

He stared at me, head cocked on one side and a small smile lifting a corner of his thin, mobile mouth. How ordinary he looked. How innocent with his straight sandy hair, his unpretentious clothes, and that open, hearty smiling face that hid such potent evil it had to have come from the devil himself.

I took a deep breath to steady myself. I longed to curse him, longed to tell him how despicable he was, how degenerate, but I knew I must not anger him. There were those rats to consider, and I was at his mercy.

"And how do you intend to get that note to Lili?" I asked, proud my voice was so calm and even. "Even if you could find someone to deliver it for you, he could not do so without the Moorlands or Alastair discovering it. And they will never let her go anywhere near you. They *know* what you are. I told them."

For a fleeting moment he looked discomposed and his cheeks turned a dull red. Then he said, "I suppose that is true. But there is no danger of that, for they will not know of the note. I shall put it in her horse's stall. Hers is the old roan mare, right? Don't bother to deny it. I have watched Lili at her riding lessons and I know she has been taught to saddle the mare herself for once young Moorland made her dismount and adjust the cinch and the stirrup. I shall simply put the note with the horse's tack."

"You are the naive one, sir," I said, feeling suddenly easier. "Everyone is looking out for you. Do you think to avoid every eye, just stroll into the stable nodding to the farmhands as you complete your errand?"

"How scornful you are! How superior your tone! I go at night, of course. I have been in the stable twice now, and no one at the manor was any the wiser. Moorland does not employ grooms. No one sleeps overhead. As for the old dog of the captain's, I like dogs. And it is easy to gain a dog's allegiance with a choice piece of raw meat. Shep will not bark at me."

I was devastated. He seemed to have thought of everything, and he certainly knew everything about the farm and its routines. There was nothing I could do to stop him. It would all happen just as he had planned.

Lili would fly to my rescue with shining eyes and a noble sense of purpose. She would make careful plans to escape the house unseen, even toy with the idea of stealing one of the captain's pistols in case she had to shoot someone to save me. Lili, who had never even held a gun before! I prayed the captain kept his guns locked away, with the powder and shot separate.

I could see her in the scarlet cloak—no, she would borrow one of the maids' gray ones so as to be less noticeable—slipping from tree to tree 'til she reached the curve in the drive. Then she would run down to the carriage that waited for her just beyond the gates. Feeling proud of herself, as dedicated as Jeanne d'Arc. Until, a short time later, she discovered exactly what Melton had in mind for her.

I could hardly bear to think of that. Lili might not be as strong as I had been, able to overcome the shame and the fear that might have destroyed me because I hated him so, and because I hated my father and brother for believing I had been the one at fault. I knew that was not true. So did my mother, but she had been no proof against my father's bellowed wrath. Still, I remember how she told me, a little while before she died, that I would find a man who loved me someday, a man I could love in return. He would be nothing at all like Gregory Paxton, and, she told me, holding my face between her hands and looking deep into my eyes, when we were man and wife, it would be wonderful—so different I would be astounded. For I would be a woman then, not a child, and that would make all the difference.

I had trusted my mother, believed her. Still, I had married the earl when he proposed it. It had seemed simpler and I was desperate to escape my father's house. I had not waited for love. I was glad of that now. My marriage had given me independence and a fortune, and in the end, Alastair had come. And he was worth any amount of waiting.

"Nothing to say, ma'am? Well, well, and who would have thought you could be silenced so effectively? Incidentally, you haven't asked, but I'll tell you anyway. I've been staying with a distant relative a few miles from here. The man's a recluse, but I forced him to take me in. That's why your precious Mr. Russell couldn't find me. No one thought to look there, since he never has company.

"Now you must excuse me. I must get back there and write a most important letter, and later, deliver it."

As he turned to go, I said, hating myself as I did so, "Are you going to leave me here alone? In the dark?" I hated the fear I could hear in my voice even more.

He paused and looked at me. "I'll be back. Later. 'Til then you must be patient. And trust the rats will not be too *im*patient."

He chuckled and I watched him as he strode down the length of the barn. As he pushed the large door open, some light streamed in. It was heartening to know there were still some hours of daylight left.

Alone, I forced myself not to give in to panic. Since

Melton had only tied my hands, I could walk. Why, I could even get away from here before he returned!

Think, I ordered myself. Think!

I had left the house shortly after one in the afternoon. The sun set around four-thirty, or perhaps a little later. Assuming it had taken an hour to drive me here, tie me up, and wait for me to regain consciousness, that left me two and a half hours. To be on the safe side, perhaps only two. Could I make my way to the high road by then? But how could I find it? In which direction did it lie? Melton must have felt this barn was too isolated for me to do that, and considering that no one from the farm had come here even when they were searching for him, it appeared he was right. That was why he had not bothered to tie me up more thoroughly. He wouldn't care if I went out and got lost and froze to death.

But the rats decided me. I could hear them more clearly now I was alone. Anything would be better than being left here in the dark with hungry rats. Anything.

It was easy enough to get up and walk to the door. I hesitated there. For all I knew, Melton might be right outside. I cursed myself for not listening more closely. I might have heard him drive away. I forced myself to stand quietly for what seemed a very long time before I attempted to open the heavy door. It was difficult using only my shoulder, but at last I got it started. As it swung wide, the rusty hinges squealed, and I froze at the noise. It was then I saw the carriage sitting abandoned beside the barn. He must have taken the horse. Perhaps to ride cross-country and avoid the roads?

I told myself to stop thinking of anything but making good my escape. If I found the road, I might meet someone who could help me get back to the farm so I could warn the others, even lead them back here to deal with Melton. That thought gave me a great deal of satisfaction, and I began to look for a lane. He had driven that carriage in here. There had to be one.

Finding it was more difficult than I had imagined. Saplings had grown up around the barn, and large bushes. At last I saw a faint track, found some broken twigs and crushed dry grass.

It was cold as I set off at a rapid pace. Whenever the wind gusted, it blew my cloak out behind me, and there was no way I could pull it close with my hands tied behind me. I told myself if I kept moving briskly, I would be all right.

The land around me was desolate, untamed. It was hard to imagine people had lived here once, using that barn, growing crops in fields that no longer existed. But they had, I discovered when I almost fell into a deep cellar hole. I had wandered from the lane a few steps and had almost found myself in worse case than I had been in the barn.

Safely on the lane again, I tried to hurry and be careful at the same time. I walked for a long time. Once I had to cross a wide shallow stream on stepping stones that were none too steady. I pictured Melton splashing through at a canter and I grimaced. Have you any idea how hard it is to keep from falling when you cannot use your outstretched arms for balance? Trust me. It is very difficult but I managed it finally.

I had to stop and rest a few times. I leaned against trees and closed my eyes. I wanted to sink down on the ground and really rest, but I was afraid if I did I would not have the will to get up again. But then I remembered Melton and what he had in mind for Lili, the diabolical plan he had gone away to set into motion, and it was easy to make myself go on.

And all the time the gray sky was getting darker, the light beginning to fade, and I could not see very far ahead of me anymore. I admit I was afraid.

At last I stumbled onto a narrow dirt road. Weeds grew between the wheel ruts. It was obviously not often used, but it was a road, and I told myself it had to go somewhere. I looked carefully and saw hoofprints turning right; wheel tracks that came from that direction, too.

I turned left. I did not want to meet Melton returning after all my struggle. I hurried until I was around a bend and out of sight. Only then did I slow my pace. I tried not to think of meandering country roads that climbed up and down dale, wound around hills, and went on aimlessly for miles before they eventually reached some outpost of civilization. And I began to wonder, with more than a little resentment, why no one was searching for me. It was late afternoon. Surely Alastair must have returned. Didn't he question my absence? Didn't anyone notice how many hours I had been gone?

I had just come to the base of a short rise when I heard the sounds of a cantering horse. I panicked, I was so afraid Melton might be coming back another way. There were no trees, no bushes near me where I might hide. And still the horse and rider came closer. Desperate, I threw myself down in a slight dip by the side of the road and prayed in the speed of his passage and the fading light, Melton would not notice me.

But what if it isn't him, I thought. What if it were someone who could help me? I raised my head and peered through the dusk. The bulky figure atop the horse who came over the rise then did not look like Melton. Afraid I might lose my only chance of rescue, I staggered to my feet, calling out for help.

The horse was almost upon me, and it shied in alarm. I heard a rough masculine voice cursing, saw the horse swung aside, and looked up into the bearded red face of a man I had never seen before. I was weak with gratitude.

"Here now! Wot are ye about ter be frightenin' the horse so?" he demanded, scowling down at me.

I do not remember what I said or how I explained the situation in stammering words. I only remember turning so he could see my bound hands. At that, he dismounted and came to untie me.

"Thank you," I said, rubbing my red wrists to ease the pain of the rope.

"This man wot tied ye, he wouldn't be named Purdy, would he?" the man asked. "I'm lookin' fer a gent named Purdy."

"No. His name is Paxton. He is Viscount Melton." I stopped then for I did not want to tell a stranger about Lili. Instead, I asked if he could help me get back to Moorland Farm.

"I can't, missus. I'm a stranger here myself," he said. "I don't know where it's at, and that's the truth."

"Have you passed any villages? Any farms?" I persisted.

"There's a small farm about two–three miles back," he admitted. I wondered he sounded so reluctant until he said, "Well, I guess I can take ye there. Night's comin' on. Best I find a place to sleep afore dark. I heard someone like Purdy had been seen around here. I'll go on searchin' tomorrow. I'll find him, y'know. Oh yeah, I'll find the blackguard!"

I introduced myself and he removed his hat and bowed as he told me he was James Fuller who kept an inn near Tetsworth on the London road. Then he frowned and said no more as he helped me up behind him on the horse. I gripped him tightly around the waist. His clothes smelled of stale beer but I did not mind. The rough homespun of his jacket was as welcome as any velvet even to my bruised wrists.

The horse must have been ridden hard, for it was only able to manage a walk, carrying both of us, and I was able to ask Fuller about this Mr. Purdy. I wondered if he had skipped out without paying his bill. I did not envy him when Fuller caught up with him. I had seen the sheathed knife at his belt, the ancient blunderbuss attached to the saddle.

"He's a no-good, low-down scum, is wot he is," Fuller began. "Beggin' yer ladyship's pardon, but there's no other way ter say it. And when I find 'im, he'll learn wot happens ter men wot hurt little girls, he will."

I froze, horrified at his words. Could it be possible Melton had attacked another child? It certainly sounded like it.

"What did this Mr. Purdy look like?" I asked carefully. "Maybe I have seen him, too, and I can help you."

"He was just an ordinary chap, friendly with everyone and quick to tell a jest. Had my little Molly laughing and playing at peek-a-boo in no time an' my Molly's shy o' strangers. He wore good clothes. You'd know 'im fer a gent. Nothin' special about his face. It were ordinary. But I'll know 'im when I see 'im. Oh yeah, there's no question 'bout that."

I said nothing more. It certainly sounded like Melton, and much as I pitied the innkeeper and especially his little daughter, I was desperate to get back to the farm. If I told this Fuller of my suspicions, he might insist on going back to the barn. It was too late for Molly. It was not too late for Lili. I had to get to her.

Only a few more minutes brought us to a crossroads and the warm, welcoming lights in a small farmhouse nearby. Fuller helped me down and went with me to the door. After the snarling dog had been quieted, my tale was soon told and we were admitted and bade to take a seat on the bench near the fire. The farmer's wife swung the kettle over that fire. Nothing had ever felt so good to me, chilled as I was. The farmer said he knew Moorland Farm well, and would take me there shortly.

His wife told me someone from the farm had been there only a short while before as she handed me a steaming cup of tea.

I knew she was anxious to discover how it was I had become lost, and why I had been wandering around the back roads in the first place, but I only drank the tea. I did not want all the world to know of Lili's dilemma. Fuller was not so reticent. He was quick to tell the two how he had found me by the side of the road, my hands bound behind me.

"Captured she were by a viscount, if ye can believe

it," he said. I saw the three of them exchange knowing glances. It was obvious the depraved ways of titled gentlemen were not unknown to them and they were not a bit surprised.

A short time later, the farmer brought his horse and cart around and I rose to go. I motioned Fuller close to tell him I thought Melton might be the man Purdy that he wanted. I also told him how he might find him if he waited along the road for him. I knew if Melton was not the man he sought, he would not harm him. But if he was . . .

I admit I prayed he would find him before Alastair did. I did not like to think of what Alastair would do when he discovered how Melton had meant to use me to trick Lili. I even shook Fuller's hand and wished him well before I climbed to my seat beside the farmer.

The drive to Moorland Farm was accomplished in silence. As we went slowly along, the farmer smoking a disreputable old pipe and only occasionally making an encouraging noise to his horse, I was content to doze. Suddenly I found it hard to keep my eyes open.

Chapter Twenty-two

Safely delivered to the doorstep by my taciturn driver, I found the Moorland farmhouse all abuzz. It was brilliantly lit and I blinked in the glare as I was embraced by a fervent Lili, who told me rapidly how frightened she had been for me. Behind her, the three Moorlands were smiling. A quick glance at Alastair was unsettling, however. He wore a black frown that would have frightened me if I had not known him better.

"But where were you, 'Nelia?" Lili demanded. "You have been gone for hours and hours!"

"Give the countess a chance to sit down and catch her breath, child," the captain ordered.

Thus admonished, Lili bit her lip, but I knew it was to be a short reprieve.

As I removed my cloak, I tired to smile at Alastair. It did nothing to lighten his mood. If anything, he looked more severe. I could tell I was in for it, but I was so happy to be back among friends, I did not care. Besides, it had not been my fault.

"Yes, but where *were* you, 'Nelia," Lili insisted. "There has been such a to-do here. All the men have been searching for you, and truly, we were all so worried. Al-as-tair has been just like a bear ever since he came back.

"Oh, you must be hungry. I'll get you some supper right away."

"Bring the decanter of brandy, Nancy," the captain said as his wife released his hand and rose to help Lili. "That's what is wanted here."

After the two left, he added quietly, "We'll not have much time to talk now, until Lili goes to bed, but give us a brief account, if you are able."

"It was Melton," I said, and the two Moorlands joined Alastair in frowning. "He was on the grounds this afternoon and he saw me walking down the drive. He overpowered me with some drug. When I regained consciousness, I was in an old barn. One of yours," I added. "He said it was a long way from the house."

Ben Moorland clapped his forehead. "The old Stiller barn! It's not been used for years, it's so decrepit. Why, I never thought to search it."

"Nor I," the captain said ruefully. "Ben, we must send some men there at once to capture this devil."

"He's not there now," I told them quickly. I had seen the way Alastair pushed himself away from the wall where he had been leaning, in anticipation.

There was no time for any more, for we could hear Nancy's voice raised to warn us as she told Lili to watch her step with the tray.

I should have been famished, but perhaps I was too tired. I made a show of eating the hot food to please Lili, and I drank two glasses of brandy and water. That warmed me deep inside and I could feel the tension begin to fade away.

"But you have still not told me where you were, 'Nelia," Lili scolded. "I am sure if it had been I who had been missing, you would have insisted on knowing first thing. And I would not have had any food or drink until I confessed, either!"

"You are right. It is just that I hate having to admit how stupid I was, getting lost. I have been wandering around trying to find my way back here for hours."

"But how did it happen? How you got lost, I mean?" she persisted. I thought she seemed suspicious as I made up a story about a bird I wanted to see closer, how I had followed it into the woods, and gone deeper and deeper until I could not find my way out. Even to my ears, it sounded like a fairy tale.

"It was only by the greatest luck I managed to get

to the road again before it was black night," I concluded. "But I was a long way from here. I was fortunate to meet that farmer with the cart. I was so tired! Don't you ever do anything so foolish, Lili. It's not only frightening, it's dangerous."

She had more questions about the bird and whether I had seen any wild animals, but she appeared satisfied now. I put my head back on the chair and closed my eyes. The warm fire was taking its toll.

"It is time for bed, Lili," Nancy Moorland reminded her.

To my surprise, Alastair spoke up then for the first time. " 'Nelia's bedtime, too. She is exhausted. I will take her up. See she is settled."

As I opened my eyes to stare at him, I saw the determination in his face. Still, I should have said I could manage myself but I did not. I did not even protest when he picked me up and carried me from the room. There was a deep silence behind us but I did not waste any time wondering what Lili and the Moorlands were thinking. Not with the heady relief I felt to be held close in Alastair's arms, my own arms tight around his neck.

He shouldered the door to my room open. The candles were lit, there was a fire in the fireplace, and the bed was turned down with my nightrail laid across it. I was sure there would be a hot brick for my feet and I sighed.

"Hot water, sir," a maid said behind us. Alastair set me on my feet although he kept an arm around me.

The maid lingered, about to ask if I needed her help, but Alastair's impatient gesture sent her scurrying away. As the door closed behind her, he put me before him and began to unbutton my gown.

"No, I can do it," I said, pulling away from him. I felt dirty in my soiled, crumpled gown and I knew my hair was a tangled mess. "Please, Alastair. I need a few minutes to myself."

"Very well. But I will be back. We have to talk."

I removed my gown and shift quickly, washed thoroughly in the hot water, and brushed my teeth and my hair. After I lowered the nightrail over my head, I climbed into bed. It was a good thing Alastair returned so promptly for I was almost asleep when he sat down on the edge of my bed.

"Now then, in more detail, what happened to you?" he began. "I'll have the whole story, 'Nelia, including any ideas you might have about where Melton is now." As he spoke, he smoothed the hair back from my forehead and dropped a quick kiss on my widow's peak. He was so gentle about it, I almost cried.

But I managed to collect myself and tell him most of the story. As I did so, I marveled at the emotions that chased each other across his face. Anger, of course, but also fear, regret—even admiration for my escape. Still, when I stopped speaking, he was frowning.

"But I don't understand why he took you," he began slowly. "Did he mistake you for Lili? It hardly seems possible."

"No," I said, choosing my words carefully. I would have to be careful here. "He was going to write to Lili with some tale about being the only one to know my whereabouts, and how only she could save me. And tell her where to meet him."

Alastair snorted in disgust before he said, "But how could he get such a letter to Lili?"

I crossed my fingers under the covers. "I don't know. When I asked him the same question, he would not tell me."

As he cocked a brow at me, I hurried on and told him about the reclusive relative's house where Melton had been staying. I could not tell him Melton intended to leave the letter in the Moorland stable tonight. I knew what would happen if I did. Alastair would lie in wait for him there and he would kill him. And then besides it all coming out—the danger to Lili, even what had happened to me long ago—there would have to be an inquiry and the Moorlands would be involved. And Alastair, even if he escaped hanging, would have the death hanging over him for the rest of his life. And the stigma that came with it. The *ton* has a long memory.

No. I wanted Melton to die as fervently as Alastair did, but not here. And not by Alastair's hand. Secretly I hoped the innkeeper, James Fuller, would do the deed for us, and we would not be involved in the investigation when Melton's body was found on that deserted road.

Still, I felt guilty. I did not like to lie to Alastair. I promised myself I would never do it again.

He leaned over and put his hands on the pillow, on either side of my head. He did not touch me. He only stared into my eyes while I regarded him solemnly, wondering what he was thinking now.

"I love you even more than I thought I did, my sweet," he said softly. "I did not know how much until this afternoon when I was so frightened for you, but could do nothing—nothing!—to help you. Don't you ever let anything like that happen to you again. I do not think I could bear it."

A singularly sweet smile lit his green eyes as he added, "As if you could prevent it. Never mind, love, we'll be married soon, and I'll see to your safety." The smile disappeared as he added, "Married as soon as I kill that damn—"

I did not care to hear Melton described, so I reached up and brought his face to mine and kissed him. Fortunately he lost all interest in the viscount. Momentarily, anyway.

Alastair did not remain much longer. He pretended to be affronted by my yawns, telling me as he stood at the door, that he was not at all accustomed to women who became bored when he was making love to them. I laughed and waved him away, but to be truthful, I had yawned on purpose. I knew I had to tell Nancy Moorland about the note Melton intended to leave for Lili in the stable tonight. The note would be there; he wouldn't know I had escaped and returned here. And it was so important Lili never learn of that note, nor Alastair either.

I made myself get out of bed and pace the floor. It was the only way I could be sure of staying awake. Finally, I heard the soft voices of the captain and his wife coming up the stairs to bed, and I opened my door softly. I waved to attract Nancy's attention, and beckoned to her. She nodded as she led her husband to their room. All this was done in the utmost silence. Captain Moorland had very sharp ears.

When she joined me finally, I told her of the problem as quickly as I could. "You do see why I could not let Alastair know of this, I'm sure," I concluded. "We cannot have him killing Melton in your stable! Why, it would mean the local justice would have to become involved, and think of the scandal!"

"Especially since my husband is the justice," she said. I was surprised. She did not seem perturbed. She sounded almost amused.

"I have another plan," I went on. I told her of the innkeeper's daughter and she looked as sick as I felt. "I told this James Fuller that Melton might be on the road where he found me later tonight. I hope he kills him. Not only to keep Alastair from doing it, but because Melton deserves to die. And I pray nothing is ever known of his death."

"It is sure to be an unsolved mystery," Nancy reassured me. "How could anyone connect Fuller to it? There won't be any witnesses, and Melton has no friends in the neighborhood. He is merely a stranger passing through who met with an untimely end.

"Don't worry. I'll collect the note the minute I'm dressed, and I'll see to it Lili doesn't have a riding lesson tomorrow either. I love Lili dearly and my husband is besotted with her although he pretends otherwise. I promise you we will not let anything happen to her."

Relieved, I went back to bed. I think I was asleep before the door had even closed behind her.

When I came down the following morning, I discovered Alastair had not yet made an appearance. Lili had gone out in the cart with Ben to deliver a sack of apples to an old lady in the village. Nancy and the captain were seated in the parlor, she busy darning hose. When she saw me, she took a note from her workbasket and held it out to me, her face rigid with distaste. I retreated to a chair by the window.

The note had been written to guarantee an impressionable young girl would be sent all aflutter by it. Written in a hasty, abbreviated style, as if the writer had had to hurry because he was in great danger, it implored her not to fail. It said she would find the carriage waiting in a small copse a little beyond the gates at two this afternoon. Melton said he would drive her to the place where I was being held. She was warned not to tell a soul of the adventure, and it was signed, "Your dear friend, Melton."

Only a semblance of rational thought would have made a sensible person hesitate and wonder. For how could her arrival at the barn expedite my release? Had the villains of the piece merely to look at her shining innocence before they tore off my bonds and fell weeping at her feet, begging forgiveness? But I knew Lili would not have been sensible if she had found the note while I was still missing, and I felt sick, as sick as I could tell Nancy was feeling.

"Now why do I sense there is something going on here," the captain mused, moving his head from one to the other of us. At his feet, his dog awoke and wagged its tail.

"Why so suspicious, dear?" Nancy asked. She even managed a chuckle. "What could possibly be going on?"

"I've no idea. Still, I would wager anything you and the countess are up to something. There are certain currents in the air . . ."

"I fear there is nothing so interesting," I made haste to say. "Tell me, when is Lili expected to return?"

As I spoke, I rose to throw the note into the fire. I watched it turn gold, then black and disappear up the chimney in small pieces of soot. I felt great satisfaction. It was gone, as I hoped Melton was gone. Forever.

We all spent the day doing ordinary things. Alastair finally came down, Ben and Lili returned from their errand of mercy. We had dinner; the captain went up for his nap. When Lili began to practice the pianoforte, Alastair and I went out for a walk.

"I wish we could leave here," I said as we started down the drive. I know I sounded fretful. I couldn't help it. All day I had been waiting, waiting, for that knock on the door that would tell of a body being found on the road a few miles away. It had never come. Several times I had caught Nancy's eye, seen she looked as confused as I, and as frustrated. I had even insisted that Alastair and I walk the drive to the road. That way I could see anyone who arrived bearing news.

Was it possible Melton had been able to avoid James Fuller? I wished I had thought to suggest a walk earlier so I might check that small copse near the gates; see for myself if the carriage was waiting. But I had been so sure Fuller would solve all my problems. It was disheartening to think that Melton might only have been frightened away when he went back to the barn and found me missing; that sometime—next month, at the first of the year—he might try for Lili again. More than disheartening. Terrifying.

"We shall leave, love," Alastair was saying and he put his arm around me to hug me close.

"But we can't go until we are sure Melton has quit the neighborhood. He is so determined!" I complained. "Yet we cannot impose on the Moorlands' hospitality indefinitely."

"It is my fervent wish we do not. Dinner at three in the afternoon? Bedtime at ten at night? To say nothing of that unspeakable fowl," Alastair said grimly. Any other time I would have laughed. Now I could not even smile.

"Besides, we have a wedding to see to, remember? Before the first real snowstorm?"

I looked up at the gray sky. A few flakes had fallen this morning but they had not lasted.

"We are both anxious to be gone. But we can't leave until we are sure Lili is safe."

"I am sure she is as safe as safe can be, now."

I stopped to stare at him. "What do you mean?" I asked suspiciously. "Have you discovered something I do not know?"

"It is only reasonable deduction, sweet. Do you agree that by now Melton knows you were able to escape the barn? I shall never understand why he did not secure your feet. So careless! Or so arrogant. Never mind. Do you also agree he has probably left the county, headed back to his own estate to brood over his disappointment and wonder how he is to face you when the Season opens next spring? And perhaps, if he is wise, to worry a great deal more about how he is to face *me*? If you do agree, you must see he will stay well away from Lili now. We know what he had in mind. He will not dare even nod to her."

I had not considered that, and it cheered me. Still, something he had said bothered me, and I thought for a moment before I said, "But Alastair, you will not kill him! Not in London!"

He shrugged. I saw his face was set, those clear green eyes intent on some far horizon. "Accidents happen everywhere, pet. Horses bolt, pistols misfire, footpads abound. Food can be poisoned, drink as well. Nobody is safe. Especially not Viscount Melton."

I shivered at the menace in his voice, and begged him to forget Melton and talk of something else.

We finished our walk in perfect accord. It was decided if nothing more was heard of Melton, we would leave the day after tomorrow. Alastair assured me Ben Moorland was well able to protect Lili and keep her safe on those occasions when Nancy did not have her under her care.

Much later that evening, after Lili had gone to bed,

Ben told us he had called on the old recluse who was Melton's relative. The man would not let him in the house, but he had assured him Melton had gone out the previous evening, taking all his possessions with him and saying he would not be returning.

"It appears he meant to leave the area as soon as he had Lili," Moorland told us. We were a rapt audience. "All I can guess is that after finding you gone, m'lady, he realized we were on to him, and fled. There's no doubt he's disappeared. I checked the Stiller barn as well."

"You found no sign of him?" I asked. "The carriage was gone?"

"There wasn't a sign he had ever been there," Ben told me. His honest face reassured me, and I relaxed, satisfied.

Chapter Twenty-three

As planned, we left the farm two mornings later after many fond farewells. I shared a special embrace with Nancy Moorland. I felt close to her now. Lili had forged a special bond between us. That young lady was saddened at our departure, but I suspected she would be laughing at her kitten before an hour had passed. She was happy here. Happy and content, as I was, for her.

It was a chilly day, and the skies continued gray, somber even for November. I settled down on the padded seat of the vicar's curricle. As we drove away, Alastair told me he had written to him earlier, to tell him the exchange of vehicles would take place as soon as it could be arranged after we had reached London. He told me Mr. King could fetch the perch phaeton. The picture of a prim and proper gentleman's gentleman seated high on the seat made me smile.

"It will also keep King occupied, and more importantly, absent, since we ourselves will be, er, occupied then," he told me with a warm, sideways smile. "We won't want King around."

I knew I was blushing so I turned and pretended an interest I did not feel in the passing scenery. Suddenly our marriage was imminent. Why, it could take place in only a day or so.

Still, even as happy as I was, Melton remained in my mind like a stubborn burr. Everyone had assured me he had left the area, and it was true we had not seen or heard anything of him. But I found it hard to believe he would just go away. No one as determined as Gregory Paxton would do that. I remember the trouble he had gone to, having Alastair's rooms watched, ferreting out the destination of the scarlet trunk, his own arrival in Oxfordshire and all his devious preparations—was that only the result of his urge to have Lili, or was it more because he could not stand to be crossed? Would not stand for it, in fact. Would a man like that just give up? It seemed most unlikely to me.

I decided I had to find out more, question James Fuller myself about what had happened the night he had waited for Melton on that country road. As casually as I could, I asked Alastair if we might not stop the night in Tetsworth. "There is an inn there I know of," I invented, praying Tetsworth was only large enough to accommodate one such establishment for I had no idea the name of Fuller's inn.

Alastair was agreeable. We could easily make London from there tomorrow, he said, and, more importantly, Doctor's Commons.

There was still an hour till dusk when we reached Tetsworth. The inn was called The Gallant Stag. I was glad to get down to stretch my tired muscles. I was sick of traveling. I suspect Alastair was, too. James Fuller came out himself to greet us, calling as he did so for a boy to take our portmanteaux. Behind us, an ostler led the tired team away.

I tried to catch Fuller's eye, but he ignored me to greet Alastair. He did not smile, in fact he was not at all the usual, jovial innkeeper. Was it because he had not run Melton to earth—killed him—I wondered, my heart sinking? And of course, now he was home, there was his little daughter to remind him of the man's treachery. No wonder he was grim!

He showed us to a private parlor and told us rooms would be prepared immediately. He promised a tasty dinner as well. I thought he and Alastair would never have done discussing it, and the wine to accompany it. I wondered how I could manage a word with him alone.

My chance came sooner than I thought, for later, as I was going to the bedchamber assigned to me, we came face to face in the hall. I was a little surprised he seemed disinclined to talk to me and I was forced to put my hand on his arm when he would have hurried by.

"Please, Mr. Fuller, a word," I said softly. Reluctantly, he stopped.

"Tell me what happened after you left me the other night," I went on, speaking quickly lest Alastair come out and discover us. "You did not see Melton? He managed to evade you?"

He paused for a moment, as if choosing his words. "No. I did not see the man, m'lady," he said, his face stony in the dim light of the hall. I sensed his disappointment in every word. "I waited a long time, but he did not come. There was no sign of him the next day either. Don't know where he got to, but if he shows his face in these parts again, I'll remember him."

"I know how frustrated you must feel," I murmured, trying hard to swallow my own disappointment. So Melton had not died. He was still free to pursue Lili and other young girls like her. My fingers curled into fists just thinking about it.

"I am sorry," I managed to say as I stepped aside. He left with only a curt nod.

I slept fitfully that night and was not awake when Alastair knocked on my door the next morning. He was anxious to be gone, and I barely took the time for a roll and a cup of coffee before I hurried to the yard. The team was already harnessed to the curricle, our baggage strapped on behind when I appeared. The day was raw, with a cold wind blowing. As usual now, it was overcast. I was sure it would snow soon. I only hoped it held off until we reached town.

Alastair and our host were deep in conversation a little distance away from me. Fuller saw me first. He clasped Alastair by the arm and said something before he called a good morning to me.

Just before he helped me into the curricle as Alastair went around to take his own seat, I took his hand. Softly, for his ears alone, I said, "Thank you for everything. It is impossible to express my gratitude for what you did for me. And I am so sorry for your Molly. I pray she may forget, in time. The same thing happened to me years ago, but I was able to put it behind me. Just love her as I know you do. She'll come around."

His eyes grew moist and he looked surprised. Small wonder. He had not known I had been Melton's victim, too.

He was not able to reply. Instead, he pressed my hand and stood watching as we drove away.

Miles later, however, I remembered how he and Alastair had stood talking together just before we left. At the time, it had seemed almost clandestine. And the way Fuller had grasped his arm. Surely that was unusual.

"What were you and Fuller discussing just before we left, my dear?" I asked. "You looked very like conspirators to me."

"Surely you exaggerate, 'Nelia," he said. Then he paused as if to consider what he might say next. I found I was holding my breath.

"I never meant to tell you this," he said finally, still looking straight ahead. "I thought it best you did not know. But I have decided there should be no secrets between us, especially on our wedding day."

"We are to be married? Today?" I asked, forgetting Fuller as I stared at my soiled, crumpled gown. Marry London's premier beau looking so unsightly? We would see about that.

"I see no reason why not, if we reach London in time," he told me. I saw he looked as handsome and neat as ever and do you know, for a moment I resented him.

"I have waited for you too long already, love. You there, get up," he called as one of the horses stumbled.

He gave me a sideways glance and I was lost. Whatever—wherever—whenever. What did it matter?

"But you distract me," he went on. "I meant to say that I know Melton is dead. I saw his body. In fact, I helped bury him."

As I gasped, he continued, "After the household was asleep the night of your kidnapping, Ben Moorland and I rode out. He had it in mind to look the Stiller barn over. Before we could reach it, we came upon James Fuller on the road. He was standing over Melton's body, pistol in hand. He did not even try to hide the satisfaction he felt that he had destroyed the man who had, in effect, destroyed his daughter."

"But he told me just yesterday he had not seen Melton! That he never came back to the barn. So did Moorland. Do you mean they both lied to me? *You,* as well?"

"I thought it better you never know. Ben and Fuller agreed. We decided to keep the whole affair a secret between the three of us."

I was in such turmoil I could not comment, and after a moment, he went on, "Fuller was grateful for our help that night, after we explained who we were. We decided it would be best to bury Melton so there would be no awkward inquiry. Ben pushed for this especially. I suspect he did not want Lili to discover Melton had been close to her.

"By the way, my dear, as appreciative as I am of all Ben's good qualities, I think Lili deserves a better husband. She's managed to bewitch him, young as she is, and I wouldn't be at all surprised if he waited for her to reach marriageable age. But it won't do. He's a farmer. He'll always be a farmer. Perhaps when the time comes for it, we might have her up to London for a Season?"

"Go on about Melton," I said coldly.

He glanced at me quickly before he said, as if anxious now to be done, "We took the body to the Stiller barn and buried it near there in a dry well. Ben kept Melton's notecase and coat. It sported a bullet hole, of course, and it was bloodied. In the spring, he will produce them, saying he found them for sale at a fair some distance from the area. Melton's disappearance will be explained. This seemed the kindest thing we could do for his wife and children. It was not right they be left to endless doubt and conjecture. Oh, Fuller took Melton's horse and carriage back to Tetsworth with him. When you saw us talking together this morning, he was telling me he had already sold them. There is no link between him and Melton now."

He stopped speaking. I was so angry, I could not.

" 'Nelia?" he asked. "What is it? Why are you silent?"

"You knew all the time," I said stiffly. I would not look at him. "All the time I was worrying about Lili, frantic that beast would come back, you knew he was dead. And you didn't tell me. You didn't even tell me when I asked you to stop at Fuller's inn."

Alastair pulled the team to a halt by the side of the road. I knew he wanted to speak, but I hurried on, "How could you do such a thing? How could you be so insensitive? How could you think me so spineless and weak, I could not bear the news? I am glad Melton is dead! Glad, do you hear? If that is wrong, I don't care. He was an evil man. The world is better off without him. I would have pulled the trigger myself, if I had been there."

I glared at him. It seemed to me suddenly there was a chasm between us I had not noticed before. He had done what he thought was right without regard for my feelings. It was pure and simple male arrogance, assuming he knew best, and I should have no opinion in the matter. And it would be this way for as long as we lived. Alastair would not change. I did not trick myself in thinking I might alter him after marriage. If there was any adjusting to be made, I was the one who would have to do it. For a moment, I wondered if I could bear it.

"I am sorry, 'Nelia. I thought it would distress you to know the gruesome details, and I assumed you would just accept his disappearance. I guess I wanted to protect you, love."

It was a handsome apology, and I could tell from his expression he was feeling remorse. I pondered anew the enigmas men were. How different in the way they saw women, our feelings and sensibilities. How strange they could be so deadly one moment, and so chivalrous the next. I realized I would never understand them, and one in particular, no matter how hard I tried. I hoped women were as puzzling to them. It would only be fair.

"What are you thinking now?" he asked, leaning closer. "Do you forgive me? You should, you know, for you are just as guilty as I am of keeping secrets."

"Whatever do you mean?" I demanded, ready to be indignant again.

"Well, you did not think to mention James Fuller when you returned to Moorland Farm, his part in your escape, now did you? Nor did you tell me about Melton's plan to leave a note in the barn."

I know I flushed, for I was feeling as guilty as any child caught stealing a forbidden sweet. "How did you find out?" I asked weakly.

"Ben told me after he had it from Nancy. Women and their secrets! I don't think you are in any position to scold me when you are just as guilty. But forget that. I have.

"Since I spoke to Ben and Fuller, asked them to keep Melton's death and the manner of it from you, I suppose I am much at fault."

No doubt we were both at fault, although I could argue the circumstances were not at all the same. But a picture of Alastair, Ben Moorland, and James Fuller as conspirators came to mind then, and it was all I could do to preserve a stern face. If ever there had been a stranger threesome, I had never heard of it. The husky young farmer, the common innkeeper, and London's nonesuch, Mr. Alastair Russell—why, to imagine them doing anything in concert was unbelievable.

Alastair reached for me then to pull me so close the white plumes of our breath mingled in the frigid air. "Say you forgive me, 'Nelia," he whispered. "Do it! Now!"

He did not give me a chance, for he began to kiss me until I stopped thinking. I was vaguely aware of a heavy wagon rumbling by us on the road, the muffled laughter of the men driving it, but I did not care. My arms were around Alastair, my hands clasping him tight, and I was lost again.

I did not feel the first snowflake that landed on my face, nor, I daresay, the twenty-first. But as the flakes melted from the combined warmth of our skin, they became icy rivulets that even passion could not overcome. Reluctantly, I drew back.

"You have snowflakes tangled in your lashes, love," Alastair told me.

I opened my eyes to see that the snow that was falling in earnest was not the big soft flakes that soon melt away, but the steady compact ones that promise dangerous roads and thick, heavy drifts.

"What a shame," I said sadly as I wiped my eyes. "Now we will never reach London today."

Alastair turned his attention to the team that waited patiently, their heads lowered to escape the snow. "I find it more than a little distressing," he remarked to no one in particular, "that the woman I am about to pledge to love forever has so little faith in me."

He slapped the reins on the team's broad backs and called for them to get up. They set gamely to work.

"I see I still have work to do to convince the lady I am not the drawling, posturing fop she has believed me to be for so long," he continued. Then he turned toward me and I caught my breath at the fire in his green eyes.

"Doctor's Commons by dusk, ma'am," he said firmly. "You may wager on it."